ISTANBUL NOIR

ISTANBUL NOIR

EDITED BY
MUSTAFA ZIYALAN & AMY SPANGLER

Translated by Amy Spangler & Mustafa Ziyalan

AKASHIC BOOKS
NEW YORK

Published by Akashic Books
©2008 Akashic Books

Series concept by Tim McLoughlin and Johnny Temple
Istanbul map by Ayşegül İzer

ISBN-13: 978-1-933354-62-0
Library of Congress Control Number: 2008925932

First printing

Akashic Books
PO Box 1456
New York, NY 10009
info@akashicbooks.com
www.akashicbooks.com

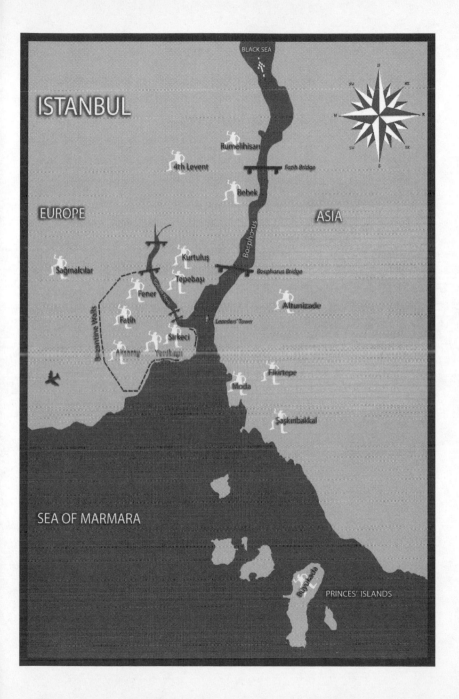

Acknowledgments

Mustafa thanks Pınar Yeşiloğlu for giving him such a good reason to live, and for not so simply bearing with him through those *Istanbul Noir* times; Cem Mumcu for encouraging him to plunge into the project; Murat Eyüboğlu for making him look good in his photographs; his aunt Nil Taneri for inspiring him with her street map of Istanbul which she autographed for him in 1967; and Refike Türker, his aunt from Kumkapı, whose death was the death of Istanbul a little bit.

Amy thanks Dilek Akdemir for, well, everything. She also thanks Tansel Demirel for being a translator's best friend; Irene Gates for valuable feedback; İdil Aydoğan for blatant honesty, bold encouragement, and Foça; participants of the Cunda International Workshop for Translators of Turkish Literature for input and motivation; Tülin Er for constant reassurance; and her mother for reading to her while she was still in the womb.

Both Mustafa and Amy would also like to thank the tough-lovin' (but not necessarily tough to love) folks at Akashic; Ayşegül İzer for the killer map; Deniz Oğurlu for the stark and striking cover photo (and Murat Oğurlu and Deniz Akkol for helping us find it); and Mel Kenne for making connections.

TABLE OF CONTENTS

PART III: IN THE DARK RECESSES

PART IV: GRIEF & GRIEVANCES

INTRODUCTION
TRANSGRESSION AND THE STRAIT: POLITICS, PASSION, AND PAIN

Istanbul is the place where East meets West, literally. It is, as convention would have it, a meeting point, a crossroads. At the same time, it marks the spot where geography is irreparably rent in two; it is a fissure in the continuum, a seething rupture, so to speak. The only city in the world to lie smack dab at the junction of two continents, Europe and Asia, Istanbul is split down the middle by the Bosphorus Strait, pierced by the Golden Horn, and caressed by the Black and Marmara seas. In short, with her "tough love," Mother Nature has pummeled and groomed this place into one of the most stunning geographical locations on earth.

Indeed, Istanbul has been the site of the collision and collusion, of the fracturing and the fusion of cultures, for millennia. Capital of the Eastern Roman (Byzantine) and Ottoman empires, the city formerly known as Byzantium and then Constantinople became Istanbul (incidentally, a word derived from the Greek term for "in the city") after being conquered by the Ottomans in 1453. Many Christian Greeks remained and even flourished in Istanbul following Byzantium's defeat at the hands of the Muslim Ottomans. Under Ottoman rule, Istanbul became known as *alem-penah*—"refuge of the universe," a haven for myriad religious and ethnic groups. When the Jews were expelled during the Spanish Inquisition in 1492 by the Spanish king, the Ottoman Sultan welcomed them with open arms. As the capital of the Ottoman Empire, Istanbul attracted hundreds of thousands of people for centuries from within the empire's vast territories and beyond. In the wake of the empire's demise, the Turkish Republic (founded in 1923) has served this legacy well. Waves of immigration, especially since the 1950s, have increased the city's population by more than tenfold: Turks, Kurds, Laz, Alevis, Circassians, Bosnians, Albanians, Macedonians, etc. You get the picture. A mosaic, a melting pot, a vat of oil and water—call it what you will, there is no denying that Istanbul has always been ethnically, socially, and religiously cosmopolitan to the core.

As submissions for *Istanbul Noir* started to come in, it became increasingly clear to us that what was taking shape was not just some collection of dark stories set in old Stamboul, but a rich portrait of the city itself—or, at the very least, a particularly revealing series of snapshots. Mind you, it is a city shaped largely by the often vicious ebb and tide of the nation's politics. Although Ankara may be the capital of the Republic of Turkey, the truth of the matter is, with a good twelve million people and thus a fifth of its population, Istanbul is the throbbing, often bleeding, heart of the country's politics. And it shows.

In a tumultuous and notoriously unreliable city where the only constant is instability, one often seeks solace in humor. You will get a dose of that in at least a couple of the stories in this collection. The humor is, we hope, appropriately dark. Rather (but not entirely) antithetical to this humor is a mood that also predominates in several of the pieces: *hüzün*. Like many of the terms you'll find in the glossary at the end of this book, *hüzün* is one of those difficult-to-translate concepts integral to the culture of Turkey and the Turkish language, and as a characteristic mood of the inhabitants of this city, several of the stories in this collection are imbued with it. *Hüzün* is a kind of melancholy, a heaviness or a sadness of heart. It is a world pervaded by gray, a state of weariness and hopelessness and lethargy. It is a word for which, arguably, there is no equivalent in English. It is an indescribable mood that you can describe for hours. And in that respect, it is a lot like Istanbul.

A sadomasochistic metropolis in equal measures self-important and self-loathing, Istanbul is rife with contradiction. It is a living conundrum: impossible to pin down and moody as hell. It is raw and human, vibrant and pulsating. It is a city of blood and concrete, a palimpsest of memorials and scars that will not be erased.

Istanbul's history has been marked by the clashing of wills, battling sometimes for life, sometimes for power, often, ultimately, for both. The last several violence-riddled decades in particular have left an indelible mark on the contemporary fabric of the city, not to mention on the minds, bodies, and souls of its people. The knife has cut deep, and the wounds may never completely heal.

This holds true especially for the coup of 1980, which marked a violent and painful rupture in the history of the Turkish Republic. In its efforts to squelch the political left, the state effectively crushed the spirit of an entire generation, extinguishing hope and erecting on its ashes an apolitical society, shaped to the mold of consumerism. An inexhaustible source of heartache and melancholy, bitterness and rage, the involuntary transition from a society fermenting with dissidence to one numbed to the point of docility has had a pervasive impact upon the Turkish people, palpable in many of the stories in this volume.

The political vacuum created by the subjugation of the left was soon filled by the emergence of new forms of nationalism and Islamism. While the history of the Republic is fraught with efforts to galvanize Turkish identity at the expense of others—such as the incitement of the "Riots of September 6-7" in 1955, during which Greeks and other non-Muslims and their property in Istanbul suffered widespread attacks, the banning of the Kurdish language, and myriad other discriminatory practices and policies targeting "non-Turks"—in its most recent guise, hysterical ultra-nationalism has become normalized. The Turkish state continues to wage a nearly twenty-five-year war against Kurdish rebels in the southeast, and a psychological war throughout the nation. With displaced Kurds heading west, Istanbul has become rife with ethnic tensions—the perfect breeding ground for paranoia. In a state that propagates its own exaltation by means of a ban on "insulting Turkishness" (Law 301), self-esteem is a shaky business, and targets for venting your own insecurity are easy to come by. Hence the assassination of Hrant Dink, an intrepid Armenian journalist convicted of 301, just two years ago—in broad daylight on a lazy day in the heart of Istanbul, nonetheless.

Together with ultra-nationalism, the post-1980 era has also seen the rise of Islamic movements, ranging from the most radical marginal groups, like Hezbollah, to the current ruling party, the "moderate conservative" Justice and Development Party (AKP). The party of a marginalized majority oppressed by the militantly secular elite cultivated by founder Mustafa Kemal Atatürk in the early years of the Republic, AKP is a nightmare-come-true for many, who believe that they will not stay "moderate" for long.

Lying at the crossroads of East and West, Istanbul belongs to neither and to both, and it is precisely this elusive in-betweenness upon which the city thrives. No matter how much blood is spilled trying to conform to Western standards, they just don't stick in this slippery city. Here, you don't break the rules, you forge a loophole through them. It is no coincidence that transvestites are generally banished to the gritty back streets of Istanbul, while one of Turkey's most popular icons is an outrageous and outspoken transsexual, cherished by families throughout the nation.

A den of sin and a bastion of virtue, Istanbul is a fog-covered playground of power and resistance, denial and repression, and if you don't know the tricks of the game, you'll likely feel the urge to abandon your marbles and go.

Some people here say that you're a true Istanbulite when you start insisting that you're leaving, but you never do. Others insist that there's no such thing as a true Istanbulite—everyone comes from somewhere, but that somewhere is never Istanbul. These clichés are perhaps testimony to this city's simultaneous push and pull, its allure—whether aesthetic, economic, mystical, inexplicable, or otherwise—and its tendency to either eradicate or repulse its own. It is a city of love and of hate, where passions ride high and often come crashing down with a vengeance.

Welcome to *Istanbul Noir:* Leave your shoes, and expectations, at the door.

Mustafa Ziyalan & Amy Spangler
Istanbul, Turkey
August 2008

PART I

LUST & VENGEANCE

THE TONGUE OF THE FLAMES

BY İSMAİL GÜZELSOY

Büyükada

How big a mistake can one possibly make? How much ruin can we possibly bring upon ourselves, our loved ones, or even strangers? Such questions would have sounded ridiculous to me when I was in my twenties. Back then, at most, you'd take a gun and empty two clips into people you didn't know from a hole in the wall. Okay, let's make that three clips. How many people can you kill at once? Or, for example, how deadly a bomb can you build on your own? That should be the true yardstick of how unhinged one is: How much havoc can you, as an individual, wreak upon the world? That was how I thought, and that was the reason, I imagine, why I was a guy who simply didn't give a damn. I was so damn sure that the highest price I'd pay for any mistake couldn't be more than my own life.

Now, as I do some soul-searching before boarding the ferry to the Princes' Islands from Sirkeci, I see how much I've changed over the last twelve years. Without understanding, or even realizing it, I have become another person all together.

I was calm and certain, as if going through the motions I went through countless times every day. As if every day I'd put in a token and pass through the turnstiles, checking over and over again whether the safety was off on the .45 caliber Beretta in my coat pocket, caressing the bag containing the painful last moments of the twelve loved ones I had lost.

I had tweaked my plans to avenge those twelve as soon as I was released from prison in my mind so many times, that by now I wasn't sure if I was living in reality, or only dreaming in the ward about the moment I'd confront the maniac responsible for their slaughter. But then, what did it matter! The truth is, there was only one clue to help me discern fantasy from reality: The setting for that scene of revenge in my dreams was a dark alley full of crime and vice, where thugs settled scores. I would imagine how he, with his graying hair, dreamy eyes, and the self-confidence of a comic book hero, would collapse at long last, his back against a wall, full of fear, finally aware that there was no escape from my wrath. The location would be a street of transvestites and pimps who knew well and good when to look the other way; when cornered in that street, Nigel's faint smirk and wistful expression would transform into a look of utter horror. Clearly understanding the end I had planned for him, he'd be able to remain standing only as long as he was leaning firmly against a wall of obscene graffiti. Finally, he would concede defeat, falling to his knees in a dirty puddle of rain.

I had been fantasizing about dozens of variations of this scenario every night, like a child who never gets tired of listening to the same fairy tale over and over. I had no choice. Then I'd plan how and where to look for him. This part worried me most of all. It was possible that Nigel, knowing my release date, had already made his escape. Yet the note he'd attached to the Polaroid that he sent with the last book (which I now kept next to the Beretta) made me think that he was as prepared and eager for the second round as I was: *Büyükada. I'm waiting for you.*

So there I was, gliding through the Sea of Marmara on

a ship rocked by a rough and humid breeze. I could see the Princes' Islands lined up in a row on the horizon, rising like the décor of a dream emerging from the fog. I thought that as I drew closer, certainly the spell would come to an end and I would be confronted with the cold reality of the island's earth. Spread over the hilly terrain of Büyükada, a dark forest shivered in the blast of harsh wind, allowing a glimpse of magnificent mansions before quickly concealing them once again. This shiny paradise that I used to visit as a child during summer vacations now stood before me in a diabolic visage, surrounded by fog and dark clouds heavy with rain. The closer I got, the better I understood why Nigel had chosen this place for our final showdown. He didn't want anyone else involved in this final reckoning. Nobody else would see us there in that little world of forests and isolated houses. We were now in the heart of nothingness. This is where we were to settle accounts. Ours was to be the confrontation of two ferocious, raging animals. Far from everyone and everything . . . But why was he dragging me all the way out here, when in his own twisted mind he'd already gotten his revenge for Xenia's death?

The death of Xenia was the result of a complicated and unfortunate game he could never buy into, he could never understand. When he was burning my loved ones alive he was righting a wrong in his mind, yet what he did indicated how hard it was for him to accept the state of things. Yes, his girlfriend Xenia was in love with me. That, essentially, was the fact he could not stomach. That was the reason why he was rubbing out my loved ones; the massacre he had carried out was not a response to my burning Xenia to death in a hotel room. I'm not fooling myself; I say it in all sincerity: The only reason Nigel killed twelve people I loved was his girlfriend's passionate love for me. If you asked him, he'd play weird games with his broken Turkish, so you'd see that his profession as an acrobat and juggler had shaped his speech too. He was an acrobat of the mind, a juggler of thought. He knew very well that he could fool others as long as he could fool himself. The way he put it thirteen years ago in Çiçek Pasajı: "If you want others to believe your lie, you first have to believe it yourself. That way you'll at least have a chance of convincing everybody else of equal intelligence." During that first lengthy conversation we had, spiced with laughter, Xenia did not look impressed by all his cunning, quasi-philosophical talk; she kept looking at me with a bored expression. You didn't have to be a genius to realize that she wasn't enjoying her lover's conversation, that she did not share the same world with him. Xenia, in stark contrast to the magnificent harmony they created on stage, was remote, disinterested, and cold to Nigel in everyday life.

When Nigel went to the bathroom, I leaned closer to the young woman and said, in way of striking up a conversation: "You don't seem to be enjoying yourself."

I expected her to say something like, *I'm a little tired*, but she kept her eyes on me for some time before finally responding: "I'm so bored of him. But that's understandable, isn't it? That I should grow tired of listening to the same joke a thousand times? Women like novelty more than men do, that's why it's the men who have always been heroes, and women the prizes."

I stared at her, my mouth agape. Back then neither Nigel nor Xenia spoke Turkish; our common language was English. I was wondering whether or not I had understood the woman correctly.

"I'm Count Dracula's homegirl, you better watch out," she said, and laughed. She placed her mouth on the red wine glass lasciviously; she puckered her lips, which were the same color as the wine, and sucked the half-full glass dry in one long sip. She closed her eyes, savoring the intense pleasure coming over her; she stayed like that for a moment, then peered at me intensely. She wasn't smiling anymore; she now looked at me with an alluring, even aggressive invitation. For an instant, her big black pupils wandered sideways; I glanced at the reflection in the windowpane. Nigel was walking back toward our table. Xenia, in a low voice, said: "You can speak Arabic, Persian, English, and Turkish. We can't possibly find anyone else like you. He is ready to pay twice as much as he offered you. Between you and me." She smiled again. She had managed to create a secret between us. And a shared secret is an invitation to further shared secrets, and sins. I was mature enough to understand that; seasoned enough to bear the consequences, however, I was not.

If I had to describe what we experienced after that night in a single word, I'd say "fun." It was a journey laced with anxiety, victory, and pleasure. Sometimes Xenia did such reckless things that I, fearful of the end of that magical dream, was compelled to rein her in. Her way of groping me, ignoring her boyfriend who stood with his back to us, planting a kiss on my lips before taking the stage, winking at me mischievously while sitting at a crowded table, well within her boyfriend's field of vision, caressing my legs under the table sometimes ... perhaps these and other dangerous games were expressions of the character traits her early Hollywood femme-fatale looks implied; but I was never as aggressive and courageous in keeping up with her as the men in those films. And that spelled doom for our relationship.

The show was to be staged in a crowded hall in Cairo. That was where I woke up from a sweet fantasy which had lasted for over a year. Nigel was moving about on the stage and in the hall in a fakir costume; he was levitating and performing some improvised exotic dance. Xenia would take the stage the moment the clarinet solo started. She'd be standing in front of the mirror which would convey the images, because the first few minutes of the show consisted of reflections. The audience would see her as an image appearing and disappearing at different spots of the stage. She'd wear a modernized version of a harem outfit, a bustier gilded with gold leaves, showcasing her fair skin with stunning generosity, and a flowing skirt, covered with glittering scales. Every time she made her entrance in that costume, an odd silence would fall over the audience, followed by deafening applause. We were used to it. Xenia was an angel, an image, an apparition which would disappear at once and materialize again somewhere else in the hall, only to disappear again. But that night when her turn came, Xenia did not go out in front of the conveyor mirror.

Suddenly the music stopped. Nigel came over to where we were. He glared at his girlfriend, who had grabbed me by the collar and was manhandling me. "What's going on here?" he asked. Just as the woman was parting her lips to say something, a deafening, defiant roar rose from the audience.

I quickly took advantage of that window of opportunity. "She's having cramps and asked me for a painkiller."

I didn't know how much of the lie Nigel believed, but he silently turned around, stepped onto the platform where his conveyor mirror was, and said, "We'll start over. Please find a more appropriate time and place to take your painkiller." His voice, strangely enough, didn't sound angry. Nevertheless, I decided to be more careful from then on and to warn Xenia that she should do the same.

As it turned out, however, I didn't have to. She managed to stay away from me for eight days following our show in Cairo. She preferred to sit next to her boyfriend, somewhere far away from me, to avoid looking at me, to avoid my eyes, all the while aware that they were on her. It seemed the love affair between the two of them had been revived. Xenia laughed with exaggeration, hugged and kissed him time and again even when Nigel was carrying on with his tasteless jokes like he had when I first met them.

As you see, everything I've told you so far fits the mold of Hollywood melodramas. I can tell you now that the rest won't be any different. At least, up until a particular point. That point is also the turning point of my short and pathetic adventure, which started with my trying to talk to Xenia backstage before a show in Jordan.

"We have nothing to talk about, I won't have anything to do with a coward like you," she said, before pushing me aside with her elbow and strutting over to the conveyor mirror platform. I followed her.

"We work together, so we should interact in a civilized manner, even if it will end soon!" I was shouting.

"Okay, so what do you want?" She had raised her voice too.

"Come to my room tonight. We should talk."

"No, I can't be alone with you."

I reached out and grabbed her arm; in the same instant the spotlight came on. Following some confusion, people in the audience started laughing. My arm and part of my face had become visible next to her.

"Let go! What are you doing? You'll ruin the show," she said.

"Tonight . . ."

"Okay," she said.

"Promise?"

"Yes! Now go," she said and started her dance. Everything was ruined.

Nigel's headaches had started again. I didn't mind much when I heard him whispering to Xenia backstage, "It's time we found someone to replace this guy."

Whenever Nigel had a headache, he withdrew to his room and occupied himself with bookbinding. He kept saying that he came from five generations of Hungarian bookbinders, bragging about it at every opportunity. Though I couldn't really appreciate his craft, I did derive a strange kind of pleasure from the books he bound, as if I was touching some sort of sacred relic. While working as an illusionist, he bound books of various sizes in his spare time, to keep in practice so that down the road he could teach his yet-to-be-born son the fine art, and thus keep the family trade from dying out. Most importantly, I recall him explaining that this occupation was the perfect remedy for a headache. I recall him saying to Xenia once: "Why on earth do you take those stupid painkillers? We should just bind books together."

That night Xenia came to my room for a few short minutes. "I can't leave Nigel alone. Let's talk in Istanbul tomorrow," she said, and then she quickly made her way, barefoot, across the hardwood floor of the hotel, back to her room down the hall.

We were in Istanbul the next day. There was a knock on the door, so faint that at first I wasn't even sure that's what it was. It was careful, reminiscent of the light footsteps on the hardwood floors in the hallway. I emptied my glass of *rakı* at once; there was another knock. It was Xenia.

She was talking with a raised eyebrow; I was trying to listen to her. I perceived what she said as disconnected words, not as a meaningful whole. I recalled images from the night she had come to my room for the first time. Scenes from our games, games she had played with increasing audacity. Now, she had knocked on my door cautiously, she was telling me what a knucklehead I was, she was going on and on about me not having the balls to face the fact that some things were finished. Perhaps she only said it once, but I kept spinning her words in my head and developed the impression that she was repeating the same thing over and over again. I was contemplating the shadows on her face. It was like watching a riveting thriller: The intimacy I once saw in those shapely eyes was fading away shade by shade, being replaced by an aggressive, shrill, even enraged, façade. The skin of Xenia's face was cracking, peeling away like topsoil in drought and yielding to the features of an ugly, cruel mythological beast.

I wanted to say, *Oh, my Xenia, even if we have to finish everything, let's do it gently; we may hurt each other, but let's not ruin all those beautiful moments.* Or something like that. Instead, a snarl escaped my lips: "You must die!"

My voice scared even me. You would perhaps deem me completely crazy if I told you what happened next, using the same words, in the same order that I did during my interrogation. In fact, the district attorney argued that I was acting the part. I can say this much: What I said and did from that moment on had nothing to do with the person I have been historically. Yes, I believe that the human being lives his or her own life as a historical subject. Every moment builds on the one before. Life progresses like the words, sentences, paragraphs, chapters in a meaningful text. Every time I recall what I did to Xenia, I believe in retrospect that I experienced a strange fracture in the flow of my life, the way we pause at an expression at odds with the flow of a text.

I wasn't the one who opened the petroleum lamp on the bed stand and hurled the liquid on her. I wasn't the one who screamed, "You've been a witch, and now you should be punished like one, you cunt!" I wasn't the one who took his lighter out of his pocket, all the while savoring the lines of horror breaking out on her face. I wasn't the one who swung the burning lighter, catching the flame on her dress. I wasn't the demon who dashed out and held the door shut as she, engulfed in flames, ran around in a frenzy. Or perhaps it was me, releasing the flames of the hell now in charge of my rage. I made a mistake; just once in my life, I made a mistake.

I was so sure the smell of burnt flesh, hair, and nylon was coming from my own private hell that I casually took out a cigarette once she had ceased trying to force the door. I remember. I was surprised not to find the lighter in its usual place, in my right pocket, and considered for the first time the possibility that these things were true, that they had happened outside my own private dark world, somewhere within this nightmare called life. I remember. I was walking backwards down the hallway, trying to understand the uneasy mutterings of the crowd gathering close by, trying to piece together a meaningful whole from whatever they were saying. That, I remember. The rest, I don't. I don't remember that I ran under pouring rain for hours, wandering with a soggy, disintegrating cigarette between my lips before finally returning to the hotel. I don't remember being arrested and put in a hospital. The next thing I remember is how someone with a long face and matty hair questioned me, keeping his deep and glinting eyes on me the whole time: "Why did you burn her?"

* * *

Nigel visited me two months after I went to prison. He looked as calm as ever, but a little worn out. He stared at me, motionless, for some time. When he parted his lips, as if struggling to talk, lines formed on his forehead and around his eyes.

"Why did you kill her?" he asked.

I had lost everything. I didn't owe him anything. I annihilated something which belonged as much to me as it did to him. I smiled.

"You watched the trial; everything was discussed there, everything I did was reported in the papers, with details even I wasn't aware of. What more do you want to know?"

"You owe me. A lot." He said this in Turkish. Although not on the same par with Xenia, Nigel too was very adept at learning languages.

"What do you think I'm doing here? I'm paying my debts," I said, smiling.

"I'm talking about what you owe *me*, not the ones running this world," he shot back, once again in excellent Turkish.

"It's all the same to me. I've lost everything. There's nothing more I can give you."

"You haven't lost everything; there is always something more to lose. Just wait. You'll see," he said. He walked away before I had the chance to truly consider his words.

Three months after that visit I received the first book. Similar to the books previously bound by Nigel, it contained thirty-six pages in a sturdy binder. The binder and the pages were made of Moroccan leather or very delicate deer hide. *One More Thing To Lose: Volume I* was written on its cover. In it were depicted the painful moments of someone's life and, on the last two pages, the person's murder and cremation in his own home. Each of the pictures occupied almost the whole surface of a page and was accompanied by a few words about the person. I thought it wasn't terribly meaningful to rack my brain over these puzzling words, which at first appeared odd and nonsensical; I put the strange volume in my suitcase. A few days later, I remembered the drawings in that book when I got the news that that my childhood friend İlhan had burned to death in his house.

I reported the matter in a letter to the district attorney with the long face and matty hair. He was good at what he did. He investigated the incident with a meticulousness that was hard to come by in those years, interviewed Nigel, and decided not to press charges. I don't know what Nigel told him, how he convinced him of his innocence, but I can't forget those four words the prison director said when he brought me the news: "He proved his innocence." It was that simple. This couldn't be the price for a crime I had committed in a fit of madness. İlhan was totally innocent here. Why on earth did Nigel kill him?

I became obsessed with reaching Nigel. It was so unfair to expect an inmate to track down an avenger roaming free outside. There were just a few things I wanted to say to him. When I wrote those down, I realized that whatever I wanted to tell him was exactly the answer to the question he had asked when paying that visit to me. How about telling him why I killed his girlfriend? The guilt that I felt for İlhan's death weighed heavily upon me.

Just as I was finally beginning to readjust to everyday life, quieting my conscience and soothing my injured ego after months of agony, a new book arrived. It was delivered to me on the anniversary of Xenia's death. Again, drawings and red ink on delicate deer hide or Moroccan leather. This time I instantly recognized the warm face of my first serious girlfriend. In spite of all those years, the curling lips, arched nose, and slightly crossed eyes of Zeynep, my first love, left no room for doubt. In the following nightmarish days I read the papers, listened to the radio, and lived in fear. It didn't take long: Zeynep had been found in her house, dead. She was charred.

I wrote to the district attorney again. I pointed out the similarity between the ways and the dates upon which Zeynep and Xenia had died. I argued that Nigel was seeking revenge and therefore punishing the people I loved in the same way that I had killed Xenia. Two weeks later the district attorney came to see me and reported that Nigel couldn't possibly have had anything to do with this crime; he had proven that he was performing on stage at the time of the murder. Astonished, I asked the district attorney, "How could you determine the time of death for a charred corpse?" He went through the files he had and hastily read the statements of three witnesses. The super of the building, a shopkeeper of the neighborhood, and Zeynep's husband, a captain, had all given testimonies clarifying the time of death.

As the district attorney was trying to convince me, I told him about the tricks Nigel performed with mirrors. I told him about how Nigel was able to project his image onto mirrors and thus appear in more than one spot on the stage. The district attorney rolled the pastel-colored folder in his left hand up into a scroll and with his right gave his knee a forceful and impatient slap; he stood up and cut me off. "Don't worry, I watched his performance three times. Even if he is doing all of it with mirrors, for him to go from Taksim to Vezneciler, to kill Zeynep, and not only that, but to burn her and then return ... how should I say it ... is next to impossible. I even arranged for a demonstration to test it. If we brought the suspect in front of a judge, he'd be released after the first hearing."

He had said his last sentence from outside the bars.

I was hopeless, helpless, and shattered. Two people I loved had been killed in the last two years because of me.

For twelve years I was forced to look on as twelve people from my life were slaughtered, all in the same way, all on the same date. Every time there was a book and there were evidence and witnesses resisting the efforts of the district attorney's office. No matter how hard I tried to get him to come, Nigel refused to see me. I swallowed my pride and sent him imploring letters, begging for forgiveness. Every time, I promised to punish myself if he'd just stop harming my loved ones. If only he would stay away from them. I tried to burn myself after the sixth murder. I had only burn marks to show for it, going from my right cheek down my neck, to my left shoulder and flank. At the end of the twelfth year, five weeks ago, that last book arrived. Drawings and words of the last living person who meant anything to me: my beloved sister, Safiye. This time there was also a Polaroid in the book, with the caption: *Büyükada. I'm waiting for you.* The photograph showed an art nouveau kiosk.

Four carriage drivers, huddling by the entrance of the coffee-house to avoid the rain, were looking at the photograph. The noise of the backgammon and rummikub games in full swing in the coffeehouse was drowned out by occasional thunder; sporadic lightning illuminated the horses on their sorrowful watch. Finally, an old driver piped up, "I know this house. It's where that foreigner stays. Toward Maden." The other drivers agreed, conceding those fateful words like the performers in an ancient tragedy. One offered a cigarette to another, and the third threw me a furtive glance before stepping into the cof-feehouse. "Let me take you there," said the old driver.

It was almost dark. We were rattling along a road under clouds blanketing the sky in increasingly darker shades of
gray. There in the green, dark forest, I thought each and every
one of the mansions, rising like ancient temples with their
pointy towers there beyond the large gardens along the shore,
must be the house where I was to meet Nigel. The dull lights
of Sedef Island were visible now. We and the weary horses
continued down the forest path, which was lit by a dirty yellow light. The waves crashing against the shore, the screams
of the seagulls, and a dog howling from afar were the only
sounds to be heard. Except for the rhythmic pattern of the
hooves flowing like a cover of fog into the hills. There was so
little left of the hullabaloo of summer; the lustrous, colorful
begonias had faded to the color of earth. The yellow leaves of
the plane trees blanketed the asphalt and the gardens of the
barren mansions, their paint swelling and cracking, covered
in wild ivy. Büyükada would wait motionlessly like a cursed,
angry, abandoned old man, wrinkled with loneliness, until the
spring, when the voluntary exiles escaping the chaos of Istanbul returned. The carriage ride felt as long and exhausting as
my entire prison sentence.

I had reached the very pinnacle of my desire to face Nigel
and avenge my loved ones he had slaughtered.

"Get off here and walk up that trail. The horses can't go
down there in this weather," the old driver said.

The moment I opened the door, the lights went out. I took a
few more steps into the pitch black. Nigel appeared. He was
just in front of me. We were facing off, like two gunslingers.
Then, another Nigel appeared out of the darkness. Then another. Then others. Each one was doing and saying something
different. When I listened closely, I understood that the ram-

bling narratives were the last words of my loved ones. Each Nigel was repeating, deadpan, the last words of another soul mate of mine.

"You have improved your technique," I said in a growl.

As the voices of those eleven Nigels faded away, the Nigel in the middle, just in front of me, took a few weighty steps, as if underwater, and spoke: "I improved not only my technique, but the content of the show as well. Seeing as we're speaking the same language now . . ."

"If you mean Turkish, fine, but you and I couldn't possibly have another language in common," I said.

"We share something else. No matter how much you may deny it, we are both keepers of the secrets of the fire, its purifying effects, its uncanny allure, its geometry. But this is the only knowledge its keeper can't convey. If you watch the fire very closely, you see that it's telling you something. You're mesmerized, and gradually the fire starts conversing with you. You crack the mystery, but can't teach it to anyone else. You are the keeper of a message so profound and poetic that it has no equivalent in any earthly tongue. We both know that now. Our common tongue is that we know the burning and purifying effects of the flame."

I dropped the bag with the books of my eleven loved ones. As it hit the floor, I removed the gun I had in my pocket next to Safiye's book, and fired. Blood spurted from three spots on Nigel's chest. He collapsed to the floor, squirming. The other Nigels were looking on, just as astonished as I was, as the man writhed. As soon as Nigel died, the images became less clear. I was searching for a light switch when a wall light on the upper floor came on and Nigel appeared once again.

"Sometimes, it is impossible to fully grasp the good or evil of your deeds, of what you've done to someone. You judge everything according to your own standards. This is the most ridiculous thing about our world. There is a price for a bottle of water. You pay and buy it. Yet to somebody else it may not mean what it means to you. It means the world to somebody about to die in the desert. In a fit of jealousy, you burnt alive a woman who you considered your plaything, but I lost the meaning of my life."

I fired again. Nigel died again, writhing in pain, again. He showed up again, spoke again of his pain. I fired again.

I loaded the gun and killed Nigel eleven times.

I had only one bullet left. I asked if he burnt Safiye. He smiled. "I sent all your friends and relatives to you. You didn't receive them? Damn! And I paid so much in bribe money!" I dropped him with my last bullet. There was a thud on the floor this time.

I picked up the bag and took the slippery trail, grasping at the puny trees that lined it. Lightning struck and I saw the blood seeping from my coat pocket. When I reached the streetlamp at the end of Maden, I took out Safiye's book. That's when it dawned on me: The pages I thought were Moroccan leather were in fact human skin, and the red ink, the blood of my loved ones. This was the first time I was walking under rain with the book, the first time I was touching the smooth, slippery surface of the wet pages.

I listened to the words of the melancholy Rebetiko song on the dock. The scent of rakı, the voices of those passionately discussing the horse races at the shore coffeehouse, the pale images of those stunningly beautiful mansions lined along the back of Nizam could not reach me. I was getting lost somewhere very, very far away, too distant for anyone to reach.

Thus Nigel managed to burn me twelve more times. Even after death. Now I understood what it meant, "the secret tongue of the flames." We walk this earth with a seed of fire within us, an infectious fire lit by a simple spark, a fire that never goes out, a fire that spreads and contaminates with a strange geometry, until it rages everywhere. There are twelve books on my shelves, twelve books I'll never ever again dare to open.

Now they've locked me up here because I was trying to feel the pain of the fourteen people I killed by putting out cigarettes on my chest. They are giving me drugs in all the colors of the rainbow; the drugs are supposed to stop my mind from working. I test the power of the fire on my body whenever I can. I smile at those who try to stop me. This is the only thing in the world that they can't possibly stop: Fire, it's everywhere. They can't keep me from touching it. But they don't know that yet.

I approach one of the visitors. "Could you give me a cigarette? They won't let me smoke here. Could you light it and give it to me, please?" Then I go to the bathroom. As I touch the concealed parts of my body with fire, I turn the bloody pages of the library in my mind; I read Nigel's books. As the smell of burnt flesh reaches my nose, I release the flames that rise from my own personal hell.

Gradually, I understand why people once worshiped fire. I hear the screams of the nurses. I worship fire.

HITCHING IN THE *LODOS*

BY FERYAL TİLMAÇ

Bebek

Perhaps all of this still would have happened, even if the city hadn't been caught up in the tempestuous lodos that night. But the truth is, that frantic wind, spinner of its own mysteries, provided justifiable motive for transgression. Strange, droning, lukewarm, the lodos keeps in its thrall not only the city, but the souls of its people as well. And Cavidan Altan was one of those people. Perhaps what would occur later hadn't even remotely crossed her mind when she left home that day. I say "perhaps," because we can never know for sure what's on a woman's mind. Now, I could pretend that I knew, but I don't want to taint the authenticity of the story by adding to it something I'm not sure about. We can safely assume the same about Tolga Güçel, and say that he, too, never would have guessed that he would experience the things he did that evening, or any other evening, for that matter.

Tolga is a computer engineer in his thirties. A few years ago, he left the company he had been working for to start his own business with a friend. They install data processing systems for companies and provide support services and solutions. Of course, he is an intelligent man—he must be, right? He's a person of high moral standards and principles, a man who likes to do things by the book. He's not married, but he has a girlfriend, a woman he met at his last job. They share a home, though theirs is a constant rollercoaster of break-up and make-up. Yes, that's right, yet another case of passion's demise and habitual routine on the rise! He works in Gayrettepe, lives in Etiler. On the evening in question, in spite of the heavy end-of-the-year workload, he had managed to leave early, thinking he might stop by Akmerkez on his way home and buy a New Year's gift for his girlfriend. A white cashmere sweater, an elegant laptop bag, or a bottle of perfume—he was still undecided. But then, what difference does it make anyway? Considering that, ultimately, he would buy none of these.

That evening on his way home from work, as he passed Zincirlikuyu and made a right onto the road to Levent, he was listening to the radio program *Women Sing Jazz*. "*Dear listeners, we continue with Ethel Waters's 'Stormy Weather'* . . ." There couldn't have been a more fitting selection. He tapped along on the steering wheel. The invasive wind whistled and shook the colored lights on the trees. Who knows, maybe everything would have panned out in another way if the weather had been different; say, if it had been snowing. After all, the New Year spirit calls for snow; and for love, hope, new beginnings, packages of presents, angels hanging on trees, the cinnamon-spiced scent of mulled wine. But it didn't happen, it didn't snow. Instead, a crazy, wayward wind kept the area convulsing for days on end, making the city slave to its whim. Though the majority suffered only mild headaches and a little shortness of breath in its aftermath, at the time, melancholy ran like a viscous liquid through the streets.

Tolga, for his part, did something he never would have done otherwise: Compelled by the sorrowful music and the feeling of benevolence that the New Year's spirit aroused, he pulled up to the curb, where a woman with shopping bags was trying to flag down a taxi. The woman, Cavidan *Hanım*, had just finished her shopping at the mall in Levent. On the window behind her, *2007* was written in cotton balls, and adorned with wreaths of mistletoe, yellow, green, and red lights, gold-lacquered pinecones, and red stars. She was a woman of a certain maturity; she held her hand in front of her face as she tried to protect herself from the wind. Perhaps hitching a ride wasn't her intention at all. Still, when she stooped and saw Tolga, she opened the back door, dropped her bags in the car, and settled onto the passenger seat without hesitation. Obviously she was cold, otherwise why on earth would she have plunged headlong into a stranger's car, especially at that hour?

While we were in Tolga's car, making our way from Levent to Gayrettepe, Cavidan Hanım was checking off items on her shopping list. She had bought a different washing detergent, something other than her usual brand, because it came with a free bottle of fabric softener. The thin peel of the tangerines had not been to her taste, and so she picked up some oranges and a few green apples instead. A bag of sliced whole-wheat bread, tahini halva, and petit beurre biscuits. Aged *kaşar* cheese, napkins, and ginger for the New Year's cookies she was planning to bake. In a last-minute dash, she had added olive oil, clotted cream, and fresh walnuts to her cart at the checkout. She realized that she couldn't possibly carry those heavy bags all the way home, and so she had decided to wait for a cab. It should therefore come as no surprise that she jumped into the car as soon as Tolga stopped. *He's young enough to be my son*, she might have thought as she got into the car. I'm not sure if I told you: Tolga has the kind of face that puts even the most jittery of people at ease.

As soon as she was in the car, Cavidan Hanım removed her beret and scarf. She swung her hips left and then right, settling into the seat and making herself comfortable. She also made sure to turn and take a good look at Tolga. He was a young man with a fair complexion, clean shaven, with longish brown hair and glasses perched on an arched nose. Cavidan Hanım didn't know much about automobiles, but still, judging from the smell of fresh leather rising from the black seats and the wooden details of the dashboard, this had to be a luxury car. Her savior, she guessed, was probably a successful young businessman. He must have been at least twenty years younger than her; Cavidan wondered if he was married. She glanced to see if he had a ring on his left hand, but her view was blocked. Tolga's fingers had stopped tapping and now clung to the steering wheel. If it hadn't been so dark inside, she could have seen how white his knuckles were. Wishing she were at least ten years younger, Cavidan Hanım let out a sigh. Fortunately, it was drowned out by the sound of the radio. *"Dear jazz fans, our program continues with Billie Holiday: 'Long Gone Blues' . . ."*

Tolga's fingers relaxed and started tapping again. "So you're a jazz fan," Cavidan Hanım said, in an attempt to make conversation. Tolga looked at her for the first time, smiled, nodded, and then turned his attention back to the road. "If you drop me off in front of Akmerkez, I can walk from there." A sudden gush of wind rattled the windshield, and shook the car even, or so it seemed to them.

"With all those bags? Out of the question! I'll drive you to your door."

The young man's polite, soft-spoken manner emboldened the woman. "I love going to the shore and watching the sea during the lodos. How about you?"

Oh no! thought Tolga to himself, wishing to rein the conversation back in. But he didn't let on. "I don't know, I never have."

As a veteran school teacher, Cavidan Hanım knew a thing or two about human psychology. This young man was clearly a victim of politeness, one of those poor souls incapable of saying no. "I'm an English teacher," she continued. "Could I possibly have had you in my class? You look familiar." She didn't mention that she was retired. She had read somewhere that the word "retired" immediately killed any spark. It reminded one of the smell of dust, wool underwear, weatherproof socks, dentures leisurely soaking in a glass at night ..."

"Oh please, I really don't think you're old enough to have been my teacher!" So she was a teacher; he should be more respectful.

Cavidan Hanım's tiny giggle drowned out the sorrowful notes coming from the radio. "Thank you, that's the nicest thing anyone's said to me in a long time."

They were in front of Akmerkez now. Tolga slowed down. A brass band was playing a merry dance tune. *Post Brass Band* was written on their red jackets. Was that what encouraged Cavidan Hanım? "How about going to the seaside? If you have time, that is."

The young man thought he must have misheard her. Cymbals were clashing, countless sticks were banging on drums, and a trumpet blared proudly, as the band battled the bellowing of the lodos. Is that what confused Tolga? "Do you have a certain place in mind?"

Cavidan Hanım gladly shut the door she had been reluctantly holding ajar. "Yes, drive straight ahead; let's go down the Bebek Slope." The jolly tunes of the brass band gradually faded away. "Cavidan," she said. It was a strange meeting, but she didn't care; she extended her hand.

"Tolga," he responded. It would be rude not to shake her hand; he realized his palms were sweaty and felt embarrassed.

The car jerked and jolted, making slow progress in the bumper-to-bumper traffic. Etiler, with its colorful, bright cafés, restaurants, and stores lining the avenue, was drowning out even the noise of the lodos.

"Would you stop at that corner?" Cavidan Hanım hopped out with the agility of a young girl, ducked into a liquor store, and returned with a black plastic bag full of beer cans.

Surprised, the young man remained optimistic. *Maybe she's planning on drinking them at home tonight,* he thought. *Maybe she's expecting guests.* He made a left turn and drove down the slope. If he hadn't turned, he could have seen his girlfriend buying flowers from a stand by the corner one street down; after all, their place was just a stone's throw away. The slope was completely dark, except for the headlights of passing cars and the blinking New Year's ornaments on the walls of the houses.

Cavidan Hanım took the sights in with a happy smile on her face. All kinds of fantasies played out in her head as she watched the dark retaining walls flow by. *All things considered,* she thought, *I'm lucky to live in this city.*

Tolga was uneasy. He had gone beyond the call of courtesy, and besides, what would he say if his girlfriend called? He could turn off his phone and tell her something like, *I was in Akmerkez, the reception was bad,* but that was hardly believable. His inner voice nagged away at him. (He was right, his girlfriend was worried. She had called his office, and they'd told her he'd already left. She'd thought about calling his cell a few times, and she almost did, and in the end, she would certainly call. Where would a grown man disappear to for so many hours?) And as if all that weren't enough already, Ella Fitzgerald had launched into another song: "Baby, Won't You Please Come Home?"

They hit traffic again once they reached the shore. The car slowed down. "Turn left, toward Aşiyan." Cavidan Hanım seemed to be in total control now. She cracked open a can of beer for herself. "Sorry, *you're* driving." At that moment, the young man felt certain this was all just one big nightmare. His knuckles were visibly white, even in the dim light. Truth of the matter was, though, this was only the beginning—he had no idea what was in store for him.

The car obediently cruised forward toward their destination. The young man turned and stopped in front of Bebek Park. Just like every evening, the Bebek meatball vendor was setting up his stand in his white minivan, in spite of the contrary weather. Cavidan Hanım took advantage of their time in stalled traffic to look around, and she did so with gusto. It was crowded, as usual; even in this weather, all the benches in the park were occupied. Cavidan Hanım took a sizable sip from her beer; it had a sour, acidic taste, and she shivered a little as she swallowed. She reached for the bags on the backseat and took out a package: fresh walnuts. She silently congratulated herself; a prescient last-minute purchase, as it were. This time she offered some to her companion. The traffic stirred a little. They barely made it past the taxi stand in front of the Bebek Café when they had to stop again. The lodos did not seem to have impacted the hotel or the seafood restaurants here one bit. The valets were constantly stopping traffic to make way for the cars of customers coming and going. Tolga was quietly eating the walnuts Cavidan Hanım kept offering to him, after removing their delicate shells. She was sure no one had skinned or shelled or peeled anything for this boy and handed it to him, ready to eat, since he was a kid. Now he was smiling too. Finally, the valet impatiently motioned for them to drive on through. *"Dear listeners, how about another tune from Ethel*

Waters? The woman says it ain't her fault—she's just living her life! That's right, Ethel Waters here and 'Don't Blame Me' . . ."

They passed Bebek Hotel, Starbucks, Divan Bakery, and then the grocery store. Even if the whole world were to go haywire, the colorful fruit-packed trays of that grocery store would be enough to restore the illusion that everything was A-OK. Cavidan Hanım, turning to her right, pointed to the olive oil specialty shop and asked: "Have you ever shopped there?"

"No," said Tolga, laughing.

Brightly lit windows, the headlights of standing cars, people going in and out of restaurants and liquor stores on both sides all blended together into one big blur; a single, gigantic organism quivering in the wind. They stopped again, where the waterfront houses ended and the sea began. The coats and the scarves of people crossing the avenue were flying in the wind. An old man laughed as he pressed down on his fedora. *Now* that's *a retiree*, Cavidan Hanım thought. She was happy, giddy; she'd never felt younger. The whistle of the lodos blew in one window and out the other.

An increasingly contented Tolga pointed to a man selling fish on the shore. "Beautiful, isn't it? How bright and colorful they are, even in this weather . . . Do you like fish?" he asked.

Cavidan Hanım looked at the round wooden trays on the stand and the neat rows of pink, white, and silvery fish displayed on them. Lamps and bundles of garlic suspended from the poles above the vendors' carts swung to and fro in the wind. The fish seller was sprinkling water on lettuce, garden cress, radishes, and lemons. "Yes, I do. I like it a lot, in fact. And how about you? Do you like snapper soup? Red snapper? I should make it for you someday."

"My mom makes delicious snapper soup." As soon as the

words came out of his mouth, the young man knew he had said something wrong; he clammed up.

Cavidan Hanım pretended she hadn't heard him. What was the point of embarrassing the poor boy? He already regretted having said it anyway. "I just learned how to make it. But Pygmy loves it."

Curious, Tolga asked: "Pygmy?"

"My cat. She loves my snapper soup." She laughed again. "She's so black, I bet you'd be scared of her if you saw her in the dark; she walks around like a pair of bodiless green eyes."

"Come on, why would I be afraid? I'm sure she's adorable . . ."

Beaten black-and-blue by the wind, the sea churned and foamed. The bus in front of them let out a hiss as it lurched forward, and they followed. Launched from the terrace of one of the seafront houses, an umbrella, a remnant from summer, blew over the road and toward the water. Spared, by the grace of God! The incident brought them closer; it was that special affinity shared by people who have survived an accident together. Just then the young man's cell phone started ringing.

"What's that, Pınar? . . . Yes, I left early, I had a few errands . . . To Akmerkez . . . To buy a present for Mom . . . Unbelievable . . . I couldn't find anything . . . What's that? . . . Pınar, can I call you a little later? I can't hear you . . ." He felt obliged to offer an explanation: "My girlfriend."

Cavidan Hanım found an excuse for joy in this revelation; so he wasn't married after all! "She was worried, I suppose. I can't blame her, I'd be worried about you too." Was that a spark of desire she saw in his eyes? No, it couldn't be, she must be mistaken.

"Should we keep going? Is there any particular place you'd like to stop?" For the first time in his life he felt the comfort of being with an assertive woman, a woman in charge, a woman who made decisions for him. But then, there were many firsts in store for him that evening. Feeling submissive to the core, he waited for an answer.

"There's a parking lot by the water, across from the grave-yard. Let's go there. It's always deserted after dark." The traffic abated. She unzipped the jacket of her jogging suit a little further, just to get some air. The medallion hanging from her neck glinted for a brief second, catching the young man's eye; Cavidan Hanım promptly took notice. The lodos was blowing through the giant trees along the roadside.

Now that they had left the noisy traffic behind, the sound of the radio came to the fore: *"We've reached the end of tonight's program, dear listeners. We leave you until tomorrow—same time, same place—with Lena Horne and 'Mad about the Boy'..."*

Cavidan Hanım felt a tingling in her loins. Don't tell me to give you a break; I'm a human being, and I know human beings have a tendency to lose it every now and then. Actually, it was pretty understandable. She'd never really had much of a sex life, other than a few rather tasteless flings with colleagues, and that was so far in the past now, her conspirators had faded into pale ghosts of her imagination. And throughout those long years, whenever she attempted to satisfy the urges of her body by herself, leaning against the cold walls of her shower stall, it wasn't those inadequate lovers but her male students that she fantasized about. She loved the way they smelled so fresh, how their voices still cracked, their unruly attitudes, and their black-haired arms peeking out from rolled-up sleeves; she loved it all, at least as much as she loved this city. She threw her head back, draining the can of beer in her hand. She'd grown silent, perhaps out of shame for her thoughts.

Tolga slowed down next to the cemetery, turned on his

right-turn signal, and then parked by the water. The head-lights illuminated the sea one last time before going out; the seagulls, caught in the circles of light, flitted about the sky like giant snowflakes.

"I can have a beer now, too, can't I?"

Without breaking her silence, Cavidan Hanım reached down into the black plastic bag next to her foot. She took out a can, opened it, and handed it to the young man. She had avoided his eyes. The jazz program ended, and Tolga switched the radio off. For a while, they just sat there, listening to the wind howling wildly.

I keep referring to the wind, I know, and perhaps you find it annoying, but there's no way around it, because for me it's the main character of the story. It was bolting through the sky in fits of madness, lunging down and surging back up, send-ing shivers through the evening lights, absorbing the familiar sounds of the city into its own roar. It dried lips, hurled any-thing and everything that failed to match its strength, weighed down upon souls, made skin crawl. Tolga sipped on his beer, contemplating Cavidan Hanım's profile, while she contem-plated the seagulls lowering themselves toward the sea. One wonders what was on their minds just then. But then, it's not hard to guess. Perhaps a jumble of thoughts coursed through Tolga's mind—how he could possibly explain this delay to his girlfriend; his eleventh grade English teacher; the fact that he had to buy a present for his mother; how awful it would be to be out at sea in this weather; whether or not Cavidan Hanım's medallion was in fact a locket, and if there was a picture in it; his girlfriend again; his mother again; even the project he'd turned in that day, and the likelihood of its suc-cess. Though these may not have been his exact thoughts, they were certainly something along those lines. He didn't try to focus on anything in particular, and that was comforting to him somehow.

He leaned back in his seat, took a big gulp from his beer, and got lost in thought again. He was back to pondering the matter of the presents; in fact, he was on the verge of actually making a decision. And he would have, for sure, if only he hadn't felt Cavidan Hanım's hand settle onto his crotch just then. At least he had finally eliminated the perfume, narrowing his options down to two: either the laptop bag or the cashmere sweater.

"Do you mind if I touch you?" she asked nonchalantly, as though asking if she could roll down the window. Moreover, she went ahead and began unzipping the young man's pants, without even waiting for an answer. And unzip them she did.

Tolga looked in amazement at the fingers pulling at his boxer shorts. *Would it be rude to ask her to take her hands off of me?* he wondered. His manhood, though, growing beneath the woman's touch, was betraying him. But she just wanted to feel around a little, right? It was hardly the end of the world now, was it? He slid down a little, made himself more comfortable. The woman's hand was brushing over the heat of his flesh; she had lowered her head and was scrutinizing the thing in her hands with the curiosity of a child observing an insect. Tolga grew uneasy and glanced around. There wasn't another person or car in sight. He tried not to think about the cemetery that extended up the hill on the other side of the road. He cleared his throat and, in a voice he thought sounded normal, asked, "Would you like me to turn on the radio?"

"Oh yes," said Cavidan Hanım, "but find another jazz program, will you?" She lowered her head and began stroking him again, picking up where she'd left off.

His hands shaking, the young man turned the radio on

and tuned in to a jazz station. The sound of a rebellious, unrepentant saxophone filled the car. Had to be John Coltrane.

At that moment, Cavidan Hanım lowered her head further and took the young man's penis into her mouth. I know, it sounds almost pornographic when I put it like this, but these things are just a part of life, they come so naturally. And as long as I'm telling you the whole story, why should I succumb to puritanical pressures and skip the details? Okay, so what was Cavidan Hanım thinking all this time? Well, first of all, she was wondering why on earth she had never done this before, and thinking how many more things there were that she had never done before, and how the world was just full of things she had never done before . . . She was intrigued by the taste; he must be a clean man, she thought, because she couldn't detect even the faintest scent of urine. Curious, with the tip of her tongue she touched the clear fluid oozing from the tip of the penis; perhaps it was due to the aftertaste of beer in her mouth, but she found it to be rather sour. She cleansed her tongue on the shaft of the young man's manhood, which was as hard as it could possibly get by now. Its skin, wrinkled at first, was now stretched tight, as if a larva inside was struggling to escape.

Tolga placed his can next to the gearshift. His hands were in the woman's black hair now.

Cavidan Hanım raised her head and peered up at him. Ignoring the pressure gently pushing down on her head, she sat up. She slipped out of her jogging pants with some difficulty, as she wasn't used to doing this sort of thing. Bodies always seemed to grow larger inside cars, somehow. She kicked off her shoes, letting them drop next to the black plastic bag. She tugged on her panties until she'd peeled herself free. The rebellious notes of John Coltrane mingling with the whistle of the wind and merging with their wetness, Cavidan Hanım climbed onto the young man's lap. She carefully gripped his manhood and placed it between her legs.

For Cavidan Hanım, the young man ceased to exist. For her, there were only the seagulls, radiant against the blackness of the night, the strokes of blue and gray against the canvas of pitch black waters, the sea in its bubbling turbulence, the hell of the lodos. She didn't notice how Tolga reached and un-zipped her top and removed it. Only when he reached around for the clasp of her bra did she move to help him. She had only her socks and her medallion on now. Her breasts, made soft by time, sagging, defeated by the pull of gravity, lunged forward with yearning and met the young man's mouth. She was rising and falling; she was taking the whole city in. This wasn't an ordinary coupling. She imagined the city's skyline, and went mad with desire. The manhood between her legs was every skyscraper of the city, symbolic bastions of power with blue-tinted windows, and crowns disappearing into heavy, low-lying clouds. That manhood was every intricate street she loved to stroll through, from Beyoğlu to Tünel. As she rose and fell, she whispered Istanbul's name. The young man held onto her hips tightly, trying to help her keep her rhythm. That manhood was the winter evenings falling early on the city, the smell of roasted chestnuts, smog, happy lights of do-mestic bliss, dim streetlamps, bright signs, decorated trees, shopping centers, polished, shiny, illuminated a thousand and one different ways. "Istanbul." She repeated the word faster and faster. That manhood was all the city's markets with their end-less spice displays, delicatessens bulging with *pastırma, sucuk,* wheels of kaşar cheese, bluefish with bloody gills lying on red trays, the vivacious hues of quinces, pomegranates, and dates; tangerines, grapefruits, oranges sold from flatbed trucks, baskets of strawberries sold by the roadside, just right for making jam; the first plums of the season, still green and crunchy in wheelbarrows; green, unripe almonds, yellow and red cherries, again pomegranates, again quinces ... tangerines ... oranges ... Cavidan Hanım let out a subdued scream and collapsed onto the young man. Perhaps she couldn't take it anymore when the warm liquid squirted out of the young man and into her. After all, we're talking about years and years of loneliness, which is easier said than experienced—and not even that easy to say. Supermarkets, convenience stores, butchers, neighborhood markets; bought, sold, cooked. Yarn shops, button shops, haberdasheries; Nişantaşı, Şişli, Osmanbey; bought, sold, knit. TV game shows, entertainment programs, bedlam, bacchanals, emotion-commerce, TV series, movies, distant countries filling one with longing, romance, sorrows, lovemaking of others, watched, until one goes numb. Loneliness is a hard business, known only by those who experience it. Has someone said that before? A sentence so trivial, anybody could have said it. But on a New Year's Eve, an evening in the lodos, in a dark park by the shore, in the cramped heat of a car with leather seats, with the seagulls dipping down and rising above the water, and the wind relentlessly battering the windows, in the extension, so alive, of a body, so fresh, loneliness could very well be killed.

Cavidan Hanım was lying on top of Tolga, motionless. Tolga stirred uneasily. "Cavidan Hanım?" No answer. This whole encounter had taken on a rather unexpected shape, granted, but even so, this dose of romanticism was a bit too much for Tolga. He tried to right himself without disturbing Cavidan Hanım. "Thank you." It sounded so raw, he thought, once the words were out of his mouth, but he couldn't think of anything else to say. And besides, the weight of the woman's body was becoming rather annoying. Finally, he became aware of the unsettling quiet. "Cavidan Hanım?" She wasn't breathing. An ice-cold shiver went down Tolga's spine. It just couldn't be, no one could possibly be that unlucky. "Cavidan Hanım?" He stumbled over the words. Just then, his phone, which was lying next to the gearshift, started ringing. He stretched, reaching out as far as the body on top of him allowed: It was Pınar. What if he just didn't answer? He did.

"Hi, sweetie . . . I'm fine, I'm okay . . ." He turned his head, away from the smell of Cavidan Hanım's hair. "Just wanted to get some . . . What's that? . . . Yes, yes, to get some air . . . No . . . I'm upset about some stuff that happened at work, that's all . . . No . . . Okay . . . Okay . . . Yes. Will do . . ." He hung up and took a deep breath. He checked for a pulse. He had to stay calm. He'd tell it exactly the way it happened. They'd believe him. There was nothing not to believe. It could happen. It could have happened. It could happen to anybody. He did his best to control the wave of panic rising in him, but it was growing too quickly, feeding off the whistle of the lodos, pulling the floor from underneath his feet. He tried to push Cavidan Hanım off of him. He grabbed her shoulders and propped her up; her head lolled to one side. In a final effort, he tried to haul her onto the passenger seat, but his foot got caught between the seat and the door. He let go of the body and tried to rescue his foot. At that point, he noticed her woolen socks. Trying not to gag, he yanked his foot free. Then the woman's foot got caught on one of the CDs in the door pocket and sent the CD flying. He deposited Cavidan Hanım's naked body onto the passenger seat, pulled on his pants, and zipped up. He was sticky all over. The inside of the car reeked of semen, but he decided against rolling the window down, with the wind blowing so forcefully outside. The woman's head first hit the glove compartment, and then the door. The gearshift stick bruised her waist. You might think, *Well, what does it matter anyway, now that she's dead?* It wouldn't matter, of course, if every mark on her body wasn't later considered evidence of battery. But as you probably guessed, Tolga wasn't the kind of guy to dump a dead body—and one which had expired with uncanny timing—on a pile of wet cold stones and just leave it there, even if it did belong to someone he didn't know, and even if he would have to pay by having his own life wrenched to pieces. After all, he had faith in the justice system.

And then . . .

I won't say what happened next. Not because I don't know, but because I don't want to bore you any further. Considering the intimate details I've already provided, I must have heard all about it from one of the parties involved, and since that obviously couldn't be Cavidan Hanım (though who knows, right?), I must have heard it from Tolga. Perhaps I'm Tolga's best friend, bearer of his secrets, his lawyer, or better yet, perhaps I'm Tolga himself. If I'm not making all this stuff up, that is. But what difference does it make anyway? Who says these were their real names? I probably changed them, right? Especially since the case still remains to be settled in court! Sharing these experiences with you—even if I don't actually know you—has, it seems to me, forged a bond between us. And that bond forces me to confess: Yes, I changed the names, and I also changed the professions and the addresses. Unfortunately, these are not real people except for their genders and ages. The only real thing is that everything unfolded exactly as I have told you. Oh, and the wind! It was every bit as powerful as I have said. Really, what a lodos it was!

THE STEPSON

BY MEHMET BİLÂL

Sirkeci

It was one of those winter evenings when the darkness descends early. His hands burned from the cold, his stomach from hunger, and his heart from longing for his mother. He looked at the kiosk in front of Sirkeci train station, at the spit of twirling meat, the *döner*, fat seeping out of it onto the fire below. He swallowed. He reached into his pocket. He had just enough money for one more night in a bachelors' room—unless he took care of it tonight, then he wouldn't need to pay for the room anymore. But what if his stepfather failed to show up again? It would mean another night of dining on *simit*, that's what.

When he had reached his home that frosty evening, the woman who opened the door was a complete stranger to him. It was from this sinister woman, with the gaping front teeth and foul look in her eyes, that he learned his mother had died. The woman was one of his stepfather's wives, and she told him that she'd moved into the house after his mother's death. She refused to explain any further. The woman started to shut the door, but he grabbed it, forcing it back open. How did his mother die? When? And where was his stepfather? The woman said nothing about his mother, only that she hadn't seen her husband in a long time. He stopped by once in a blue moon to drop off some cash, but he never stuck around for long. That was all she could tell him. She shut the door.

The roots of his hair were damp with sweat, there was a tingling in his knees, and the tips of his toes had gone numb. He sat down on the wet concrete step in front of the house. He was frozen in a state of shock and grief. His facial expression, the thoughts and questions running through his mind, the entire flow of life, all of it was frozen in a state of temporary coma. At every door he knocked on that night, he met the same response: "I don't know anything about it!"

Both he and his mother were outsiders in this place, his stepfather's hometown. Something had happened, someone had done something to his mother, and now everyone was keeping it from him, as if they'd made some kind of pact of silence. There was a sternness in their answers, a chilliness in the voices, and an unbreachable distance in their faces. They didn't want him, didn't want him wandering the town's muddy streets like some stray shadow, didn't want him asking questions, didn't want him knocking on their doors; they wanted him to evaporate, to get lost, and for good. It was as if his mother had been erased from their memories all together. So where was his stepfather?

With no place to go, he spent his time behind the neighborhood coffeehouse, shivering and whimpering like a dog in a graveyard. At the end of the second day, he was getting a drink and washing his face at the fountain behind the mosque, when the sound of the *imam*'s frazzled voice sent a chill down his spine. Though only a few years older than him, the imam looked like a ghastly old man, what with his turban, robe, and beard, and squinty eyes behind dark glasses; in a voice that sounded like something out of the netherworld, the imam was saying something about his mother's death. He approached the imam timidly so that he could hear better. It had been months since the young man's mother had died, the imam explained. It was the young man's stepfather who had informed the imam of the woman's death one evening, asking that she be buried the next day following the morning call to prayer. It is only for Allah to judge, it is true, the imam said, and as a sinner the stepfather bore the weight of his own sins. But he had to admit that he did not like the look of the step-father that night. Instead of sorrow for the departed, his eyes had shined with raw sparks of fear, sated flickers of rage. Of course, only the dearly departed, the man's stepfather, and Allah knew what had happened that night, whether the woman had passed on naturally, or due to an accident, or whether she was the victim of a malicious deed.

"So, you mean you have no idea why or how my mother died?" the young man suddenly asked.

Unfazed by the interruption, the imam told him that other than the suspicious look in the stepfather's eyes, there didn't appear to be anything out of the ordinary. Maybe she really had died of natural causes; maybe she'd just run out of breath or her heart had just stopped beating.

It was obvious, however, that the imam had not taken a liking to his stepfather, a man who in his entire lifetime had not once donated a dime to the mosque, attended anyone's *mevlit* service, or gone to Friday prayer, or *any* of the *bayram* prayers for that matter. Or maybe the imam simply felt a twinge of pity for this desperate, suffering young man.

There would be no peace for him, and he would not be able to mourn properly, until he knew the why and how of it, and the imam was aware of this. And so he told the young man that his stepfather had gone to Istanbul, that he was there in a neighborhood called Sirkeci, that there the young man would find a coffeehouse run by his relatives, and that he could ask his stepfather to tell him the truth of the matter himself once he found him. The young man felt an urge to hug the imam, to kiss his hand, to wipe his skirts on his face. But he was out the door before the imam could even finish saying, "May God pardon his faults."

There was no doubt in his mind: It was his stepfather who was responsible for his mother's death. That tyrant, that drunkard, that asshole with the many wives had consumed his mother, whose very hand the young man held in such high esteem that it seemed too precious for his lips. He'd taken her life. Sent her to the grave much, much too early, without even going to the trouble to tell her son about it.

He knew that if he did not get his revenge, he would be defiling the memory of his mother, damning her love for him, betraying the breast whose milk he had craved since his first breath of life.

When he first disembarked, the crowd and noise that he found in Sirkeci had sent his head spinning. The tram siren, the honking cars, the people scurrying along the muddy sidewalks, all of it had unnerved him completely, and so he ran, straight to the sea with its billowing waves a few hundred meters in the distance, sprinting, as if toward some kind of miracle. While catching his breath he stood looking out at the ships rocking back and forth in the water, the greedy seagulls squawking in the air, the men fishing from the Galata Bridge, the larger bridge connecting the two sides of Istanbul, and the misty beauty of the opposite shore, which extended before him like a living, breathing postcard. He was hungry, as usual. It was then that he purchased his very first simit in Istanbul and quickly devoured it, right down to the last sesame seed.

Finding the coffeehouse that the imam had told him

about proved quite a task. In the narrow streets crammed full of jostling pedestrians, salesmen screaming out their pitches, store on top of store on top of store, heaps of merchandise piled high upon tables, and dark office buildings, he was looking for a coffeehouse with a certain name but an uncertain address. "Walk straight ahead, turn right, then go uphill . . ." "You're at the wrong place, brother. You gotta go down this street until you see a kiosk on the corner, then you turn left there, and then . . ."

The cigarette smoke stung his eyes and seared his nose the moment he stepped into the coffeehouse. He scanned the room, searching for his stepfather. There were men yelling, playing cards, rolling dice in a game of backgammon, watching television. He looked at each face. When the apprentice carrying tea on a suspended tray asked him who he was looking for, he told him. But why was he looking for him? "I know him from back home," the young man said, and gave him the name of the town. That loosened the apprentice's tongue up a bit. He told the young man that the latter's stepfather wasn't there at the moment, and that he only stopped by every once in a while. There was a hotel where he hung out sometimes though. He could tell him the name of the hotel, if the young man wanted to try there.

It was nearby. It wasn't nearly as difficult to find as the coffeehouse had been. He passed through a number of dark, narrow, muddy, potholed, lookalike streets before arriving at the hotel. It had single and double rooms, as well as twelve-person rooms with bunk beds, what the receptionist referred to as "bachelors' rooms." He asked about his stepfather. Perhaps he was staying there? "What you want with him, huh, boy?" the receptionist snarled in response. He repeated what he had said to the coffeehouse apprentice. He wasn't up to no good; he was just hoping to find his friend from back home. The receptionist told him that his stepfather did stay there, but that he didn't show up every night. Now, did he want a room or not? He whipped out the money for a bed in one of the bachelors' rooms.

Toward morning the door opened, startling him so much that he nearly bumped his head on the iron bars of the bed above. It took him a few moments to recall where he was. He wasn't in the army ward, or in the infirmary at the barracks—then he finally remembered. He had to keep watch. Shivering, he got out of bed and with slow, silent steps made his way to the toilet. The odor was suffocating, and so he held his breath as he peed, for what seemed an interminably long time. He washed his hands and face; there was no soap; he took a piece of tissue paper from the nail in the wall and dried his hands. Quietly, he descended the stairs.

He exited the hotel and walked across the street; there, he knelt behind a large garbage can. His empty stomach was raising hell and his eyes burned, desperate for sleep. He saw a crumpled newspaper on the ground and reached out and opened it. Maybe some reading would wake him up; besides, it was a decent way to pass the time.

RUMORS END IN MURDER

A woman in Bayrampaşa shot and killed a man whom she claimed had spread rumors about her . . . Another transvestite murdered. The transvestite, who was staying at a hotel in İzmir's Konak district, was found dead, having been stabbed in the heart with a knife . . . When his neighbor started making passes at his daughter, the man chopped him up with a meat cleaver . . .

It was a rude awakening: Who sought revenge empty-handed? Well, he did, apparently. How was he going to take out his stepfather? He didn't have anything, not a knife, not even a shiv. He heard footsteps and sat up. A tall, bald, pot-bellied man with a mustache and a long beard was approaching the hotel. He tottered drunkenly. That was him; that was his stepfather, his mother's murderer. The young man's heart began racing, beating like a machine gun. He was glad to have found this man, but he was suddenly furious at himself for having shown up empty-handed. Still, he stood up and ran across the street, stopping his stepfather in his tracks.

"What did you do to my mother?"

His stepfather was startled at first. But then he looked closely at the face of the pathetic figure standing across from him, and scowled. Try as he might, the young man didn't know how to interpret the expression oscillating across his stepfather's face. Was he an innocent man who had been wronged? Or a sinner whose sin had been uncovered, a petulant drunkard, his mouth and nose twitching unconsciously? Though he reeked of alcohol and was shrouded in a mist of sleeplessness, the man quickly snapped to. He was looking down, in both senses of the term, upon the scrawny body before him, his snot-nosed stepson, who stood screaming at him in that puny voice of his.

"What the hell are you talking about, snot-face?"

In a reflex he wiped his nose with the back of his hand. He felt weak and helpless, like a peeled onion, like he'd been ground to a pulp. With all his weakness, he grabbed his stepfather's collar.

"Did you kill my mother?"

His stepfather swayed slightly before grabbing him by his

wrists and throwing him to the ground and kicking him over and over again. The more the young man struggled to get up, the harder the kicks became.

"What the fuck are you talking about? Huh? You little fucker and your fucking mother. Too bad you couldn't be a man and stand up for her, huh? Fucking faggot!"

As he lay on the ground being kicked, he recalled the house where his mother and stepfather had lived. A house that he could never, not even for a second, call home. He was the last to bed and the first to rise. He recalled his sofa bed, which he couldn't unfold until his mother and, especially, his stepfather had left the living room for the night. Drunken hands some nights, under a shield of darkness, would touch his shoulders, his chest, his cock, pretending to tuck him in.

He was making his way down Mercan Hill, from the Covered Bazaar to Sirkeci, filled with shame. He had lost his past, his present, his entire life. Because he had lost his mother. He was incapable of taking his revenge. And even at this moment, feeling so useless, he imagined himself embracing his mother, weeping and sobbing, and telling her all about what his step-father had done.

Beneath drops that resembled neither rain nor snow, he dove into the streets he had wandered through when searching for the coffeehouse. He was looking for the display tables with the knives which had caught his eye earlier. Most stores were closed at that hour and the streets were largely deserted. The peddlers with their socks, lemons, chestnuts, "whorehouse sweets," smuggled cigarettes, alcohol, mobile telephones, fake perfume, fake Viagra, lighter fluid, pirated CDs, videotapes, and DVDs seemed to all be in a silent daze, moving about like a slow-motion film. Finally he saw a stand with meat and bread knives and cleavers. But the goods on display weren't what he was looking for; sure, they'd do the job, but they were too difficult to carry. As he looked blankly upon the wares, the peddler asked him knowingly: "So whatcha need, brother? A jackknife, a dagger, a switchblade?"

He felt much stronger after pocketing a switchblade, one that opened just like that—*chaak*—with the press of a button. He was no longer afraid. He wasn't thinking of the hunger he felt, or his yearning for the warm embrace and sweet milk-scented breast of his mother; he was thinking about vengeance, and hate.

He'd taken up position behind the trash can again, in that same sheath of darkness across from the hotel. He put his numb hands to his mouth and blew warm air into them. Then he slipped his hands back in his pockets and ran his fingers over the switchblade. It was even colder than his fingers.

He came to when he heard a woman scream: "Give me my money, damn it!" His hand went to the switchblade in his pocket and he pressed his back against the wall to conceal himself further.

"Where you goin', you bastard!"

He stuck his head out a little, still shielded by the trash can, and saw a tall, young woman with golden-blond hair thrashing about on the ground at the corner opposite the hotel. Then he saw the man who was kicking her. He took out his switchblade and darted toward the woman.

"What money, cunt? What fucking money?" the man screamed back at the woman.

"You think you get to fuck for free, bastard? Go fuck your wife for free, asshole."

The woman was dressed much too lightly for this cold

weather; it was beyond the young man's comprehension. Her long, thin legs gleamed from the ground where she lay, and her black panties and ass were visible beneath her skirt, which was now up around her waist. He was shocked at the woman's determination, as she fought the man's legs by kicking right back at him. As if she were asking to be killed.

"You asshole, leave her alone!" he screamed.

Both the woman and the man looked over at him, stunned. The man turned away from the woman and furiously stomped toward him.

"What, you her fucking pimp or something? What's it to you anyway, fucking scumbag!"

With a showy press of the button the switchblade opened—*chaak*. He liked that sound. The sparkle of the blade, there beneath the streetlamps as he moved it around in his hand, dazzled even him. By the time the man had begun to make his silent escape, the young woman was already on her feet.

"Thank you sooo much. You came just in time."

The young man looked at the woman with a stunned expression as she said these words. She had a very deep voice. In fact, it wasn't like a woman's voice at all. Moreover, she was at least half a foot taller than he was. She put on quite the show as she coyly straightened out her skirt and hair. There was almost nothing left of the woman who'd just had her ass kicked moments before.

"Allah must have sent you to me. My hero. So tell me, where are you from?"

Now he was sure. The protrusion on her throat, her Adam's apple, moved up and down as she talked.

"Goddamn you!"

His eyes were wide with disgust and he was looking for a

hole, any hole, to crawl into. As he ran back toward the hotel, he saw his stepfather walk out and step into a taxi, which then disappeared down the street.

"Hey, where you goin'? Wait a minute!"

The woman man, the woman-like man, that blond-haired faggot in the miniskirt, just wouldn't shut up. He, or she, chased after him, adjusting her clothing along the way. The young man ran after the taxi, cursing his bad luck, cursing his fate. He'd missed his prey. He had hoped that he wouldn't have to wait another day, that he wouldn't have to spend another night out on the cold stone pavement, that he would take care of this matter that evening, but now, because of some faggot's ass-fucking money, his prey had gotten away.

Undaunted, the transvestite continued to chase after him. "Where are you running off to, sweets? You some kind of idiot or what? I won't take any money from you. C'mon," she said, her feminine wiles back in full gear.

He stopped and turned around; he glared at the transvestite, furious. But the look the transvestite was giving him was that of a smitten schoolgirl; she smiled bashfully.

She tottered backwards a step or two when the fist hit her chin. The amorous sparkle in her eyes was quickly replaced by something else entirely. "Are you crazy, man? Why are you hitting me?" she screamed. She glared at him, not like someone who'd just taken a punch to the chin, but like a disappointed lover. "I just thought I'd pay you back for your help is all."

He was about to unleash another punch when he thought better of it. It occurred to him that he had never talked with a real woman, besides his mother. If it were a woman standing across from him, and not a man who looked like a woman, would he still beat her? Would he still have run to the woman's rescue if he'd known when she was being beaten that she wasn't a woman, not really? He didn't know, his mind couldn't handle it, couldn't process it. He'd let his stepfather, his prey, that bastard, he'd let him get away! And for what, for who?!

"Come on, let's make up, sweets," the transvestite said, extending her hand.

His fists landed on her shoulders. The look in her eyes said she'd put up with anything, anything from him; with each blow to her shoulders she took a step back, but she didn't resist. She didn't say a word.

"Get the fuck out of here . . . Go! Don't get me messed up in your fucking bullshit!"

Late that night, he lay in a cold bed in another bachelors' room when his dick, the existence of which he was almost completely oblivious to except for when he had to pee, stood straight up in some kind of rebellion. It was screaming, defying him like some neglected child. The transvestite's thick lips, painted blood-red, her sullen eyes peering out from beneath those long lashes, her legs shining beneath the streetlamp, her panties and ass peeking out from beneath the skirt that rode her hips, were all frighteningly real, right there before his eyes. That look she'd given him, as he'd been shoving and tormenting her, he thought it might rip a hole in his thin skin. Perturbed, he rolled over.

There he was, never having slept with a woman, never even having held a girl's hand, and though there were dozens of female models, singers, artists that he could be dreaming of, it was the dream of some faggot that had awoken his lust, and this infuriated him. No matter how hard he tried, he couldn't banish those stubborn thoughts from his mind, couldn't make his cock, which stood rock-hard before him as if to question his authority, submit to his will. A saying he'd heard during his military service came to mind just then: *A soldier is like a cock: If you pet it, it stands up; if you beat it, it sits down.* As the image of the transvestite danced before his eyes, he wanted to beat the shit out of his dick. But his sperm sought release; it wouldn't stay put. In a huge explosion, the sound of which he could have sworn he heard, he came onto the transvestite's face, his liquid flowing in streams like blood from a bullet wound. As the semen, its stifling scent rising to his nostrils, flowed down between the transvestite's fake eyelashes, her entire body trembled in small spasms.

The next night, he had positioned himself at the corner of the street where the hotel was, feeling the malice in his bones, and the switchblade in his pocket, when he took a nasty blow to the neck and fell to the ground. Before he could even open his eyes, two thugs had beaten him unconscious, sending him on a slow descent into a deep well, lulled by a barrage of expletives.

In a dream, wrapped in tulle-like desire, he was innocently kissing and sucking his mother's breasts, as he lay on her chest. Until the warm, peaceful dream was interrupted by the pain in the back of his neck and a salvo of bitter curses.

When he opened his eyes, he couldn't tell right away if he was in the lap of reality or still in the lap of the dream. A hand with long red fingernails was wiping away his tears. His head was on the chest of the transvestite he'd wrestled with the other night, and his hand was on her breast. He looked at the transvestite's large hands, her blond hair, and her eyes, both excited and content, radiating the confidence of a lover who only a few hours before had unveiled her repertoire of sultry games. Then he saw the transvestite's naked body, and the shriveled cock in a mass of long pubic hairs. When he saw that he, too, was naked, he leapt out of bed. He wasn't dreaming!

When had he gotten naked? Who had he ever shown his body to? To his mother, when he was a child and she used to wash him, and to the nurse at his physical before doing his military service. He'd never been naked in the presence of anyone else. Now here he was, the sparse hairs on his chest, his stomach shrunk with hunger, his loins all sticky.

He was both in pain from the beating he'd taken the previous night and in agony over finding himself in bed with a person who had a cock. He could have killed that transvestite right then and there. But first he had to find his switchblade. Where was it? Where were his clothes? His pants, his military underwear and undershirt . . . He began searching the room like a madman. The transvestite quickly pulled herself together; she drew the red bed sheet over her body and tried to explain. She said she'd found him near dawn, close to the hotel, in a pool of blood and urine, on the verge of freezing, delirious and mumbling. Of course she recognized him right away. She picked him up and carried him straight home. She figured since he'd been wandering around that hotel with a switchblade in his hand for days, he must have an enemy, a score to settle, someone he was after. And so that's why she didn't take him to the cops or the hospital. So . . . what? Had she done something wrong? Could he just calm down a little?

But there was no calming him down. "Where are they?" he screamed, spewing a muddled list of demands. Where were his pants? His shirt? His jacket?

"I washed them. They haven't dried yet."

He'd lost his virginity. Inside he was still raw, pure, naïve. And he was yelling at the transvestite like a rabid animal. But the transvestite, for whom every day was virtually an act of suicide, didn't seem at all frightened by this comely young man; on the contrary, he brought a flutter to her heart. She was only too willing to play the role cut out for her in this performance, or so it seemed. She immediately brought him his damp clothes.

First he put on his pants, then he realized he'd forgotten to put on his underwear, so he took off his pants again. This time he put them on in the appropriate order. Then his T-shirt, his shirt, his jacket ... He ripped his switchblade out of the transvestite's hand.

He was walking out the door when the transvestite yelled after him, like a desperate mother to her stubborn child, "Don't leave like that! You'll catch cold!"

His past was a fog, his future a dead end. The gaping hole within him continued to grow. While his mind was busy thinking about how to take care of one dirty mess, his body had been sullied by another. Now no matter how much he scrubbed the damp clothes that clung to his body there in the winter cold, the dirt would never wash off.

And now, in that bone-chilling cold, his head spinning with hunger, in the face of a browbeating storm, and still without anyone to fend for him, he was walking amongst the crowd on Mercan Hill, going forth, unable to protect his feet from the melting snow, his ears from the boisterous salesmen, his shoulders from the blows of passersby, his eyes from the umbrellas.

And you can't be a hero when you don't have a dime to your name. It was a moment when he wished to die. But he couldn't. He could not possibly pass from this world without first killing. He owed it to his mother. If he didn't do it, what would he say on the other side? How could he possibly look his mother in the face?

"You still want to pay back your debt?" he asked when the

transvestite opened the door. With his weakness he betrayed his masculinity, with his tongue he betrayed his soul. His body was full of defects, his self was full of the transvestite, and his tongue was vapid.

"I thought I did," the transvestite responded flirtatiously. She stepped aside, inviting him in.

When, chilled by the morning frost, he entered the living room, a wave of cigarette smoke and incense sent his head spinning. Why had he missed the transvestite? Why did he want her? Because she stirred his juices? Because she was the only person in his life who had ever reached out to him? Because her home, her bed, her food was warm? Or was it because he was actually dealing with himself for the first time?

They made a pact. They made a pact with the wordless knowledge and the profound pain of being alone in this world from which they had long ago been severed, and which would never take them back.

He was waiting in the darkness of the bedroom, the switchblade in his pocket.

Several days and several nights had passed, but his stepfather had somehow managed, again and again, to avoid falling into their trap. Either the transvestite's timing was off, or the stepfather just wasn't drunk enough when she made her move. Sometimes he ignored her because there were others with him. The transvestite devoted all of her time, her energy, her concentration, and her care to seducing the stepfather, seeking out every opportunity to make the big catch. Finally, that night, she'd collared him, drunk and eager.

When he heard the key turn in the lock, he held his breath and ran his fingers over the switchblade again. The light came on. The transvestite didn't call out to him, which meant that the old man was with her. This time, tonight, she had brought him. God willing, she had brought him. He sat up straight again, swallowed, held his breath. He heard some voices, some laughter; he pricked up his ears, but he couldn't understand a word. Just some drunkard spouting expletives, and the transvestite's trite responses. Then, footsteps. The living room light seeped under the bedroom door. The footsteps stopped. The living room door squeaked but didn't close. Every now and then the transvestite burst into laughter.

"Would you like something to drink, sweetheart?"

"Do you have any *rakı?*"

He quietly opened the door, having taken off his shoes so they wouldn't squeak on the parquet floor in the hallway. He pressed down on the switchblade's button—*chaak.* Making his way down the hallway, he counted silent prayer beads in his head: *Kill him, kill him, kill him* . . . On the inside he was now like a small child poisoned with hate. He felt neither the fear of death nor the fear of killing. He was flushing the poison of fear out of his system by taunting death, by challenging it. His fear would be dulled to the point of irrelevance once he'd finished the job and disappeared into the night, light as a bird.

He approached the living room, leaning his ear in closer. He could hear his stepfather's voice. "Oh baby, yeah, go on, bitch—faster, faster!" Tormented, he wavered there before the door of decision. Finally, he slithered through the half-open door, silent as a snake. That's when he saw his stepfather sitting on the couch, legs spread wide, head thrown back, eyes closed, and the transvestite kneeling in front of him sucking the head of his cock, which she held firmly in her hand. She was raising and lowering her head in a swift motion, doing all she could to revive the dead.

He watched his stepfather sitting there in a state of complete and total submission. His throat stretched back, bared, the thick veins popping out, begging to be cut. Just a few steps later, with a swift motion, he thrust the switchblade into his stepfather's neck. Dark red blood spurted out impatiently. He stuck the blade in again, and again, twisting it firmly. With each stab the blood continued to flow, though never quite as much as at first. It was as if he could hear the blood draining out of his stepfather once and for all. Then, still holding the switchblade, he stepped back and observed his stepfather. The old man made a wet wheezing sound, and his eyes shined, no longer with hate, but with amazement at the courage of his namby-pamby stepson.

The young man held the bloody switchblade and continued to look his stepfather right in the eye, as if wanting to be absolutely certain that he had paid his debt, that he had finally avenged the loss of his mother. Across from him lay a hairy, disgusting, cowardly slab of meat that had nothing to do with the mother in his mind, and all of the values that he attributed to her.

One last wheeze and the body became a corpse.

It was only then that he paid any attention to the transvestite, his loyal partner, his quiet helper. The transvestite had abandoned the stepfather's shriveled one-eyed snake and turned her head, with an expression of submission and blood splattered all over her hair and face. Her eyes shined with both fear and regret, but all the same, they told him: *We are partners in destiny, made of the same clay—we are one.* It was a look that proclaimed to him, *If you want, we can run away from here, together—you hold the reins in your hands, I don't care if the disaster you've created for yourself consumes me too . . .*

He looked at the transvestite's messy fake-blond hair, at her determined eyes, seeing the threatening gleam of her gaze that contrasted with her compassion; he looked at her bloody face, and at the blood-red lipstick smeared all around her full lips. Her scorching honesty, which aroused a sense of gratitude, and of indebtedness, stirred something else inside him—an unsettling truth. It was now obvious to him that he had walked through that door, and that there was no going back, and that now he stood on the threshold of yet another point of no return. It was a horrifying moment, when he realized that he derived pleasure from pleasures he had never experienced before. A moment when he surrendered to his true desires, the ones he had run from and hidden, hidden from and ignored. A moment of defeat at the hands of the realization that this startling, frightening, abhorrent passion existed within him too.

AN EXTRA BODY

BY BARIŞ MÜSTECAPLIOĞLU

Altunizade

Hasan took a puff from his cigarette. "Have you ever seen an anthill?" he asked. "I love ants. They're just so damned hard-working, those little creatures. They can keep walking up and down the same path for hours, carrying all kinds of shit to their homes—twigs at least twice their size, things to eat, all kinds of stuff. And they never, ever get sick of it. Put your foot down in front of them and they stomp right over it, or walk right around it. It doesn't faze them, not one bit; they never get tired of obstacles. I adore those little bastards."

Just then, an ant zigzagging along the stone floor paused, as if aware that it was the topic of conversation; its legs trembled slightly, then it continued along its way.

Murat scratched his cheek and licked his chapped lips.

"They're just animals, man. They don't have a choice; they just do what they've always done, what the rest of them do. They've been around forever, but have they tried to figure out an easier way to carry those twigs? Pick it up with your mouth and carry it, just like your daddy did—geniuses, fucking geniuses! I mean, shit, man, thousands of years and the dudes haven't made one bit of progress."

Hasan scowled at the younger man. He felt an odd rage build up inside of him, a rage that he himself couldn't understand, as if he were the butt of some nasty joke. "Ants are not common animals," he said, stressing each word. "They're a lot smarter than many of the assholes I know."

Murat gave him an uncomprehending look and shrugged.

"Fuck it . . ."

Murat chuckled good-naturedly. "You want another tea, man? Your glass is empty."

"No thanks," Hasan replied. "I've had enough today. And you shouldn't drink so much of that stuff either. You're gonna get sick."

"It's not like we'll die from drinking tea, man," Murat said with a chuckle. "We'll be dead long—"

"Whatever," Hasan said, cutting him off mid-sentence. "Just don't drink so much."

Murat's eyes moved to the bed where Hasan was perched. "This is so fucked up. How are we gonna get this guy out of here?"

Hasan turned and looked at the figure lying on the bed. He was a bulky man in his thirties, with thick black hair, naked except for a pair of boxers. He had a chiseled face, the kind a lot of women find attractive. The hole in his head hasn't cramped his style at all, Hasan thought, like it's some beauty mark or something. His face was perfectly clean below the nose, but his eyebrows were crimson with blood, and his legs and one of his arms were covered in it too. Hasan's hand went to his waist, out of habit, just to check on his reliable old Glock 35 and the silencer next to it. He'd never been able to shake off the anxiety he felt after a hit—fear that he'd forgotten his gun at the crime scene and the police would trace it back to him and nail his ass. The scenario had plagued him ever since his very first job.

It's been decades, and I still haven't made one bit of progress.

"You sure there's no saw or anything up there?"

"No, man, I looked all over. I looked up there too. Not even a bread knife. I looked for a sack, but there's nothing except these grocery bags. Barely big enough for the dude's head. I've got me a good pocketknife here, but ..."

Hasan smiled at the younger man's joke. "So if we can't cut him up, we'll just have to lug him out like this. Let's just hope Ali brings an extra sack."

"Ali's gonna be pissed ..." grumbled Murat.

"Well, fuck that. What the hell can we do about it? It's not like we did it on purpose."

"Yes, I want him dead. I've never wanted anything so much in my entire life. No matter what, you absolutely must finish him off, not just wound him. He'd know I was behind it and that would be the end of me. You will make absolutely certain that he's dead, right?"

"Don't you worry, Zeynep Hanım. We've been doing this for years."

What a fine woman, Hasan thought to himself. If I had a woman like that, I wouldn't even think about cheating on her. Some guys just don't know what they've got. Hasan felt jealous (and he knew it) of the man who'd managed to nab this tasty side dish. As the old proverb goes, money attracts money, and one woman attracts more women; it was like some kind of law of nature.

The young woman touched the bruise on her cheek with her index finger. Hasan liked her red lipstick.

"You see what he did to me? Bastard. Abuses me just because he can. But would he ever beat his wife? Of course not; he wouldn't, couldn't do it. He can only get away with beating me."

"You should break it off with him, Zeynep Hanım." Hasan let out a heavy sigh. "The best thing for you to do is get out of here, hide somewhere far away until we're done with this."

"*My job, my life, everything I have is here,*" *said Zeynep, with an audible crack in her voice.* "*Besides, he would find me. There's nothing, nothing that's beyond his reach . . . You don't know him. No, he would never let me leave him. I've tried, I've told him so many times. Why do you think he beats me? He won't leave his wife, and he won't let me leave him . . .*"

She reached out and took the man's hands in her own.

"*He's the one who made me do this.*"

Hasan looked down at the soft hands resting on his wrists. He felt a slight stirring between his legs.

"*Just three more days and it'll all be over,*" *he said, looking the woman in the eye.* "*I swear.*"

"We gonna get a bonus for this?" Murat asked with a laugh. He scratched at his palm; the surgical gloves were making him itch, as usual. He wished he was as lucky as Hasan; the gloves never made Hasan itch. Why did his skin have to be so sensitive? The next day his palms would be covered in a rash, and they'd probably swell too. "That's the first time I've knocked somebody off for free in a long time."

Hasan snapped back to the present.

"What? Oh, right, well, let's just pick off a few more folks on the way back and give the lady a bulk discount! You shitting me, man? This guy ain't shit to her. She only hired us to knock off the husband. It's just bad luck is all. Our bad luck."

Murat glanced at the man in the bed. "More like *his* bad luck . . ."

"It's his own damn fault. If he'd left on time, he wouldn't have had this problem," said Hasan deridingly. Again he slid his hand over the pistol at his waist. "This place was supposed to be empty. The man should've kept his word."

"And he shouldn't have gone pulling a gun like that, right?"

Hasan nodded. That was true too.

"I'll tell him to meet me at the hour you say," said Zeynep. She took a puff from her cigarette, blew the smoke out to the side.

Hasan thought what beautiful lips the woman had. So smooth, full, neither too thick nor too thin. And that dark red lipstick that made them all the more alluring. It seemed that his words had helped to put her at ease. The cloud of smoke grew paler and faded away into the air.

"He'll be right on time. He's careful about that. Besides, we haven't had sex in a week, he'll be impatient. Wait for him at the house. And when he comes . . . you know what to do."

Hasan didn't respond right away. He was stuck on what she'd said about not having had sex in a week. For a few seconds he imagined taking the woman into his arms and laying her down on the carpet, pumping in and out between those tender thighs. His eyes moved to her lusciously full breasts. He really was jealous of that bastard.

Maybe he'd have a chance once that asshole was out of the picture?

He gave her a suggestive look, and was glad to see her smile back at him. Yes, he might have a chance, maybe just a slight one, but that was better than nothing. He inhaled the scent of perfume that filled the room.

Once he got this job out of the way . . .

Then again, with a shared secret like this, she'd hardly want to play hard to get, right? Besides, she'd need someone to look after her, to protect her and take care of her. Women—they're so damn sexy when they're helpless.

"Do you have any extra keys to the house?"

"Yes. I'll give you one before you leave."

"And you're sure it'll be empty?"

The woman nodded. "There are three couples who use it. We don't know each other. We let the landlord know when we're going to use it, and he tells the others, or he suggests another time if it's not available. He makes sure there aren't any scheduling conflicts. Everybody keeps their word; confidentiality is essential to all of us."

"I'll call you when we're done, Zeynep Hanım," Hasan said with a smile. "You have nothing to be afraid of. You've got me now."

The young woman took another puff from her cigarette. She crossed her legs and her skirt hiked up, but she didn't move to pull it back down.

"Zeynep," she said, with a slightly warmer smile this time. "You can just call me Zeynep."

Murat walked to the window and looked outside. It was dead quiet, not a soul in sight. He glanced over at the "Culture Palace" construction site, where he saw a pack of four large dogs walking by, like some kind of inner-city gang; the big white Labrador that appeared to be their leader walked with a limp, one of its legs shorter than the rest.

The house must have looked calm and peaceful from the outside. Who could have guessed what was really going on inside—that a man had just been shot dead between these very walls? And that the same fate awaited another? But then, Murat couldn't tell what the darkness outside concealed either. Who knew, maybe at that very moment someone was being strangled, raped, or tortured inside the walls of the silent construction site. A bird alighted on the roof of the half-finished building. A dog barked from afar, and another howled in response.

"Nice piece he's carrying," said a voice from behind him.

He turned around. Hasan was standing next to the body, checking out the deceased's gun.

"SIG Sauer. Loaded."

"Probably afraid of some jealous husband," Murat guessed.

His partner didn't respond.

"What if he's an undercover cop or something?" Murat continued, with a scowl.

The two friends looked at one another anxiously.

The man's clothes were piled carelessly on top of an armchair. Hasan started going through them, his fear growing as he searched, until finally he uncovered a wallet. He took out the man's ID, and an expression of relief spread over his face. He looked at Murat. "We're all good," he said.

Just then Hasan's phone rang. He removed it from his pocket and looked at the screen. Just as he had expected, it was Zeynep. It rang one more time before going silent.

"Our prey's on his way," he said in a low voice, but loud enough for Murat to hear.

"A white Ford Focus. Let's take our positions."

"You got it, man," said Murat. "Ali's on his way too."

"What exactly is it you idiots want me to do?" Ali asked. He took a swig from his beer and rolled the liquid around in his mouth before swallowing it. An old Turkish folk song played on the radio.

"You just need to get a clean vehicle," Murat explained from the backseat. "Nothing that's hot. Get it from someone reliable. But nothing too expensive either. We may need to get rid of it. Once we've nailed the guy, you come and get him. Then we'll dump the body."

"Your real job is to be our guide," Hasan added. He looked at his partner out of the corner of his eye before turning his attention back to Ali.

"We're not from around here, you know that. If it were Ankara

or İzmir, we'd know the place like the back of our hands, but we're new in Istanbul. Our client's talking about a house in Altunizade. On Sultan Selim Avenue. We don't have time to go scoping out the area. And then we need to find a place where we can dump the body once we're done. Someplace far away, you know, safe. That's what we need you for."

Ali nodded. He took another swig of his beer. They were parked along the side of the road. A van drove by.

"That street's crawling with police. In cars, on foot, in armored vehicles even. The Riot Police headquarters are over there, and the Juvenile Police Station is right next to it . . . How are we supposed to get a body out of there? It's too risky."

"Find a truck," said Hasan. "We'll take the body out in a trash bag and toss it in the back. Nobody'll suspect anything. Besides, it'll be the middle of the night. One of us'll keep a lookout, for headlights and stuff."

There was a short silence.

"I don't like doing a job when I don't know who I'm doing it for," the young man mumbled.

"Man, but you know us," said Murat. He was about to say something else, but then Hasan shot him a look and he decided against it.

"Our client doesn't want too many people involved. She found out her lover's married, she wanted to leave him, but the bastard won't let her go. He beats the woman day and night. The poor thing's all messed up, her face, everything. It's kind of like charity work. You'll get your money straight from us. You trust us, don't you, Ali?"

Ali turned and looked at Hasan. He'd done a lot of jobs with these two cronies, and he'd always been dealt a fair hand. He thought the plan over for a moment, and then nodded. It wouldn't take him half a day to get them a truck. Easy money, he thought.

He remembered the tip he'd received on the following week's horse
races; he could really use that money right about now.
  "Okay," he said. "Let's do it."

The Ford Focus pulled over in front of the house and the
driver took a quick look at himself in the rearview mirror.
These rendezvouses still got him all worked up. They'd had
sex probably more than a hundred times in this house, on
the stone floor, in bed, in the tiny bathroom, breathless, their
sweat mingling, but here he was with butterflies in his stomach, as if it were the first time all over again. He was in a
good mood. The last time they'd met, he'd really roughed the
girl up, taking his rage at some two-bit cheat out on her. But
tonight he would be gentle, win her over again, mend her broken heart. And of course he would be duly compensated for
his kindness.

Deciding that his hair looked okay, he smiled. He ran his
fingers over his goatee.

It's going to be one fine night, he said to himself.

As he walked toward the house, he thought about what
he'd say if she brought up the whole divorce thing again.
He was determined not to leave his wife—no way. Fire ran
through his veins at the mere thought of her moaning beneath another man; no way that was going to happen. His
lover had to accept him just the way he was, period. If she
insisted on whining about it, he'd simply remind her of the
beatings she'd already been given. He'd shut her up, somehow.
But hopefully it wouldn't come to that; he didn't want to beat
around the bush, so to speak, with such unsavory topics. He
imagined his little angel looking at him amorously, like she
used to when they first hooked up. He missed that.

He slipped the key in the lock. So let's see if she's been a good girl and done as I said, he thought. Or maybe she had another surprise in store for him? He looked at the bed, hoping to find the young girl there, naked, as he had instructed her to be. A roguish smile spread across his lips.

But there was something else waiting for him on the bed, something unexpected. A stranger, a guy, oddly contorted and, holy fuck, covered in blood from the waist down!

The man just stood there, dumbstruck.

Even the two bullets that sent him collapsing to the floor failed to erase the stunned look from his face.

"You sure we're at the right place?" Hasan asked.

Murat shook his head. "Of course, man. I came here twice and checked it out. This is it." He turned the key in the lock; the door clicked open. "See, the key fits."

The two partners quietly slipped through the door. They held onto their guns, just in case. The woman who had hired them was going to invite her lover, their target, here for sex, and they would be waiting. It was a simple but solid plan. This house, which was used by several couples in rotation, was supposed to have been empty at that hour.

But it wasn't.

When he heard the door open, the half-naked man lying in bed looked up, a stupid smile spreading over his face. He was obviously expecting someone else, probably a woman. A second later he reached under his pillow, pulled out a pistol, and moved to raise it at them. It was a big mistake. Two bullets each from two silent guns nailed him to the bed.

Hasan and Murat turned to one another and cursed.

"Fuck."

The truck turned the curve slowly, careful not to scrape

against the cars parked on either side of the road. It was still the middle of the night; in a few hours, the streets would be packed with vehicles bound for the Bosphorus Bridge. One of Istanbul's more fashionable neighborhoods, Altunizade was home to modern office buildings with glass façades and shiny apartment complexes reserved for the upper crust, all surrounding the grandiose shopping center, Capitol. The truck passed first by the apartment complexes, then by Capitol, then by the office buildings, before driving through an underpass and emerging at the top of a hill that led down to Üsküdar and the Bosphorus shore.

Ali knew this street well. When he was a kid, he used to come visit his grandfather here, in a house in the Gypsy neighborhood behind the riot police building. He was fond of his grandfather; in fact, Ali was the only person in his family whom the man really liked. A generous Istanbul gentleman with a dour face but a heart of gold, he had always had a big soft spot for his grandson. Disowned by his daughters, the old man had taken his final refuge in this neighborhood. Ali would come here alone to see him, usually without even telling his mother. He felt safe, as if he belonged, there amongst the Gypsies, who sat on the sidewalk chatting, and amongst the slovenly children and the old, wrinkly faced women watching the passersby, and even amongst the trash that littered the street from one end to the next. Poverty had always had an allure for him; he felt more comfortable in run-down neighborhoods like this one than he did in fancy restaurants or upscale hotels.

The avenue was every bit as fascinating now as it had been back then. It was like the crossroads of two civilizations, with police buildings situated like a border control between two different cultures, splitting the avenue almost right down the middle. Below the riot police building was the Gypsy quarter, which was always rowdy with weddings or brawls, while above it stood rows of two-story houses, each with its own garden, all left behind by the Greeks, all still standing calm and silent amongst centuries-old plane trees.

It was in front of one of these houses that the truck slowed to a halt. Its walls were painted dark green, unkempt grass overran its front yard, which was home to a single, paltry tree, and its borders were marked by stones and surrounded by an iron fence. Next to the front door was a chair facing the street, and a folded-up picnic table. Ali pulled on the parking brake and got out. He looked left and right and then, seeing that the coast was clear, started walking toward the house, with a large black sack in hand.

He didn't need to knock. He'd called Hasan on his cell phone before he parked. He figured they'd be watching for him through the peephole in the door, and he'd figured right. As soon as he reached the door, it opened up. He silently stepped inside. He'd just parted his lips to greet the other men when he saw the two bodies lying in the middle of the room, and so he let out a curse instead.

"Fuck!"

The young woman waited excitedly for several minutes after the man got out of the Ford Focus. That asshole, who was inevitably late for every appointment, couldn't have been more punctual this time around; he must have been hungry for his lover's skin. If it had been me who had called him over here, would he have come? If I were his mistress, and not his wife? She couldn't be sure, and so she banished the unpleasant thought from her head. Time was passing at a maddeningly slow pace. The fact that nobody was emerging from the house was a good sign. Or was it? What if something had gone wrong? God forbid . . . Her phone rang and she looked at the screen; she was relieved to see that it was Hasan. Still, she answered, just to be sure.

"*Everything okay?*"

"*We're all good," replied the confident voice on the other end.*

She hurried over to the car at the corner, got in, and wrapped her fingers around the steering wheel. She waited like that for several minutes. She felt her body trembling, but thankfully, it didn't take long for her to calm back down. A smile spread over her face. She turned the key in the ignition.

She quickly made her way down the hill to Üsküdar. It was still dark out. Slightly anxious, she glanced at the gigantic tank and the police armed with machine guns standing guard in front of the station. A group of boisterous Gypsies gathered around a large bonfire turned their inquisitive eyes to the passing car and the attractive woman inside.

When the woman reached the pier, she parked in a spot that would allow for a quick exit. She didn't plan on sticking around for long. She guessed that the truck would be pulling up to the house right about then. She took great delight in imagining the body being dragged along the ground, stuffed into the sack, and then tossed into the back of the truck. The sleazeball had finally gotten what he deserved.

The coolness and the soft breeze of the Bosphorus quieted her nerves. Finally, she was free.

She walked across the street, over to the girl standing alone in front of the Beşiktaş motorboat pier. Looking at her, Zeynep found it hard to believe that this babe in the woods was only eight years younger than herself. She watched her, affectionately, for some time. The girl was lost in thought, gazing at the Bosphorus and the lights of the opposite shore. What was she thinking? Was she afraid? Worried? Probably. The girl didn't notice the woman approach her.

"It's all over," she said in a gentle voice.

Startled, the girl turned around. For several seconds, they just stood there looking at one another.

"Zeynep . . ."

"Neşe."

"Are you sure? I thought maybe he wouldn't show up . . ."

She reached out and gently caressed the girl's cheek. "Yes, dear. It's all over, finally."

"Is an extra body going to be a problem?" Hasan asked the now ashen-faced Ali in a low voice.

Ali continued to stare at the bodies. Hasan was a little surprised that Ali, a veteran of the business, seemed so flabbergasted by this minor glitch in their plans, but he didn't make a big deal out of it. Actually, he could understand where the guy was coming from. After all, they were all in this unexpected mess together.

Ali didn't answer Hasan's question, so the latter continued.

"It was an accident, I swear. It wasn't planned. The goddamn guy was here when we arrived, just lounging in bed. Then he made his move—he pointed a fucking gun at us, the idiot. You can guess the rest. There was nothing we could do. We thought the house would be empty; we were taken by surprise."

There was a brief silence.

"We're not trying to fuck with you, Ali. You trust us, right?"

Ali snapped to, as if suddenly awaking from a bad dream. First he looked at Murat, and then at Hasan, who was waiting for him to respond. The bewildered look in Ali's eyes had been replaced by the resolute gaze of a man who knows exactly what to do.

"Okay, it's all right. What's done is done. Like you say, what's the difference? So it was one body, now it's two. You guys bag one of them, and I'll go get another sack from the truck."

Hasan and Murat glanced at one another. They could both tell that they were thinking the same thing: *He's gonna make a run for it ...*

"Let me come with you," said Hasan. "I could use the fresh air."

His suggestion was clearly not open for debate, and so Ali did not object. They didn't speak at all on the way to the truck. Their eyes darted right and left, scoping out the surroundings, but there was no one to be seen. A taxi swiftly passed the truck and continued along its way.

When Hasan and Ali returned with the other sack, Murat had already tied the arms and legs of both bodies. It would be easier to bag them that way.

"I couldn't care less how it happened," Ali grumbled. "You got us into this mess, so you carry these bastards out of here. Anyway, I have a bad back."

Hasan laughed. "All right, Ali. No problem."

Murat wound the remaining string into a ball and stuck it in his pocket. The extra body was heavy; carrying that sucker wasn't going to be easy. "Should we make two trips?" he asked, though he doubted Ali would agree to it.

He was right. "Let's not take any chances. It's almost morning."

"I agree," said Hasan. He glanced around the room, saw the tea glasses and the cigarette butts. "Plus, we've still gotta clean up the blood and all this other shit. You go first, Ali, make sure the coast is clear, and then we'll bring 'em out."

Hasan and Murat loaded themselves up with one sack

each and walked to the door. They figured Ali would open it for them, but he didn't. A few seconds passed before they turned to look at him. What the hell was he waiting for?

They froze stiff. He was pointing his pistol straight at them. A Glock 17, with a silencer. Hasan's mouth fell wide open. Their guns were at their waists. But their hands were full.

"What, you take me for some kind of fool or something?" Ali said.

He sent the first bullet into Murat's forehead. The young man toppled backwards like a felled tree beneath the weight of the sack he was carrying, hitting the wall before collapsing with a thud onto the floor. In a reflex Hasan opened his arms, releasing the sack from his hold. He cast a glance at Murat's lifeless body before turning to meet Ali's gaze, the latter's eyes blazing with inexplicable rage.

Just one extra body . . . We didn't do it on purpose . . .

He took a bullet right between the eyebrows and collapsed to the floor next to Murat.

Ali had a sour taste in his mouth when he slid in behind the steering wheel. He coughed up a ball of phlegm and spit it out the window. He cursed those fucking bastards who'd gotten him messed up in this bullshit. What the fuck—to knock off Kâzım *Ağa*'s one and only son? Talk about gall . . .

They make a man sorry he was born . . .

He was glad now that he hadn't met the client. Four bodies would be found in that house come morning. Four men who'd shot one another. Nobody would ever know he'd even been there. Nobody.

Especially not Kâzım Ağa.

Close call, he thought as he pressed down on the gas pedal.

Houselights had already begun to dot the twilight sky as the truck made its way downhill.

* * *

The young woman was standing with her face to the strait, watching a gigantic ship float by. Its lights looked so beautiful. She wondered what it was like to be inside, watching the shore from out there. Actually, all she wanted to do was go somewhere far, far away, someplace so foreign that everything she had experienced here would cease to exist for her.

"How are we going to pay those guys?" she said, her voice heavy with concern. "I can't stop thinking about it, Zeynep. If we don't pay up, those guys will never leave us alone. I mean, they're murderers for God's sake. I've scraped together a little here and there but . . . it's not very much."

Her voice grew slightly shrill and she seemed to turn into a little girl, like she always did whenever she got excited.

"I'll get some from my Dad too. I'll lie about what it's for, tell him it's for school or something. Or that I'm sick. I don't know. But I'll come up with more. I promise."

"There's no way we could've afforded it," Zeynep said, shaking her head. "You can't even imagine how much they were asking for, sweetheart. Even your father couldn't have gotten us out of it, believe me."

She thought of Hasan's expression, the way he had drooled when he stared at her legs. She doubted the asshole would've made do with just the money, but she didn't tell Neşe that.

Neşe turned around and gave Zeynep a frightened look, all the blood suddenly drained from her face.

"Don't worry, baby. I took care of everything."

Zeynep took a puff from her cigarette.

"I told you about that mafia godfather, the one our asshole did business with—Kâzım Ağa. Well, I had a little talk, a little more than a talk, with his son last week, and invited him to the house. An hour before your appointment. He's no different from all the

other assholes. He wanted me to be his mistress, to make me part of his harem. He would've taken care of my husband, too, if I'd asked, I'm sure of that. But for what? Why save myself from one animal just to go and be a slave to another? Believe me, from now on nobody's going to make me do anything I don't want to.

"Anyway, our boys wouldn't recognize him; they're new in Istanbul. And I'm sure that when our boys burst in, he reached straight for his gun. He's the panicky type. So he wouldn't have left them any choice. He keeps a gun under his pillow even when he's making love, can you believe that? They'll never be able to show their faces in Istanbul after this, trust me. Kâzım Ağa would skin them alive. They either hightail it out of here or they're finished. Simple as that."

She took a deep breath.

"If they do cause us any trouble, I'll make sure the ağa gets wind of their names. I'm sure he'd believe me and not them. I've even made up a story already, just in case."

Her eyes wide, Neşe peered at the woman standing next to her. She felt extremely grateful, but also ashamed. And now, after what she'd just heard, she felt a slowly growing sense of admiration too.

"I'm so sorry, for everything," she said in a low voice, like a child who's just broken a toy. "He told me you would get divorced, that your relationship was over. But when I learned the truth . . . I hated him. I swear, I was going to be out of your lives, if only he'd left me alone."

"I know, sweetheart," said Zeynep, smiling. She reached out and ran her hand through Neşe's long red hair. Neşe gently leaned in toward her.

"You weren't his first lover. I couldn't even count how many there've been. But even I wasn't able to leave him, so how could a little angel like you possibly have done it?"

She thought of all the beatings she'd taken, all the slaps to the face, for some bullshit reason or another. But now, all that was over.

Zeynep slipped her arm around the waist of the younger woman, who snuggled up next to her, resting her head on Zeynep's shoulder.

Two large seagulls passed in front of them, so closely that if they'd reached out, they could have touched them.

PART II

PUSHING LIMITS, CROSSING LINES

PART II

THE SMELL OF FISH

BY HİKMET HÜKÜMENOĞLU

Rumelihisarı

Cemile *Abla* had a bad habit. It was a habit that tormented her so much it gave her stomach cramps. But other than that, she was a fairly carefree woman. No one had ever heard her complain, not even when her knees ached on rainy days. She was just grateful to have friends who came knocking at her door frequently enough to make her forget her loneliness. She had enough money to buy meat twice a week, and a house with a roof that never leaked in the winter. In fact, according to Nalan, if Cemile Abla would only, finally, sell her two-story wooden home, she'd have plenty of money to squander for the rest of her life.

"Your house stands out like a rotten tooth in the middle of all these new ones," Nalan had told her. Nalan was a tiny woman whose hair had begun to thin out a couple of years before, but her skin was still as smooth and shiny as could be. She and Cemile Abla had been best friends ever since they were kids. Their mothers—may they rest in peace—had been neighbors for fifty years. When her oldest son got married, Nalan sold her house in Rumelihisarı and bought a new three-bedroom apartment in a faraway neighborhood—and, as she had told Cemile Abla, she'd made enough money off the deal to pay for her son's lavish wedding to boot. Nalan's was the one and only house on her street that hadn't changed hands to be demolished and replaced by an expensive apartment building with a view of the Bosphorus.

Cemile Abla's wooden house stood all alone, tall and proud at the top of the stone stairs, a bastion of the past. The neighborhood real estate dealer was constantly at her heels, yapping like a newborn puppy. If he could just convince her to sell, he'd make a small fortune on the commission alone.

But no matter how suffocated she felt by the profusion of restaurants along the shore—a new grand opening every week!—the throngs of graduates of the nearby university storming in for Sunday breakfast with their entire families in tow (Nalan complained, saying they probably didn't have any eggs of their own at home), and all the automobiles jamming the avenue, Cemile Abla was determined not to sell her house—no matter what. Luckily her friends' and the real estate dealers' insistence never went beyond harmless banter; she knew deep down that if they'd pressed her just a bit more, there's no way she could have said no.

Cemile Abla had gone shopping at the supermarket to get ready for the guests she was entertaining that evening. For her everyday needs she went to the little ant-infested grocer down the hill, but on special days like this one, she preferred browsing the big stores with their wheeled carts and long corridors illuminated by glaringly bright lights. It gave her that same dizzying sense of exhilaration that she used to get back as a senior in high school after a reluctant visit to the amusement park, at the insistence of friends.

She had decided to offer her guests chocolate cake and canapes on white bread with tea. Having bought a jar of the most expensive cocoa, a container of French mustard, and a few of what the man at the deli counter told her were the best cheeses of Italy, she headed home, inhaling the scent of the Bosphorus along the way. From a short distance away, her eyes met with those of Captain Hasan, and she smiled. Captain Hasan must have come back from fishing early, for it was uncommon to see him on the shore at that time of day. He was sitting on a low stool on the edge of the sidewalk, an extinguished cigarette stuck in the corner of his mouth, leaning over, trying to teach the scrawny boy he'd recently hired how to tie knots. His red and blue boat rode the gentle waves just behind them. ("A person who has a ship, not a boat, is called a captain," Cemile Abla had complained at the age of seven. Her father had patted her head and replied, "If that's the way Hasan likes it, then what's it to us?")

"I've got a three-and-a-half-kilo bluefish for you," Captain Hasan said joyfully. "Caught him at the crack of dawn, he must've been drunk, fell for it hook, line, and sinker!"

"Thanks, but my refrigerator's already crammed full," replied Cemile Abla, placing her bags on the ground on either side of her. "Give it to someone else, it would be a sin to waste it."

"No way, it's for you. Nobody else knows how to cook it right. They'd make a mess of the poor thing . . . So, you want me to bone it or you want to do it yourself?"

Cemile Abla took a deep breath, turned her eyes to the clouds, exhaled, and answered, "I'll take care of it. Thanks."

It was said that nobody along the entire Bosphorus could clean a fish as well as Cemile Abla. It was from her father that she'd learned to work a fish so deftly. On her way home from school, she used to stop by the stand that once stood on the right side of the pier. There she would remove one squirming, restaurant-bound fish at a time from the shallow tubs of water and cut off their heads and tails before scaling and skinning them; the bigger ones she would bone as well. When she was still too short to reach the counter, she'd prop herself up by standing on an old cheese tin. Then she'd run home and watch cartoons for half an hour, munching on some bread and jam that her mother had prepared for her, before starting on her homework. Actually, if she'd gone straight home instead of stopping by the fish stand, she would have had an extra hour to watch cartoons. But she was more fond of the knives and the fish than she was of TV. With each day her fingers grew a little more used to the tools, her wrists stronger, her movements more graceful. Nothing could take the place of that odd feeling she would get. Every now and then her teachers would scold her because her hands smelled of fish, but it was worth it just to see the proud smile on her father's face as he watched her working at the counter. And it wasn't only her father who held her in such affection; she'd become the apple of everyone's eye, all the way from Ortaköy to Sarıyer. Awed by her love of fish and her skilled mastery of the knife, each and every fisherman, young and old alike, saw Cemile Abla as his own ideal daughter, sister, or even wife. And the fact that her father was the famous Ali *Reis* didn't hurt either.

The scrawny boy was off in his own little world, watching a sports car drive by, when Captain Hasan slapped him on the back of the neck. "Get off your ass and help Cemile Abla with her bags!" he yelled. "You some kinda idiot, boy? Do I have to tell you everything? And wrap that fish up."

"There's really no need, Captain Hasan, I can carry the bags myself," said Cemile Abla. "They're not heavy anyway."

But she knew what would happen. The man would insist, and once again she wouldn't be able to say no. Cemile Abla was annoyed with herself. Sometimes she even hated herself for giving up so easily, for acquiescing to things she really didn't want to do. But no matter how hard she tried, she could never manage to say no when people persisted with her. She became horrified, thinking that if she said no she'd be thought rude, or that she'd insult the other person, or hurt their feelings; she'd get a lump in her throat and her palms would grow sweaty. She wouldn't be able to look the other person in the eye; she just couldn't stand the thought of how that person's eyes would dull with disappointment as soon they heard the word "no." And so that was her constant dilemma. She'd have to drink that third cup of coffee despite her heartburn, go shopping with the girls even if she preferred to do so alone, go picnicking at Kilyos with her old neighbors even though she really didn't feel comfortable wearing a swimsuit.

Simply because she loved them so much, because they made such a fuss, because they insisted.

Actually, these things were the least of her troubles. What really got on Cemile Abla's nerves was how her friends pressured her to get married, how they were constantly introducing her to potential grooms.

In her youth, Cemile Abla used to love to walk to Bebek and get a cherry-vanilla ice-cream cone, sit on a park bench with a dog-eared Sait Faik book, and just relax. But nowadays, in front of the ice-cream stands stood long lines of bronze, blonde-haired girls, pot-bellied boys, and odd, shaggy dogs of a sort she had never seen before. Cemile Abla had begun to feel like a stranger in her own land, as if at any given moment she might be caught and deported. But instead of worrying herself over nothing, she'd made a resolution not to venture beyond the cemetery, the boundary of white marble separating Rumelihisarı from Bebek, during normal waking hours. She would go for walks in the wee hours of the night, once the fancy dining high-lifers and the bar brawlers had hopped into their cars (which were usually parked on the sidewalk and nearly toppling into the sea) and gone home, once all the apartment lights had been turned off, once all the dogs had stopped howling.

What she liked most about these walks was the fishermen. Because of the wall of wedding boats blocking access to the shore, not many fishermen, other than Captain Hasan, stopped by these parts anymore. But there were a few who, as if by some unspoken agreement, would draw their boats ashore in the shadow of Hisar on moonlit nights and, if they happened to be in the mood, reminisce about the old days for hours on end. Sometimes they'd lean on the old cannons at the base of the towers. It made Cemile Abla happy to see them as she walked along the deserted sidewalks and the asphalt roads now devoid of passing cars. She'd join them when invited; there was no need to insist. She would join them not because she couldn't say no, but because their conversations reminded her of her father. She'd sit down on the old blanket they'd have spread out on the ground, sticking her legs out to the side and bending them just so, and then she'd cover her knees with the edge of her topcoat and sip on the half-full tea glass of undiluted *rakı* that they'd offer. It was during those hours that the fishermen, so reticent during the daytime, would wax talkative; they'd discuss sea currents and schools of fish, they'd tell stories about the adventures of Ali Reis, ask Cemile Abla how she was getting on, and then, when dawn began to break, they'd get back into their boats, their minds at ease, knowing that they had done their duty and tended after the daughter of the great man who preceded them. Then they would head out into the foggy waters of the Black Sea.

Cemile Abla had one condition for the potential grooms who

came to meet her. They had to meet at her home, not outside. And they had to come after dark (she had no intention of falling prey to the tongues of those pint-sized gossip mongers playing ball out in the streets), but not too late (She didn't know yet if these new neighbors of hers were the snoopy sort or not). *Sure he can come over, we'll drink some tea and chat and get to know one another,* she'd say. *And then we'll see.* Having so thoroughly enjoyed their first visit, the gentlemen would want to meet a second time. By the second visit, however, they did not have to be told: It would become blatantly obvious that Cemile Abla had absolutely no intention of marrying. Disappointed and resentful, they'd go back home, and after a few days, all they would recall was the delicious cake, the tarts, and the faint smell of fish.

Luckily, Cemile Abla had so far encountered only two obstinant potentials. The first was a lawyer with a single, long eyebrow. He drank his tea warm with four heaps of sugar. For some reason he just hadn't been able to find a proper companion and, because his heart could no longer bear his mother's griping, he had decided to take care of the matter as swiftly as possible. After all, his mother—may she live long—was on her deathbed (as she had been for years). And so from now on he was not going to be picky; he was willing to overlook small defects. On his second visit he informed Cemile Abla that he was going to take her to kiss his mother's hand and discuss engagement plans. An apartment in Üsküdar was ready and waiting for them; they could sell this ramshackle house with its creaking wooden planks and put the money in the bank. The three of them, mother, son, and daughter-in-law—may they live long—would come together and build a happy little nest of their own.

The second one was a handsome, bright-eyed, bushy-tailed man. He was at least ten years younger than Cemile Abla, well off, and apparently had a hankering for older women. So much so that by their second meeting he had two plane tickets in his pocket and had already booked a room at a hotel in Bodrum. "Are we going to stay in the same room?" Cemile Abla had asked. Was it such a bad idea for them to slip under a blanket and get to know one another better for a few days, seeing as they were about to share the same pillow for the rest of their lives? The worst part about it was that the man's smoky voice and the sparse hair on his fingers up to the first joint actually turned her on. "I'm not going anywhere until you say yes," the young candidate had announced. When he smiled, his lower lip protruded ever so slightly.

Today's guest didn't look much like a mama's boy. And he had no intention of locking Cemile Abla up in a hotel suite or anything of the sort. He was very polite; his first wife had died of breast cancer (—*What a pity* / —*Yes, it was truly a pity*); he was Nalan's brother's army buddy, so he wasn't really a stranger. His eyes were red, as if he cried all the time (—*I think I need to change my glasses prescription* / —*Oh my, yes, you should get that looked at right away*); he was a retired history teacher (—*Yet you're still so young* / —*But I just can't deal with teenagers anymore*); he suffered from gastritis and ulcers; he couldn't have salt because of his blood pressure; and he was very lonely.

Cemile Abla was too happy with her own life to settle for alleviating some guy's loneliness. The thought of growing old and dying in a home full of stomach pills and history books gave her goosebumps. (—*What's the matter, Cemile* Hanım? *Are you okay?* / —*Oh, it's nothing. Just a little chill.*) Besides, she'd made her decision as soon as he told her that he hadn't had a bite of fish since he was a child, and that he held his nose whenever he walked by a fish stand.

"You see, I had this accident once when my mother tried to force me to swallow fish oil," he'd explained, and just as he was about to go into the details, Cemile Abla excused herself and went to the kitchen.

Cemile Abla had long ago reconciled herself to the fact that she would never be able to find a husband like her father; and deep inside she was relieved about this. But at the same time, she didn't want to be rude to her matchmaker friends, or the eager potentials who came to visit. At some point in the middle of their first meeting, she would get lost in thought and weigh the possible match thoroughly, sincerely, without prejudice, and with a clear head. But there was no need to waste any time considering the possibility of a man who couldn't tolerate the smell of fish.

Timur Bey (—*My father was a great admirer of Tamberlaine, that's how I got my name. / —Won't you have another piece of cake?)* was so excited that he failed to notice Cemile Abla's evasive answers, her distress, her constant escapes to the kitchen. His mind was elsewhere: He had one foot in the grave, he was certain that this was his last chance, so he had promised himself that he wouldn't give up until he had resolved this matter once and for all.

When Cemile Abla returned from the kitchen with fresh cups of tea, she found Timur Bey standing there expectantly. He took a small box covered in red velvet from his pocket, opened it with his thin fingers, and removed a diamond ring.

"It was my grandmother's. My late wife, may she rest in peace, wore it all the time, and I hope that you, too, will like it."

"Timur Bey, I'm shocked," said Cemile Abla. She placed the tray on the coffee table. "I don't know what to say."

"Please. Please, I beg you, don't say no." He took a deep breath before continuing. "If you reject me, I don't know what I will do, I don't know how I will survive. Believe me, I couldn't bear it, I don't think I could possibly go on. I've waited so long, only the thought of the day I would once again give this ring to a woman I love has kept me going. But I swear, I'm at the end of my rope. If you don't . . . life for me will be meaningless . . ." He took the fingers of Cemile Abla's left hand into his own and squeezed them so hard he nearly broke them.

Cemile Abla stared ahead blankly, hoping that this response would put an end to the conversation.

"Forgive me . . ." said Timur Bey. "I'm so terribly excited, I don't know what I have to say to convince you. But I can tell you this—I'll talk for as long as it takes, for hours if I must. I'll do whatever, whatever it takes . . ."

Waiting for the cake in the oven to rise, Cemile Abla laid her knives out on the marble counter, which smelled of detergent. She still used her father's set of knives. Those ebony-handled, steel blades had become an extension of her own body; they were more familiar to her than her own hands, her own fingers. She laid the five knives out according to size, the smallest of them the length of her pinky and as thin as a razor, the largest bulky enough to split a soda can in half. The chopping knife which she used to cut the heads off of larger fish she placed lengthwise at the top of the row. Next to the chopping knife she set the scissors that she used to remove their fins; they were sharp enough to cut off a tree branch as thick as her wrist. She caressed each of them, a sweet shiver of pleasure running through her as she felt their metal upon her flesh, and then like a nurse preparing for surgery, she conducted a final inspection of each.

She could see the towers of Hisar from her kitchen window. Who knows what went through the minds of the war-weary janissaries as they leaned upon those rocks and rolled their cigarettes five centuries ago, she thought. Was there a woman watching them from behind the tulle curtains of her kitchen window on the hill behind them? Was there a seaside road for the carriages, or did fields covered with trampled grass extend to the edge of the Bosphorus? Could you look into the water and see the bottom back then? Did they ever imagine that years later the Turks would be selling tickets to "infidels" so that they could climb up those steep stairs and take in the view from above? That concerts would be held right in the center of the towers, behind those high walls? Or that college students would play backgammon and drink tea on the slope where heads used to roll? It frightened Cemile Abla the way everything changed, incessantly, over time. Actually, she was rather fond of the small innovations, like color television, markets selling hundreds of varieties of cheese, and hot water every day; she had no objections to these. But she knew that if things were simply left to take their course, soon there wouldn't be anything familiar left around her, and she would find herself caught up in the wheels of a way of life utterly foreign to her. But she had no intention of changing *her* way of life just because everything else had changed.

She washed the bluefish thoroughly before laying it out on the counter. When she had to deal with a really big fish, first she'd cut it up into pieces in the bathtub, roll it in newspaper so as not to make a mess, and then carry it to the kitchen before she set about boning it. This time she wouldn't have to go to so much trouble. She used the sharp side of the mid-sized knife to scrape off the fish's scales. The crisp crunchy sound of the fins as she cut through them always gave her goose bumps on the back of her neck (according to her father, these very scissors were responsible for slicing off four fingers of a careless apprentice). She removed its gills. She made a shallow cut into its belly with the thin knife and plunged her hand in to remove its intestines. The gooey mass that clung to her fingers no longer made her sick to her stomach. With two swift swings of the meat cleaver she separated the head and the tail. She suddenly got the feeling that the fish was stirring beneath her hand, struggling to escape; but she just took a deep breath and proceeded with her task. Using her pinky and ring finger, which were still clean, she turned on the faucet and cleaned the blood clots off the fish. With the razor-sharp edge of the small knife she sliced the fish open along the length of its spine, from where its head had just been moments before, all the way down to its now absent tail. She used a large knife to pry into the fish horizontally and in a series of rapid movements separated out the bones, gathering them together in a pile on the side. Throwing out the bones of the fish would be a sin; she'd boil them for soup in the evening.

Once she'd washed and thoroughly dried them off, she applied a thin coat of olive oil to the steel of her knives, meat cleaver, and scissors before wrapping each one up in a piece of cloth and placing them in their respective drawers.

Timur Bey was still on his feet, holding the wedding ring out to Cemile Abla.

"Please sit down, Timur Bey," she said.

"Please don't say no," said Timur Bey.

"I can never say no, I just can't."

The man's face suddenly lit up. "So that means you say yes. I haven't misunderstood, right? You accept?"

"If only you had chosen someone worthy of your grand-mother's wedding ring. It would have been better for both of us, really."

"I'm sure my grandmother would have gotten along with you wonderfully, if she were still alive," said Timur Bey. He then plopped himself into the armchair, as if he'd only just realized he was standing up. Reaching for his tea, he seemed perplexed by the ring in his hand, not knowing where he should put it. But, thank goodness, he did not stand up again; instead he reached out, extending the ring to Cemile Abla from the armchair.

"I know from the films on TV how it's supposed to be done nowadays, but . . . such things really don't suit me. I apologize. The truth is, I was planning to get down on my knees to propose, but now that I'm here I just . . ."

Cemile Abla stared ahead. It would all be so easy, if only she knew a way to say it without hurting the man. But at the moment, she couldn't think of anything at all.

"Please, I beg you, don't turn me down, don't do this to me," he said. "I swear on my honor that I will do everything in my power to make you happy. Who knows, maybe you'll grow to like me once you get to know me better."

"There's no doubt in my mind that you are a very good, kind person, Timur Bey."

"Besides, the important thing is to have a life partner to share your loneliness with, isn't that right?"

Cemile Abla shook her head faintly, as if to say, *I suppose so.* The more the man talked, the more uneasy she became, and the greater her desire to open the windows and take a long, deep breath. She was horrified at the ring so stubbornly forced upon her, dangling there beneath her nose. As if completely unaware of how odd he was acting, Timur Bey remained still as a statue with his arm in the air, the faintly trembling ring held between his thumb and forefinger. Cemile Abla panicked at the thought that his arm might grow frozen in that position, remain airborne like that forever. She couldn't stand it any longer, and she quickly grabbed the ring, thus rescuing the man from his perilous position.

Unable to come up with a better idea, she politely placed the wedding ring on the edge of the table.

"We should celebrate," the man said.

"But you haven't drunk your tea," Cemile Abla quickly objected. "It must be ice cold by now."

The man downed the tea in a single gulp and excitedly began making plans. "Let's go out for a nice dinner, if you'd like. Look, we're in luck, there's a full moon out tonight. We have to celebrate, and we have to do it right. We can't go just anywhere. Let's go to your favorite restaurant . . ."

She had to wait a few more minutes before the medicine began to take effect. But Cemile Abla was tired of talking. "Have you ever thought about what happens to us after we're dead, Timur Bey?" she finally asked, desperately wanting to change the subject.

Though thrown off guard by the question, Timur Bey did his best to respond, as courtesy demands. "Unfortunately, I'm not really able to perform the duties of our religion as well as I should. But still—"

"I think it's going to be wonderful. We'll float in an endless sky like white balloons. Now and then we'll come together and form great big, even more beautiful clouds, then we'll split up into small pieces again and glide off in different directions. We'll wander in circles around a soothing light, and nothing will have a beginning or an end."

Timur Bey struggled to keep his eyes open, fighting the dead weight of his eyelids. He tried to spring to his feet, but failed. When he asked in a barely audible voice where the bathroom was, Cemile Abla got worried. If the man locked himself in the bathroom, she would have a nasty situation on her hands. She would have to break down the door. But Timur Bey was already on his feet, staggering toward the dining room door.

"I just need to wash my face," he mumbled. "It's just because I'm so happy, I guess . . ."

As soon as he reached the hallway, he collapsed to the floor. Cemile Abla, who was just a few paces behind him, took a deep breath of relief. How nice that Timur Bey had already made it halfway to the bathtub all by himself.

Two hours later, as she once again wrapped her knives, scissors, and meat cleaver up in their cloths and returned them to their drawers, three large, black trash bags stood in front of the kitchen door.

The mother of the first of the two stubborn groom candidates had somehow gotten Cemile Abla's telephone number and called less than a week after her son went missing. Her voice undulated with concern; she found the situation humiliating, that she had to talk with Cemile Abla under these conditions, when they hadn't even met, but she had no other choice. "Well, I tell you, I've been really worried myself, ma'am," said Cemile Abla. "I made all these preparations. I thought to myself that a man like your son, a man from such a good family, would at least call and let me know that he couldn't make it. But unfortunately, I haven't heard from him at all. And I had to give all those pastries and cakes to the neighbors' kids."

That night, she thought that she'd be able to carry the bags, which stood lined up in front of the kitchen door, by herself; she might not be able to carry them all at once, but certainly she was strong enough to take them out one by one. But her knees were so sore that she gave up after dragging the first bag down the hill. "There must be an easier way to do this," she mumbled, when the solution struck her—Captain Hasan. She headed down the shore and found him sitting on a stool just on the other side of the pier, puffing on a cigarette as he gazed upon the lights of distant ships. Just as she had guessed he would, Captain Hasan got up from his seat without asking a single question, without waiting for any explanation, in fact, without even the slightest glint of curiosity in his eyes. He ground his cigarette beneath his foot and followed Cemile Abla over to the bottom of the hill. First they carried the bag she had brought down to the captain's boat, then they went to her home and grabbed the other two bags. Even Captain Hasan had run short of breath; using the sleeve of his shirt, he inconspicuously wiped away the beads of sweat that had gathered on his brow from all the climbing.

"Don't you worry, Cemile Abla," he said with a grave expression once they had made their final descent. "I'll drop these straight into the current at the mouth of the Bosphorus. Nobody will know."

When they ran into one another around noon three days later, they didn't mention it; Captain Hasan just shook his head as if to say, *Mission accomplished*. And though she could hardly conceal her curiosity, Cemile Abla never asked: Had he simply dropped the bags into the strait, or had he untied them and dumped out the contents?

Thankfully, nobody called to ask about the second potential

groom. And this time around Cemile Abla was more experienced; she didn't even attempt to carry down the three large, black bags she'd set in front of the house. She went straight down to the shore and found Captain Hasan. She didn't need to say a word; she gave him a certain look, and he immediately understood that she needed his help once again. Captain Hasan seemed to handle the bags with more ease this time; in only fifteen minutes he had taken all three down and loaded them onto the boat without shedding a single drop of sweat. "I should set off before sunrise," he said. "I'll take care of these and then come back and pretend I forgot something and pick up that lazy-boned boy." The car-fanatic apprentice had just started work earlier that week.

When Cemile Abla got down to the shore, she found four fishermen settled in front of one of those hollows in the Hisar walls covered by iron bars; they were conversing in low voices, their eyes turned to the waters painted orange by the moonlight. When she reached them they greeted her as joyously as ever; she accepted their invitation to join them and sat down on the edge of a blanket. They chatted about this and that as she sipped the rakı in her tea glass. For a moment her eyes met those of Captain Hasan. Cemile Abla turned her head before anyone noticed, and began telling a funny story about her father. She was sure that the captain understood.

When she got home, she began trying to tape the cover back onto an old book, just to pass the time. It was an hour before sunrise when she heard the light knock at her door.

"You've got some packages that need to go down, Cemile Abla?" Captain Hasan asked. His cheeks were red from the rakı.

"I hate to trouble you . . ."

"No reason for you to come out, I'll take care of it."

Because she knew that he was too bound by the rules of etiquette to come inside, Cemile Abla dragged the bags to the front door herself. She was in a cheerful mood, relieved at not having to climb repeatedly at the crack of dawn. When she went to the living room to open the curtains, a tiny glinting object caught her eye. She had picked up the tea glasses, plates, forks, and knives earlier, but the wedding ring was still there on the edge of the coffee table. She thought about what she would tell Nalan. She was sure her telephone would ring before the clock struck noon; in fact, she wouldn't be surprised if Nalan came all the way over here just to gossip face to face.

"I guess I'm just not meant to marry," she'd tell her friend. "They all just slip right through my fingers. It's as if, just when it's all about to happen, *poof*, they evaporate into thin air, just like that. Don't get me wrong, I'm not taking you for granted, but please, let this be the last one," she'd say. "Don't introduce me to anyone else. Really. You think I'm not saddened by this, but really, it weighs so heavily on my conscience."

ALL QUIET

BY JESSICA LUTZ

Fatih

Privileged, that's what I am. I pray in the Conqueror's Mosque, the most honored one in the whole of Istanbul. Look at its simple, vast courtyard. There's nothing to distract a man from his mission, just the sober beauty that reminds one of the Greatness of God. Of why I have to perform my difficult duty.

At the fountain I have just completed my ablutions, a ritual that soothes me. A little cat came up and licked the water drops off my bare foot. I thought it to be a good omen even if I had to wash again. I love cats. I thanked God when I was praying inside, surrounded by the thick walls laced with five rows of arched windows that support a dome so high, it must have been a miracle half a millennium ago. Fatih Mehmet, the Conqueror, built this tribute to Allah after the greatest city of the infidels surrendered to the relentless blows of his army. *Our* army! We, the Muslims, arrived, and Constantinople became Istanbul. Some claim the architect failed to make the first mosque of Istanbul higher than the infidel's biggest church, the Hagia Sophia. They say the Sultan ordered his hands to be cut off, but I think that's just malicious slander invented by the infidels.

I must go now. No time to linger. I'm quiet inside, focused. I have the address written on a piece of paper, but I don't need it. I know where to go. I leave the outer courtyard of the mosque through the gate at the right, which brings me into Darüşşafaka Avenue. Isn't that a beautiful name, Abode of Dawn? I walk past Wednesday Market with its small shops. Dried fruits and nuts, frilly dresses for little girls, a toy shop—didn't have those when I was small—the *tulumba* shop. Maybe I could stop for some of those sweet syrupy balls. I'm sure my assistant would like to. But no, I mustn't indulge.

Evil tongues say I know little mercy. That's not true. My assistant will testify that I find my task hard. He's a reliable young man. But it must be done. God's soldiers must be tough. We cross the Yavuz Selim Avenue straight into the Manasyazade Avenue past the İsmail Ağa Mosque. I know that at the back of its courtyard, the old *medrese* is still being used for teaching. One of our finest Quran courses is given there. Perhaps on my way back I could pay a visit. The teacher is a friend of mine.

Look at the pretty ladies in the sun, their faces framed by headscarves and reddened by the icy wind that's blowing. I disapprove of those young, slender girls who wear their long coats so tight that a man needs no imagination to know what's inside. They send my blood racing. Very bad. They're asking for something to happen to them. We're nearly there, I think. Left off Fethiye Avenue, at the end of this street we go right, and then left again.

Here's the place. First on the left after the big grocery. Its stands of vegetables nearly blocking the pavement. As I expected, a decent, modest street. Is it surprising? If you remember, back in the Conqueror's time this was the first neighborhood of the city that was populated by Muslims. No fancy houses, no showcases for wealth, just as God commands. Behind these metal-framed windows live good folk. My assistant knows the address too; he's spotted the door already. I let him press the bell. He likes that.

"Who's there?" I recognize Zekeriya's drawling voice.

My assistant announces our arrival. It takes awhile before the buzzer sounds. I'm not worried. I know our friend will let us in. He has erred, but he's not lost. I'm here to bring him back to the flock. Third floor. My assistant presses the button. He likes that.

I suspect Zekeriya hesitated before opening the door because he thinks little of me and my assistant. There are some who think the boy is retarded, but I can tell you he's not. And of course Zekeriya's wife hates me. I guess she's at home. She once criticized me for my black beard that makes me look much older than her husband, even though I'm ten years younger. She said I was faking, despite my skull cap, my pious robe. She said I'm not a real Muslim. The nerve.

I showed her what a woman's place is. She's never said a word to me again, but her eyes tell me enough. Ha. I laugh at her.

I bet it's she who has persuaded Zekeriya to leave the brotherhood. She would, with her poisonous tongue. She can expect something from me too. But my priority is Zekeriya. He is, after all, a good Muslim. I know he prays at the little mosque we passed on our way here, an old Byzantine church with its typical flat dome. No better place to be reminded of our superiority. Yes, he's a good Muslim all right.

There he is. Look at him, wringing his hands by the door. He clearly doesn't want to let us in, but of course he will. What's he saying? Oh, his oldest daughter came home today. She's in her first year at university. Just finished her first term. They were about to sit down for a special meal.

No, don't worry, we won't join. In fact, we won't be long. Tell your womenfolk to eat. I'll have a little word with them later, but you don't need to know that.

On our way to the living room, past the kitchen, I catch a glance of his wife. Her frown makes me smile.

Yes, Zekeriya, shut the door behind us.

Bang!

Ha. He didn't expect that. I must say, my assistant does a great chop. It always takes them by surprise. Poor Zekeriya. On his knees. I bet it's all black before his eyes. He's not moving while my assistant ties his hands behind his back, but I can see he's coming to. Time for me to examine the bookcase. What have we got here . . . wise sayings of the Prophet, may God's blessing be upon Him. Wise sayings of the Prophet Jesus. More wise sayings. Ah, and now he's about to say something himself. Time for me to leave.

Through the door I hear his surprised yelp.

"Hey, what is this . . . all . . . about?" The last words he whispers, because the kid has put a knife on his midriff. I know. We've been through this routine before. The sun must be reflecting on the blade as he presses its sharp tip through Zekeriya's clothes. Very gently at first. Then he'll twist it slowly. A hole in Zekeriya's sweater. It looked new. Perhaps he's wearing it for his daughter.

I'll check out the ladies in the kitchen.

Hmmm. No daughter in sight. Where is she? Gone to visit a friend, says the bitch. Too bad. But I must concentrate on what I'm here for. I pick up an ashtray and some matches. That's all right, isn't it? Of course it is. I knew it. No. No tea yet. See you later.

Poor Zekeriya. He looks at me with such hope when I enter the room again. He's trying to move away from my assistant's hand, but it follows him, keeping the knife firmly in place. I wonder if he has already pierced his skin. I see no blood yet.

"If I push up . . ." he hisses, and pushes, "I could pierce your heart. Open your mouth."

"Please," Zekeriya says, looking at me. I smile back, while my assistant stuffs a rag into his mouth. He always carries a piece of towel in his bag. You never know what you might need it for.

Ah, that assistant of mine is so fast! I hadn't even seen Zekeriya move—perhaps his shoulder is in pain—but there it is. His hand shot at the knife and with lightning speed stuck its tip in Zekeriya's nostril. Muffled sounds. Fast breathing. His tongue must be bone dry. He's getting scared. Good.

"Get up."

My assistant doesn't help him. He pulls up his legs and rolls over onto his face. Now he can smell whether his wife cleans the carpet properly or not. I feel like kicking that chubby ass up in the air there. Instead I tell him to sit down on the chair my assistant has placed in the middle of the room. Meekly he does so, and then he gives me that begging look again. I smile. He makes a sound and widens his eyes.

Ah, it's the knife he sees coming. My assistant slashes downward, rips straight through his sweater. This time his skin bursts. The cut isn't terribly deep. It might not even hurt. It will though, just you wait. I've lit a cigarette and I wave it under his nose. He doesn't smoke, I know, but he recoils because he can feel the heat of the red cone. I like this bit.

He tries to move further away from me as I confront him with his betrayal. Don't you know, I ask him, that you can never leave the brotherhood? And I stab the cigarette butt onto his chest, on the edge of his bare nipple.

His howl triggers my assistant. The tip of the dagger immediately on the stretched upper lip. Zekeriya closes his eyes.

Oh, come on, stay with it! Aren't you listening? I plant the red-hot stab in his ear and I can see his eyes water. And look at those swollen veins on his throat. That's a scream that wants to come out. Good boy, he's not uttering a sound. Ooops. But he nods.

The glistening blade slides upwards on his lip; its cutting edge touches the cartilage between his nostrils. My young friend is clearly angry too, and I inform Zekeriya of this unfortunate fact.

My assistant nods to the rhythm of the loud jingle from the truck that sells propane tanks. It's a rather funny sight. The amplified tune penetrates the room. I bet it always comes around the same time. Must be one of the rare neighborhoods that don't have natural gas yet. I hear a voice call out to the street—the woman next door? I wonder if she hears anything going on in this living room. The thought excites me. Someone calls the elevator. Must be the truck driver's boy. With a squeak it departs from the floor we're on.

What's that smell? Faintly metallic, familiar . . .

Ah. Blood. My assistant is getting carried away. It trickles all over Zekeriya's front, onto the carpet. That stain will always be there for him to remember. Ah, blood on rugs. No way to get it out.

I tell Zekeriya I am thinking about letting my assistant cut off his nose for setting such a bad example in the eyes of the community, especially the youngsters. I love the way his eyes widen. Suddenly I think of my father. I shudder. I want to shake off his image.

Zekeriya gags. He can't stand blood either. I lift my hand, and my assistant takes the knife away. Zekeriya's gaze turns to a picture on the end table. His parents. I strike. I hit him so hard he falls over onto his side, chair and all. Bang! That bloody, filthy little prick! He infuriates me! I remember going to his petty stationery shop to invite him over. I sweet-talked him, told him about making the world a better place. I sent customers to him, to prove that God's brotherhood does good. And now that his business is going well he wants to back out, the selfish coward. He couldn't stand to share his wealth? Didn't want to help out the odd apprentice we sent him? Or, ah yes, I remember, he reminded us once that there is no force in Islam, only persuasion. Ha! I'll teach him what persuasion is. I kick him in his stomach. He pulls up his legs. I kick his shin with the ball of my foot, a little trick I learned from my father. Maximum effect without shoes.

Zekeriya moans.

My assistant is quick to silence him, but . . . what's that? I hear shuffling on the other side of the door. There's a soft knock. We all look up. Is it the wife?

I open the door with a creak. Look at that. A boy, bringing a tray with tea. Thank you, and now get lost. Oh, you want a little peep? I allow him a glimpse before I shut the door. No harm in educating the young.

I tell my assistant to put Zekeriya upright again and give him his tea. I watch as he undoes the gag and pours the scalding liquid into the man's mouth. Zekeriya squeaks. What a brilliant idea it was, that tea, whoever thought of it.

I ask him if he will continue depriving us of his contributions and company. He whispers something that I can't understand. I slap him in the face. I notice his eyes go to the door, he must have heard something. With one jump I'm there, while he tries to shout, "No!" through the rag in his mouth.

When I pull open the door a crack, I find opposite me the Mrs. of the house, holding the little brat by the ear. My fingers fold around his other ear while I look her straight in the eye. Eavesdropping, was he? She doesn't lower her gaze as she should. I'll deal with her in a minute. For now, yes, of course we'd like some more tea.

When she walks away—I spot a little hesitation in her gait—I drag the boy to the bathroom, take the key from the inside, and push him in. Before I lock the door I tell him how quiet he has to be if he wants his father to live.

I think I might take a little look in the kitchen. She looks up from wiping off the table when I enter. A shadow darkens her face when she sees it's me.

"Is my husband with you?" she asks. I think I see faint moisture appear on her upper lip. It makes me feel good. I tell her we're discussing business of the brotherhood, but I know she must be wondering why her husband hasn't come out of the room, why he isn't here instead of me. It's quite inappropriate for us to be together in the same room like this, and she should angrily send me away. But I can taste her fear now.

She's turned her back to me, to close the window above the counter. Quite right. You don't want anyone to hear what's coming, my dear. Through the white nylon curtain I can see the next building near enough. I move forward and stand next to her. She blabbers something about her father-in-law who is asleep. The water boils. She pours it in the teapot. And lets out a cry when I grab her arm. The tea glasses clatter on the tray.

She tries to pull away, but my grip is like a vice. I can't help but grin at her feeble attempt to break free and soft laughter escapes my throat. How satisfying.

"Where is Zekeriya?" Her question comes out as a whisper.

Nothing will happen to him if you keep quiet, I say.

"What have you done to him? What have you done to my son?" She shrieks and scratches my face with her free hand,

and she kicks my shin. I love it. I pull off her headscarf and grab her hair.

When I bring my face close to hers, she spits. I don't care. I slowly wipe my face with my sleeve and hold her head at the base of her skull. Her eyes become big like saucers while I bring my lips to hers. They're firm and warm. My tongue finds its way between them.

Ouch! The bitch, she bit me!

I slap her face. Anger burns in the pit of my stomach. I shake her head with her hair in my fist. And tell her my assistant is holding a knife to her husband's throat. All he needs is a word from me.

That's better. Her movements become kind of mechanical, but she follows my hand obediently when I pull her to the kitchen table. She doesn't move when my hands disappear under her sweater. I feel her skin. Her soft, bouncy breasts. I can't control my hands. They grab, they squeeze. Pull. Pinch.

I want to see them. I push her shirt up. Fill my mouth with flesh. Suck. Bite. Smell. For a moment I feel deeply happy. I sigh.

Then my mind switches on again. I tell her to get ready for me, and watch as she takes off her slippers, her tights, and her panties, and neatly folds them into a bundle. She leaves them on the floor by the armchair in the corner and comes back to me. I push her onto the table.

There is something sacred about this body that has never been touched by anyone but that misery-guts tied up in the living room. It makes me singe with excitement. I ride. I gallop. To a height I have never reached.

I can hardly stand on my legs anymore. My chest feels all relaxed. With my eyes closed I quickly say a prayer, although

I know I should ablute myself first. Thank you God. Thank you.

Privileged, that's what I am. I walk over to the living room, where my assistant is keeping an eye on Zekeriya. The door is wide open. Poor Zekeriya. He has more blood on his face and chest than when I left him. Actually, there's quite a puddle around him. He doesn't look too happy. In fact, I'm not sure he's conscious. My assistant has found another rope in his bag to tie him to the chair, so he stays upright, but his head is hanging to one side. I sit down at a distance on the sofa. I feel good. Look, Zekeriya is coming to. His head jolts back and forth, and he opens his eyes. They're swollen. Did my assistant punch them? Well, our friend asked for it. He'll think twice about leaving us again. I'd be surprised if he doesn't show up at our next meeting. I've raised his contribution a little too. That'll teach him.

Oh look! I can't believe it. Is my young assistant getting a hammer out of that bag of his? Yes, yes, look at him. He puts a nail on the middle of Zekeriya's head. Right on the top. Zekeriya is not quite aware yet of what's going to hit him. Ha ha, that's a funny pun. One, two, three, bang! Now he knows. I think I'd better stop my assistant. The nail is for the next time. We must give him a chance to repent.

I sense reluctance, but my assistant puts his tools away. He's a reliable fellow. Someday I'll show him what else can be done with a hammer and nail. Amazingly effective tools, actually. My hand still hurts from that time my father nailed me to the doorpost, and how many years has it been? But I'll keep that for later.

Before we shut the door behind us I hear blubbering from the bathroom. I tell my assistant to get the elevator. He presses the button. He likes that.

* * *

Author's note: In the year 2000, the Turkish police carried out a major operation in Istanbul, raiding cells of an illegal organization and killing their leader at the end of a four-hour armed clash. The organization called itself Hezbollah, which means Party of God. Buried in safe houses scattered throughout the country, the police found nearly a hundred bodies of Hezbollah's victims, including women. Most of them were small businessmen who had been supporting the organization, but had lost faith in its cause. All victims had been severely tortured.

AROUND HERE, SOMEWHERE

BY Algan Sezgintüredi

Şaşkınbakkal

By the time he reached the Marmara shore, his lungs were about to explode. He darted across all four lanes of the coastal road, its white stripes shining beneath the orange glow of towering streetlamps, the cars racing by as if speeding were some kind of prerequisite for driving in the wee hours of the night. He had neither the time nor the courage to look back. And rightly so, for just a few yards later he heard someone yell out, telling him to stop. He'd heard it the first time, as he began hightailing it down from Baghdad Avenue, and he knew well and good what the third time meant. Back in the day, he wouldn't have had to run at all. But these guys were new to the job, they didn't know how to grease their palms. Yet. Right? Or maybe they were just idealistic kids who refused. Once upon a time, I would've refused too. Once upon a time, money wasn't everything. Once upon a time. But Teoman was no slacker, he had his boys' backs. Right? Or maybe these guys aren't idealists, just a little slicker than their predecessors? A little too greedy, pushing for five instead of three? Run. Run, goddamnit. Then again, what the hell if I get caught? I'll just get roughed up, grin and bear a couple days of questioning, and be out before you know it. Nothing new to me. Besides, it's not really me they're after. They know who I am, the shit I'm up to. I'm a little fish. It's only been two years since I started, though I'm no rookie. I'm not falling for it; I know exactly what those guys dish out, and how much. And those laws that are changing as Turkey tries to get its eager little foot in the door to the European Union, well, they're in my favor. Their beef is really with Teoman, not me. And damned if they'll ever catch him. None of you guys have ever even seen him, let alone know where he is! That man's got your daddies on a leash!

Should I ditch the bags? Ditch 'em, get rid of 'em, then plead your case before that asshole Teoman. Right! "You know how much that shit's worth, huh?" "Of course, boss." Fucking heartless dwarf! No way you can explain. The man won't listen. Better to risk it.

I nearly stumble. Not far now. The lights over on that side are out. What luck! And right at the breakwater too. C'mon, Tufan! Run. Keep it up, boy. Dude, if you go and fill up a shore with sand, then you doll it up with some fucking fast growing trees! That's what you're *supposed* to do. Damn city . . . Now I'm just a sitting duck. It's all in the legs. My lungs are gonna explode. I can't breathe.

The third warning came just a few steps from his destination.

I don't know how, but I feel it; these guys don't give a shit about the law; they're not gonna just fire into the air. Fucking rookies! Into the air, dudes, into the air!

A shot rings out. He thrusts himself between two high-speed boats docked inside the breakwater. Man, that hurt. Knee, elbow, pain from head to toe. But don't move. This place is dark enough. Maybe they won't see you.

He waited, his breath bated. He didn't budge. The pain, it would pass. It was all about not getting caught. Actually, it wasn't so much about not getting caught as it was about not getting caught *right now*. Because tomorrow is Sunday. And that means Yeliz is coming over. The girl's only got one day off a week as it is, and I can't spend that day in custody. Keep it up, just a little longer. I'm wearing black, and I'm surrounded by darkness. And there's no moon. Lie down flat. Hide your face, don't let it shine. Maybe they won't see you. They might think you've escaped.

Damn it, quit prancing around! Fuck off already! Go look for me somewhere else!

Wait! Best to crawl between the boats. I learned this crawling thing back in the military. Don't raise your ass; keep your knees to the ground, go easy on the cartilage. On your knees, that's right. Just like they got you doing in civilian life too. Well, damned if I can't crawl with the best of 'em. Oh yeah, that's it. Slowly. Right there, between the boats.

Tufan, a dealer on Baghdad Avenue, slithered his way between two canvas-clad boats, and continued on all fours.

Just a little further. That's it, right there. There are more than twenty boats here. And it's dark. They'll never find you. Ha! They're not even coming. Stupid rookies. Wait a minute. Let me just stick my head out here a bit. Aha. They're gone. Idiots! Wait, maybe they've gone down below?

He leaned over and looked down at the concrete path along the coast. All clear. Well fuck me! Those guys really are rookies. Man, it's not like I disappeared into thin air, the least you could do is come down and take a look.

I can't believe it! I lost them! The suckers are gone. Yes! Tufan, my man, just wait a little bit, and then go home and reward yourself. You deserve it. Seems I ain't such a bad sprinter after all!

What? Wait a second. What's that? Hold on, there's someone there. Over there, way at the end of the breakwater. Holy shit! They're not gone after all.

Tufan quickly crouched back down, his heart racing once again.

How did I miss them? They must have slipped by me, hurried all the way down there. Impossible, but . . . Wait a second.

He held his breath, poked his head out, slowly.

There were two of them. But this guy's alone. And he's just sitting there. What the . . . ? At this hour? Maybe he's one of those winos. Or some guy with the blues, got himself a bottle of wine, swinging his legs over the sea. Maybe he's about to drown himself. Maybe he's trying to decide, right now. But then that's everyone's predicament in this country, right? Sucked the life out of every damn one of us. Wait! Maybe he's got some money on him. A swift kick to the head, take the money, and run. Better than showing up at Teoman's empty-handed.

Still doubled over, he slipped out of his hiding place and started weaving his way through the boats. He'd forgotten all about the fuzz; his hand went to his pocket and he pulled out his switchblade.

He approached the man in complete silence, deftly, carefully, but then, just as he was about to assume his position, the man turned his head.

And Tufan, there before a face he recognized even in the dim light of a distant lamp, did not know where to hide his knife.

"Ekber *Amca?*"

The old man squinted at him. His eyes searched the face of the younger man, who swiftly moved to conceal his weapon behind his back. Ekber Amca's eyes, wrinkled around the edges, sparkled at finally having found what he was looking for, and a smile immediately spread across his face.

"Tufan?"

"Amca, what are you doing here at this hour?"

"I'm waiting."

"For what?"

Instead of answering, the old man motioned for Tufan to sit next to him. Come, sit down. Don't stand there, I don't know how long we'll be waiting. Tufan looked at him, puzzled.

"Come," the old man said. "Don't be afraid, they can't see you anymore."

"Who?"

"Weren't you just running from the police?"

Tufan continued to stare at him with uncomprehending eyes.

"Just come here and sit down. It's good that you've come. We can have a chat."

Tufan didn't know what to say. It was their downstairs neighbor, Ekber Amca.

Oh man, Ekber Amca was on my case all the time when I was a kid! Don't play in the garden, watch out for the flowers, don't pick the plums until they're ripe . . . He'd yell at me all day, and go tattle to my daddy at night. Got plenty of ass kickings thanks to you, huh, Ekber Amca? But then, can't really blame you much. You don't really get it when you're a kid though, do you? Your wife had passed away, your kids had grown up to be useless ingrates, and nobody ever called on you anymore. You were screwed, nothing left, nothing but your house. Loneliness. I didn't understand it at the time, of course. Crotchety old man just looking for somebody to yell at, that's what I thought. My mom, may she rest in peace, she stayed out of it most of the time, but my dad, he'd beat the crap out of me, just 'cause I'd ruffled your feathers. Probably because he was sick of your nagging. My dad was a crank anyways, had no tolerance for me getting on anybody's nerves. A call from the principal's office, and *whap*. Someone in the neighborhood ratted on me and it was, "Come here, boy!" Ekber Amca, man, you know what, you were the freaking bane of my existence; you still like that now or what, you son of a—? I was a kid, man, how could I know what you were up against?

"Of course, how could you?" said the old man, his eyes still fixed on the horizon, which was covered in a sheet of darkness, pierced only by the lights of the Princes' Islands. "You were a child."

Ah fuck! Is this guy reading my mind?

"Of course I am. What's wrong with that?"

Fine, then read this!

"Shame on you, Tufan. All grown up, but still the same old good-for-nothing punk."

What the hell do you know about what I am?

"I know you got mixed up in drugs and whatnot, dropped out of college, and made a royal mess of your life. And I know that you deal out on the avenue. That enough for you?"

Oh, c'mon! Man, what's going on here? Is this some kind of dream or something?

"Dream . . ." The old man peered intently at Tufan. "A dream, of course. What did you think it was? I'm sitting here at the breakwater, by myself, at some ungodly hour. It's dark out. I'm alone. You run away from the police and come here. Yep, a dream. All of it. Life, etcetera. It's all one big dream . . . What? 'Cheap-ass philosophy,' you say? Now look here, you little twerp!"

"Not swallowing it, Ekber Amca. I don't get whatever it is you're up to, but I'm out of here." He started to get up, and the old man smiled again.

"Sit down. What kind of a man are you anyway? Aren't

you the least bit curious? Shouldn't you be wondering what
the hell some old man like me is doing out here like this?
Sheesh."

Tufan turned and stared at the head of the breakwater.
Shit! Those guys are still here. There, over there, where I
jumped into the breakwater.

"Don't bother, son. They can't see you."

Tufan frowned. What do you mean?

"I mean, they can't see you. Forget it. Now look here,
I've got something to tell you: I think heaven's around here,
somewhere."

"Wha—?"

"Heaven, I said. I think it's around here somewhere."

Tufan glanced over his shoulder again. The two plainclothes narcs who'd just been chasing after him, and who a
short while before had tried to bust him as he was passing the
goods to some upstart, were still standing in front of the two
boats he'd slid between after jumping into the breakwater.

"What do you think?"

Tufan looked again at the man sitting next to him. Okay,
so this is definitely Ekber Amca. So . . .

"Calm down now, son. Like I told you, they can't see you.
So now, tell me, what do you think?"

"About what?"

"Boy, would you stop looking around? They can't see you.
So?"

"So what?"

"You know, heaven."

"What freaking heaven?"

"Heaven heaven." He motioned vaguely toward the sea. "I
think it's somewhere around here."

"Heaven?"

"Yes."

"Around here?"

"Yes."

"You mean, in the sea?"

"No, son. I mean in Şaşkınbakkal."

"Heaven? Heaven, like, paradise? In Şaşkınbakkal?"

"Yep."

Tufan laughed. Heaven? You've had a little too much to drink there, have you, amca? I mean, if you're talking about hell, okay, but Ekber Amca, if this haven of lowlifes is any kind of heaven, at best it's a heaven for rich bastards.

"Shame on you, Tufan."

What, you saying it ain't true? What middle-class stiff can buy anything from those stores on the avenue? How much is the rent? But never mind that, you know how nuts they go for these worthless pills? No, of course you don't.

"How could I know, son?"

Well, then who are you to talk? What kind of heaven could this place possibly be?

"What's heaven like then, Tufan?"

"Shit, I don't know ... *Huri*s, *gılman*s, all that stuff."

"So, let's start with the huris. You mean to say there aren't any girls here? But what beauties there are on our street alone!"

"Uhh, for example ... ?"

"Esra, Arif's daughter, on the third floor?"

"Who? That slut Esra?"

The old man pursed his lips together and gave Tufan a stern look.

"What?" Tufan said. "You're not going to tell me about Esra now, are you? Oh man, Ekber Amca ... kids these days ain't what they were back in your day, you know!"

"I know," the old man said. He sighed, shook his head. "I know."

Tufan felt his stomach knot up. Man, did I say something wrong?

"No, son, why do you think it's wrong? If you say so, it is so."

"Look here," Tufan said, trying to cheer the old man back up. "Your whole heaven business already went belly up."

"How's that?"

"I mean, you're talking about beautiful girls, and you fell flat with that first example."

"How so? You mean Esra isn't pretty?"

"Of course she is. She's beautiful, but—" He paused. Man, you can't just come up and tell him the chick puts out to everyone and his brother just for a couple of grams of powder. But then you did already blurt out the whole slut thing . . . C'mon now, amca, you sit at that window all day. Don't you see that girl coming and going? You think those sunken eyes are from studying all the time? Can you really be that fucking naïve? Man! He raised his head and looked at the old guy. "You were reading my mind again, weren't you?"

"I was, son. But there's no need, I already know about Esra's predicament. Like you said, I sit at the window all day, and I'm not blind. But anyway, my claim remains."

"What claim?"

"About heaven."

"You mean, even if she's a slut?"

"What exactly are huris supposed to do, Tufan?"

Tufan tried to recall what he'd been told in religion class back in school, or the things he'd heard during his childhood. He hadn't had anything to do with God for some time. After his father died and he'd gotten the apartment all to himself, he never went to prayer, not even on religious holidays. He could hardly remember a thing. But okay, the duty of huris ...

"That's exactly it, Tufan."

"What, you mean about them being some kind of whores, right?"

Ekber Amca burst out laughing.

"Nooo! What kind of language is that now?"

Well, what then?

"Theirs is a holy duty."

"Oh, so you mean if she spreads her legs for every Tom, Dick, and Harry *here*, she's a slut, but over *there* ..."

"Slut's a term we use, son. A label we slap onto people when it suits us. Look up. We can't know who's what in His eyes, now, can we? Look, for example, back in Sumer, it was the responsibility of priestesses."

"Now you're messing with me."

"It's historical fact."

"Well," said Tufan, laughing, "then you're right. Şaşkınbakkal's crawling with huris."

"And handsome gılmans too."

"If it's like you say, then yes." Tufan was in a good mood now. He'd forgotten all about the police. But wait, what about the abundance, all that milk and honey in heaven?

"You said it yourself."

"Said what?"

"That Şaşkınbakkal could only be a heaven for rich people. I mean," he said, spreading his arms out, "you want abundance, well, here you have it."

"Like that abundance is for *us*."

"Why not? You get your share, don't you?"

"Selling drugs?"

"However. The fact of the matter is that there is abundance here, and you benefit from it." The old man laughed again, then stopped and shook his head. "No, I haven't lost my marbles from loneliness, or from sitting at the window all day. But, well, yeah, when you've got nothing else to do, you think . . . a lot."

"So, you mean you thought and you pondered, long and hard, and you found heaven, here?"

"Not yet. But it's around here, somewhere. Or at least, it seems like it to me. Look around you: the sea in front of us. Look at those lights coming from the islands, like a necklace of jewels there on the dark sea. Where else can you find such beauty? This is one of the most beautiful seas on earth."

"You mean the Sea of Marmara?"

"Of course."

"That sea in front of us? The one teeming with germs?"

"It didn't used to be like that."

That's right, it didn't. Tufan remembered going swimming here back when he was five or six years old. Right over there was the sailing club. And a little farther down, Suadiye Beach. A long time ago. Before they filled in the shore and built the road.

"Besides," said Ekber Amca, "they've reopened Caddebostan Beach."

Tufan laughed again. That's right, they had reopened it. And the masses had rushed in to get their feet wet. The municipality claimed that the pollution level had fallen. Bullshit. Just pulling the wool over the people's eyes. But Tufan didn't want to draw this out any longer than necessary.

"All right, fine. A beautiful sea before us. What else?"

"Tufan, you ever walk around?"

"What do you mean?"

"Here. Not on the avenue, in the streets."

"Like, when?"

"Anytime. Spring, summer, winter, whenever. Tell me, when was the last time you took a walk though the side streets of Şaşkınbakkal? Those treelined roads, quiet, calm, so far from the chaos of the avenue, with the occasional breeze caressing your hair? It's been a long time, hasn't it? Probably back in middle school, with your girlfriend or something? And now, ha, only when you're running away . . . or when Teoman calls . . . By Teoman, I mean your boss. And a dwarf you say? . . . All right, okay, why are you getting all riled up?"

"Ekber Amca . . . man, this just ain't right."

"Why not?"

"I mean, I don't know. This shit's got me feeling so naked, so exposed. This, that, everything . . ."

"But you can read mine too."

"How?"

"I don't know. Just try . . . No, son, you're not high, you're clean . . . No, no! Ha ha ha! . . . No way! You haven't hit your head or anything either."

Tufan didn't get it. He didn't get it, so he tried. How he tried, or how he did it, he did not know, but in no time his head was spinning from all the images, scents, tastes, sounds that filled it. He heard the leaves from the plane trees rustle in the wind in the side streets in the middle of winter. He saw children running through the alleys in the spring. He saw fourteen-year-old Ekber, in the middle of summer, drinking cognac and smoking dope with friends in the hut of the older Emin, who rented out boats on the shore, before the road had been built over it. The day he married Hilmiye *Teyze*, may she rest in peace. Ekber becoming a father. And then his son slamming the door shut behind him, cursing. How his daughter married a hard man who, yes, was just like him. His departure for Germany. Hilmiye's Teyze sudden death. Pain. Loneliness. Growing old. He saw him growing weak. He felt it.

"Focus," said the old man.

It was so easy.

I just learned how to do it myself. You came up next to me, you know, when I turned around and looked at you. And you were about to attack me. No, don't worry, it's okay. I'm not angry. There you go, calm down. Just like that. You understand me now? . . . Oh, come on, don't get upset. The loneliness is my loneliness, it's no fault of yours! My wife's death, the way my son and daughter up and left . . . How were you to know that I had no other friends but you and those other kids out on the street? I got up early every morning and waited for you guys to go out into the garden and play—what did you think? . . . Oh, now, son . . . No, no, you didn't get on my nerves. I couldn't have cared less about you messing up the flowers. You get it, don't you? The reason why I got so upset, yelled and screamed at you guys . . . Oh, now, son, I know, you're lonely too. There are lots of us. C'mon now . . . . Shhh . . . Don't cry. You got used to it back in law school, so much hope, so much ambition . . . How proud dear Mehmet *Bey* was that you were going to become a lawyer. But then, well, you became a filthy drug dealer . . . Ohhhh, please now, son! Well looky here, so there *is* a special someone. Oh, but she doesn't know, huh? That's all right.

Tufan couldn't stop crying. I've already hit thirty, Ekber Amca, and just look at me, man!

Okay, son, now just calm down. It's all over now.

What do you mean *all over?* Can't you see? I sell poison to kids! I wait for them in front of school, sell to kids as young as fucking fifteen! Everything I've ever stood against . . . Don't you understand?

We don't have to understand, Tufan. You don't have to understand me, and I don't have to understand you. Or the world, or anything else. We don't have to understand. We're children. All of us. His children. We don't have to understand. It's over now.

The old man threw his arm over Tufan's shoulder. The latter let it all out, leaning against the old man, weeping loudly. Teoman. Beatings. Fear. Escape. Police. Drugs. Yeliz. How can I tell her? I'm screwed! I'm fed up with this shit!

"Ohh, look at that view."

Both of them swung around.

It was a short, energetic-looking young man, standing about two meters behind them, his hands at his waist. He had curly blond hair and his eyes sparkled with joy. He was wearing a black T-shirt with *Annihilator* written across the chest.

Tufan instinctively leapt to his feet; he didn't know who this guy was, but he knew his type. His hand went for the switchblade in his back pocket. At the very same moment, Ekber Bey grabbed Tufan by the leg. Hold on, son.

"Looks like you guys have been chillin' out," said the new arrival. "That's good. Honestly, I can't stand those high-strung types." He stuck his hand in one of the pockets of his baggy hip-hop pants and removed a folded piece of paper. "Okay," he said. "Let's see what we've got here." He unfolded the paper, mumbling to himself as he read it. "Ekber Şen, right?" The old man nodded. "Great. And you, you must be Tufan Tokgöz."

"And who the hell are you?" asked Tufan.

"Shhh," said Ekber Bey. "Excuse him, your Holiness, Azrael."

The young man let out a giggle. "No, Ekber Bey. The big boys don't do the bookkeeping." He took out a pen from another pocket. He looked at it, then at the paper, and then he motioned for Tufan to approach.

"So who the hell are you?"

"Who, me?" He scrunched his brows together in thought. "Oh man," he said, finally, "you guys rule. Not many of you hotshots think to ask me my name. Hmm, what shall I call myself this time?" A smile spread across his face, he looked to the sky. "Okay. Fine. *Cheese.* That's right, my name is Cheese. How's that?"

Perplexed, Tufan looked from Ekber Bey to the young man, who was again motioning for him to come over. Tufan didn't know why, but he was gripped by a sudden fear; his knees quaking, he walked over. From behind Cheese's shoulder, he could see the two cops still standing by the boats. Cheese noticed the expression on Tufan's face.

"Don't mind them," he said. "Now turn around for me."

Tufan stared at him blankly.

"I said turn around . . . Ha ha ha! You nasty little thing, you. That's a good one. No, that's not what I had in mind. I'm just going to use your back to write something, if you can stand still for a minute, that's all. All right? Now turn around."

Tufan turned around. Cheese placed the piece of paper on the dealer's back. He started writing. He stopped, looked at the pen, shook it up and down, and started writing again. Then he stopped again. He brought the point of the pen to his mouth and blew a few warm breaths onto it. He tried writing again. He let out a swear word. He looked over Tufan's shoulder.

"I don't suppose you've got a pen on you?"

The old man shook his head.

"I'm not even going to ask *you*," he said to Tufan. "Well,

there's not much to write anyway. I can just punch a couple of holes next to your names." He shook the pen once more. "Fucking supply department . . ." He pressed down on the pen and punched two holes in the paper. "All right, you can turn around now."

"What the hell's going on?" asked Tufan. Not that he couldn't sense it, he just wasn't quite ready to admit it.

"What's going on?" Cheese opened his eyes wide. "What the hell's going on, you ask? Wait, let's see now, what's going on." He moved his hand to his chin, squinted his eyes. "Hmmm. There's going to be a car crash on the avenue in a little bit. Classic midnight drag race. I've got one more pickup there." He sighed. "A father on night duty out looking for a pharmacy. Unfortunate case, that one. Just became a daddy. The punk who hits him survives though." He sighed again. "Five minutes after that I have to go down to Kadıköy; a wino on the docks is going to have a heart attack. Now wait a second . . ." He looked at the paper. "That's right, then I have to cross the Bosphorus. A whore in Beyoğlu . . . What? . . . Haaa haaa haaa! A huri? Oh, that's a good one. I'll have to tell the sisters about that. But anyway, then I have to go to Etiler, and so on and so forth. Ah, but if you're asking what's going on in the world, now that's a tough one to answer. There are tons of officials, and they're all fully booked.

"Oh! Wait! I'm sorry," Cheese said suddenly, interrupting himself. He covered his mouth in feigned surprise. "You still don't know what's going on here, that's what you're asking about. Oh, sweetheart! Innocent babe in the woods! But c'mon . . . you're on to us now, right? C'mon, say it."

Several moments passed before Tufan finally managed to croak out the words, "I . . . I'm . . . dead?"

"Bravo!" replied Cheese.

"B-but . . ."

"See there, the ambulance has arrived."

Tufan spotted the vehicle parking along the coastal road, about fifty meters away. Its lights were off. You could only tell it was an ambulance because the orange light on top shone beneath the streetlamp. They weren't in a hurry, of course. That's why they'd taken their time, cruising to a halt, no siren. Tufan watched as two people waltzed out of the ambulance, opened the back doors, and took out the stretcher.

"You mean . . . I . . ."

"I mean *you,* boy," said Cheese, placing his hand on Tufan's shoulder. "You took a bullet in the back at the end of that chase a little while ago, as you jumped onto the breakwater. And the guys who shot you have been waiting by your body over there."

At a loss for words, Tufan turned to Ekber Amca.

"Ekber Bey had a heart attack ten minutes before that, and collapsed into the sea. Someone'll find his body in the morning, I suppose."

"Cheese, son," said Ekber Bey, as he stood up, using his hands to push himself off the ground, "I want to ask you something."

Cheese smiled. They've always got questions. Sooo many questions. He folded his arms. He looked at the old man approaching him, and then at the dealer. "Yes, Ekber Bey," he said . . . No, I'm not the one who's going to do your account. Yes, you can rub the heads of people walking in the streets, they'll let you do that . . . Sure, why not? . . . Nah, it's not that bad. Of course, it depends on how things add up for you . . . No, I have no idea when Yeliz is coming; they only give us the lists of the people we have to pick up . . . Well, I'd love to stay and chat, but I'm in a bit of a hurry. Work, you know. Ha ha ha! I'm lying, of course. Why would I want to stay and chat with *you* guys? Well, you know, I can't always act as formal as they want us to, but then, who can, right? He looked up again. Besides, even He knows this job's unbearable if you play by the Book all the time . . . What's that? . . . Yeah, right, of course, of course, it's around here somewhere. Whatever.

THE SPIRIT OF PHILOSOPHICAL VITRIOL

BY LYDIA LUNCH

Tepebaşı

Some days you just want to fuck shit up. Spread the misery around. Louse up somebody's life. Even the score. Find an unsuspecting, but not undeserving mark and dump a truckload of shit on his head. Because you can. Because some perverse mean streak needs exorcizing before it contaminates the whole of your being and you in turn do something horribly ruthless to a public building, a strip mall, a shopping center, a city block, an entire neighborhood, the necropolis you're stuck in and all the mindless zombie breeders and their greedy offspring who roam this parasitic planet as it spirals toward its imminent extinction, when the bomb in your head wants to explode in your hands and take a couple hundred thousand people with it. I get ugly like that sometimes.

I was burned out, bitchy, and bored. Again. Had a couple of hours to kill before the train to Athens would signal the close of a month-long low-rent aimless ramble instigated in a spastic fit of dementia. I started the journey suffering under the delusion that my rotten moods were the by-product of stagnation and lethargy exasperated by routine and monotony. Doesn't matter what you do or don't do to earn a living, to pay the rent, to keep the lights on and the wind out, the same job done over and over again for any period of time becomes a mind-dulling prison sentence which sends sensitive nerve endings into a St. Vitus dance of agitation. Brain dead but spastic. Numbed of all but the most negative emotions. A harvest of superhuman willpower and extreme focus the only defense against a scorching desire to flail arms and legs blindly like a punch-drunk boxer shadowboxing in the dark, hellbent on murdering the invisible enemy which has become an all-encompassing surround. As if allergic to the air itself. Day in, day out will do that. Truth was, I was just as much of a miserable cunt when there were no responsibilities, deadlines, headlines, nosy friends, or dying relatives to ruin my day. Bitter. I was praying that a break in my routine would break me of my bullshit.

Keep dreaming.

Twenty-nine days ago I purchased a cheap ticket from a Midtown bucket shop specializing in no-frill flights. I landed in a city I had no intention of visiting. I bought a bargain train pass good enough to get me a seat on the off hours. I did not consult an atlas. I packed nothing. I told no one. There was no one to tell. I needed to disappear from the city, state, country, culture, global stranglehold of hypocritical doublespeak, corporate slave trading, universal insanity, and my addictive predilection to the minutia of every possible encroaching disaster, which was leeching precious energy from the wellspring of my being. I thought by playing a stint of runaway fugitive with a strain of wandering-gypsy shape shifter that I could outmaneuver a vindictive part of my personality which had become increasingly hostile and was battling for dominance as a natural reaction against the world at large. I assumed that divorcing myself from negative elements, information overload, satellite TV, the Internet, radio, newspaper reports, telephone updates, and local gossip, I could somehow purge myself of this overwhelming need for retribution, revenge, violence. I needed to physically remove myself from a world that was making my psyche sick.

Tramping through Belarus, Poland, Slovakia, Romania, Bulgaria, night stalking dead zones, stopping in crusty post-industrial villages free from the ravages of tourists, football hooligans, vacationing families, hen parties, business men. Rummaging for an hour, a day, thirty-six hours, just long enough to explore the haunted remains and ghostly remnants, the garbage and wreckage of life dispossessed. A deserted farm house, her roof collapsed under the weight of a century and a half of blustery winters, rotting wood, and termites. A dilapidated factory, a victim of her own contaminants, battered blood-red by rust and erosion. At one time a proud workhorse spitting out spare parts for armored tanks and land rovers, now a decayed orphan whose guts had been ripped out and sold for scraps. Slivers of copper wiring scattered like auburn gossamer refracting sunlight. Empty hollows which had sucked life into their vortex and existed now as a testament to mystery and disappearance forming a beautiful vacuum devoid of humans. This was bliss.

And therein lies the problem. I was almost completely depressurized, left alone to moon vacantly into the ruins of collapsed architecture, rambling absently through dusty towns and half-deserted villages, mingling with humans only long enough to request a bottle of water, something to eat, a place to sleep. The joy of not understanding any but the most rudimentary of foreign phrases turned even the most grating of native tongues into a brutal symphony of discordant melodies. The dull ringing in my ears, a revolt no doubt from overexposure to the chronic chattering of Western mouths in love with the sound of their own voices, had vanished. The palpitation of my jugular, a sure sign of the thickening of my arteries filthied by the poison of close proximity to the contagions which overpopulate every city, had quelled. The painful spasm in my left pinkie, a simple decades-long nervous twitch, had within the space of four weeks subsided. I felt a renewed vigor in my bloodstream. My head didn't hurt. My eyes no longer stung from the endless dribble of Visine or their perpetual narrowing into slits as thin as razorblades in an attempt to filter out the grotesque barbarity that passed itself off as humankind.

I should have folded myself into a tiny package, hid under a rock, and relished the last remaining unfettered breaths before catching the night train that would deposit me at an inhospitable airport en route back to the overcrowded necropolis from which I had escaped. I could have remained firm in the conviction that although each day is indeed riddled with innumerable aggravations, I had now conquered enough distance, squandered enough time, to outrun the demons who are forever forcing the execution of that Herculean battle between control and desire. I could have ambled quietly into the nuclear sunset of a fading Eastern European hamlet and patiently awaited the arrival of the next train out. But I needed to reacclimate back into the real world before boarding my impending nine-hour trans-Atlantic flight stuffed between screaming children, grubby teenagers, talkative grannies, and inebriated single men. Newfound Zen be damned! The potential for strangling a stewardess, rushing the cockpit, screaming "fire in the hole," grabbing the controls and taking the whole seething mass into a watery grave was a preoccupation I fought every time my brain cells began to tweak on pressurized cabin air. I opted instead to stop in Istanbul.

The dense heat slaps my head like a wet blanket soaked in

urine. I disembark just in time to be serenaded by the haunting sickness of the midday call to prayer. My irritation returns
twofold as I'm jostled by a gaggle of terminally old women
scurrying like lizards, overloaded with wicker baskets full
of rotting fruit. I scamper aimlessly ahead of them, no clue
where I am, where I'm going, or what the hell I was thinking
when I decided to just drop in for a few hours of exploration.
In order to truly understand this freakish divide which both
straddles and separates the East from the West, Asia from
Europe, would take the most astute detective decades of investigation. Ripe with intrigue, filthy with an undercurrent of
sexy repression, her sinister underbelly shrouded in aromatic
blossoms whose fragrance can never fully disguise its festering malignancy. Istanbul is a beautiful bitch languishing on
a hotbed of winding passageways steeped in sleazy mystery
where crusty cousins with dirty fingernails wheel and deal
anything that yields a price tag. The art of bartering, bad-
gering, and hustling, if not invented in Constantinople, was
long ago refined here and is now practiced by nearly all of its
estimated fifteen million sweating bodies. If I hadn't already, I
was about to lose my fucking mind.

A petulant gang of six-year-old boys had been following
me for blocks, barking with insistence that I purchase a pack
of their ratty Kleenex. Their skinny arms and legs encouraged visions of tiny morsels of grilled meat slathered in chili
sauce and served on a stainless steel skewer sharp enough to
puncture tires. With blood pressure skyrocketing, blood sugar
plummeting, I needed to eat before adding cannibalism to my
lengthy resume of hate crimes.

I ventured up a dusty side street in search of libations. A
scattering of mismatched tables offered miraculous refuge at
a deserted café. Empty save for a litter of dirty tiger kittens

frolicking after a cloud of iridescent horse flies at the feet of two outstanding specimens of hyper-sexed American stupidity. The twin towheads sporting sun-kissed cheeks, broad shoulders, and aviator shades intensified my hunger. Now it was more than food I craved. I slid into a grimy seat at the next table.

I summoned the waiter, placed my order, and sitting within earshot of their inane conversation felt my blood pressure hike itself up another notch even before the lamb chops arrived. I started getting itchy. My pinkie began to twitch. My eyelids burned. Spoiled shits with Mommy's money pillaging through Eurasia stoned on hash and horny as hell flipping through incriminating photos on expensive cell phones while relaying a running commentary of their recent female conquests: "Anal in Varna," "Organ Grinding in Odessa," "69 Plus One in Sarajevo." Sounded like a laundry list of bad alt-porno, further evidence of which I was sure could be found on the palm-fitting camcorder coyly snuggled against the blonder of the two's semi-erection.

"Shit, she's a gaper," the bulging one sidelined, inching closer to the phone.

"I'll give you that one, holmes, but Dirty Sanchez be damned! Two can ride for the price of one!"

"That's right, cowboy!"

The bosom buddies knocked knuckles.

Although I didn't feel a moral obligation to avenge my sex-starved sisters in absentia for the randy reminiscing of these gloating globe-trotting Lotharios, I couldn't resist the festering urge to retaliate like a frontline crusader in the war where the battle of the sexes never ceases to rage. Hell, I didn't need an excuse, I just wanted to blow off some steam. At their expense. Play them at their own game. And a perfectly ex-

ecuted act of meaningless cruelty does momentarily relieve
the predator of built-up aggravation much the same way a
good dose of gruesome pornography can temporarily abate
the unpleasant urges of a weekend pervert. Fuck being quaint.
I wanted to do some damage.

I overheard them discussing the need to go back to their
hotel to recharge their camera before that evening's outing.
Mr. Still-Half-Hard was complaining about the slovenly conditions of the dump they were forced to check into until their
room at The Bentley was ready the following afternoon. "Yeah,
the Palas is crusty, man," the genius to the left muttered. They
had to be referring to the Pera Palas. A faded yet glorious old
whore who in her day had housed dignitaries, pop stars, and
spies, but was now a dusty relic renowned for her ancient history and tainted splendor. Soon to be condemned to rehabili-
tation. I wasted no time inserting myself into their salacious
conversation. I beamed an undetectably phony smile in their
direction, wiped the sarcasm from my palate, and asked with
as much sincerity as I could stomach if they were from the
West Coast.

"Malibu," the smart-ass offered.

"Miami," I lied.

Gratuitous small talk follows. I pile it on. Feign interest
in their himbo babble. "Must be great taking a year off before hitting film school at USC." My stomach churns bile. I
continue the charade, insisting they look me up if they ever
make it down to South Beach. I scribble a fictitious e-mail
address on a napkin. They give me theirs. I close in for the
kill. Tell them I overheard their plans to go back to their hotel.
Would they mind if I tagged along to charge my cell phone
before facing the terminal nightmare of a slow train to the
crowded plane back home? I must've forgotten to do so last

night. Surely they could understand how impotent one feels when their lifeline to civilization short circuits. Naturally, they bought my lie. Exchanging a bemused smirk. I chortled to myself. I didn't have a cell phone. Or an e-mail account. Or a post office box. Or a permanent address. I hated the thought of being tracked.

I suggested we order a couple of Tuborg tall boys to take back to their room. "Cold brew on a hot day," Einstein mutters.

I'm growing murderous. Visions of duct tape and Thai tattoo tubes drown out the mundanity of their nonsensical dribbling. We round the corner and enter the lobby with only seconds to spare before my cool evaporates and I stab them both with the steak knife stolen from the café.

The Palas was perfect. Truly. Tarnished, tattered, down at the heels, and haunted. The ghosts of illicit romance, espionage, and dirty deeds painted the lobby in a milky film. The marble columns were cracked. The carpets were sticky. The lobby stunk of cigarettes, booze, overripe broads, and men old enough to overlook their own halitosis. Nobody batted an eye as three twenty-somethings (okay . . . I'm lying again) scaled the massive staircase up to the third floor.

Blond and Blonder opened their flimsy door to reveal a shitty room with a spectacular view. Two ratty queen-sized beds bookend the massive window overlooking the breathtaking Bosphorus, that magnificent river of mysterious origin that slices Istanbul in half. Her glistening shores flanked by glorious monuments erected centuries before in praise of egotistical kings who worshipped at the feet of false gods. The late-afternoon haze refracted heat and light, creating a gauzy mirage. The madness below was temporarily suspended, silenced. A frozen moment, postcard perfect. And rudely interrupted by the staccato pop of a beer can cracking open.

Which reminded me why I was there. I needed to leech a little blood as purgation against my own incurable sickness. I winked and took the can.

I soon excused myself and entered the sprawling bathroom. Beautiful tiles of lapis blue, ivory, carnation pink, scuffed with soap scum. I set the beer on the edge of the tub. Opened my purse. Removed a small ornate brown bottle whose faded label promised *Spirit of Philosophical Vitriol*. I had to chortle. Such a poetic name for Algarot, a trichloride which induces vomiting and diarrhea. Purchased with half a dozen other outdated bottles of hazardous pharmaceuticals at a small flea market outside of Satu Mare. Now hidden in a locker at the train station. The key tossed down a sewer grate. Squeezed a couple of milliliters into the can's mouth. Flushed the toilet. Washed my hands. Adjusted my lipstick while pinching myself, trying to ease my rictus grin into a sexy smile.

I joined the little party in the corner rolling hash joints. Probably game planning where to hide their camcorder. Let 'em wet dream all they wanted. I'd grab it on my way out. As well as their wallets, cell phones, credit cards, passports, and airline tickets. I passed the poisoned brew to the high baller on my left. Still didn't know their names. Didn't want to.

Suck guzzling half the can, the wonderfully hunky idiot burps proudly and raises the beer in a toast in my direction. I wink, blow a kiss, and purr, "Good little donkey . . . gobble gobble," while the mark does as expected and finishes off the can. A witchy giggle tickles my throat. I get giddy when someone is about to shit their pants.

"Music!" asshole number two insists. "We need some tunage!"

"I'm on it, soldier," his nutty buddy mutters, taking a deep drag on the soggy joint. "Bro, this shit is silk."

Now I wanted to puke. Turkish tobacco mixed with a bullet of black hash which still stinks of the mule's ass that smuggled it in. The moronic tub thumping of watered-down West Coast gangsta rap bleeding out of crappy portable speakers. The juvenile camaraderie. Their good looks. Perfect teeth. Their sense of entitlement so indicative of a generation bred to measure merit in net worth, success with fame, importance by how many like-minded dimwits have visited their shitty web page. Their fratboy sexuality and everything they stand for is about to fall. Another beautiful victim of gastrointestinal poisoning.

Two minutes and thirty seconds later an outrageously harmonic eruption of wet sulfuric gases explodes from the rear of the stoner to my right who's frantically yanking on his belt buckle near the entrance to the bathroom. He clutches the door knob in one meaty fist but lacks the strength to pull it open. "Man, was that joint laced? I think I'm melting." His legs give out. I laugh out loud. Another soul-shattering anal skronk. A wet greasy stain spreads across his backside. Shit. That was quick!

"Christ! Take it in the shitter, dude, you're making me sick," heckles his compassionate traveling companion. No sooner said and he's also done in by a violent spasm which suddenly doubles him over in what appears to be a one-man football huddle. Hands on knees, head bent down. Choking, spitting, drooling. "What the fuck? I told you we shouldn't drink the water . . ." He doesn't get it but I'm cackling like a madman. His head thrashes from side to side. Explosions of yellow and green bile spraying from his mouth and nose, soaking the bedspread and mattress. A Jackson Pollock rendered in puke.

"Fat joint," I snicker. "Never touch the shit myself, the smell alone makes me sick."

He continues to retch.

I reach for the hidden camera which they had strategically placed on top of the old chifforobe angled in the corner. It's petite red eye aglow. Unwavering. I zoom in for an extreme close-up of the beautiful wreck's puckering maw, capturing every intoxicating minute of his award-winning regurgitation. I'm a bloodhound in heat, the camera my snout. I follow the chartreuse trail as it cascades over the side of the bed and mingles with the toxic brown effluvium of his ailing twin, who's crawled out of his dirty drawers and into the sanctuary of the bathtub turned toilet. A shroud of steam haloes his gorgeous grimace. I tower above the ruined puppy, a psychotic paparazzo, focus trained on his heavy lids, parted lips, limp prick. He stinks. I zoom in.

I imagine the credits artfully rolling up from the mist announcing my latest contribution to the vast library of reality porn on that slagheap of American culture, the Internet. *The Spirit of Philosophical Vitriol*, a.k.a. *Dirty Dicks and the Chicks That Love Them: Volume 6*.

PART III

IN THE DARK RECESSES

ONE AMONG US

BY YASEMİN AYDINOĞLU

Sağmalcılar

"**I** will flog the piss out of you, you hear me, you mother-fuckerrr!" he bellowed above me. I thought my eardrums would burst. I was begging, dying, my knees trembling. The bones, the joints of my hands, had turned to putty.

"Brother, I swear to God, it wasn't me. It wasn't!"

They were yanking my head back by the hair on the scruff of my neck and dunking it into the bucket. I couldn't count how many they were. Each time I held my breath as long as I could. I let it out bit by bit, but it was no use. I couldn't take it anymore. I inhaled some water through my nose. The salt singed my nostrils, scorched my throat. My eyes burned. They were dunking my head into something, something heavier than water, oilier than water, saltier than water, but what was it? It was like seawater, like tears, what they were trying to drown me in. This time he pushed me hard, harder, into the water, by the back of my neck. I struggled, I cried. You could drown in a fucking spoonful of water. What the hell did I know? What the hell was I doing here?

A crackling sound exploded in my ear. Suddenly, I woke up. I was in the prison ward. The music broadcast had started. Orhan Gencebay buzzed through the speakers: *"May I be damned if I've forgotten you, if I've found another lover."* A dream? It was all a fucking dream, goddamn it. I touched my face, felt the tears still there. My balls and my chin ached from the spasms, from the crying. I'd never been so happy to wake up in this ward. I headed straight for the toilet upstairs, cutting a path through the pungent scent of urine. I didn't want to let on that I'd had a bad dream. Sixty of us all living together in the same room; sixty people under the constant surveillance of fifty-nine. Somebody's bound to catch on to your soft spot. My biggest fear, ever since I was a kid, was for someone to be able to read my mind.

But then I really shouldn't be surprised. I've got a penchant for finding myself in the craziest situations. I remember the day I arrived here, for example. They unloaded us from the van, I raised my head, and, *Goddamn it, Ahmet!* I say to myself. *You just stepped in a pile of shit! Now lift your fucking foot.* The walls of Sağmalcılar Prison lay before me. Surrounded by white houses, the place sticks out like a bruise on the skin of a pale lady. Shit had gotten real serious real fast. And to think that dude I jumped with a knife was only packing a hundred bucks. Asshole! Hardly compensation for the price I'd have to pay. Made an absolute fool out of me. And if things keep up like this, I'll be a disgrace until the day I die. But there's one thing I've learned in this life, and always failed to do: Never ever trust your feelings and the reasons behind them. 'Cause they change so damn quickly, leaving you with nothing to do but lick your wounds.

The music stopped all of a sudden. They announced Sinan's name. The same Sinan I'd just killed in my dream, and then got all choked up about swearing to my interrogators that it wasn't me. He's trying to get transferred out of here, but he keeps turning up empty-handed. You can't just go wherever you want whenever you damn well feel like it, now, can you? As soon as he heard his name announced, Sinan made a dash for the hallway. With a noisy rattle of the keys the door opened, and out Sinan went. Then Orhan *Abi* picked up where he'd left off, crooning away.

I waited for him to return to the cell. I was sure he'd get rejected. The aftershocks of my dream slowly wore off. I'd never been so frightened by a dream since I was a kid. It'd been on my mind for a long time. I had asked, but Sinan's lips were sealed.

"You think killing someone's gonna earn you stripes or something?" he had said to me once. He talked with a whistle through his broken front tooth.

I said nothing.

"Don't ask me then, go ask your master," he said.

"The master's situation's different," I said.

"What about it? Self-defense or not, you deal with the consequences."

The man he called my "master" was a prisoner we worked with in the carpentry shop. Sinan didn't like him, not at all. He was respected by the other men, like he was some kind of ward *ağa* or something. Two plainclothes flatfoots tried to rape his wife one night when they were coming back from Kumkapı, and he butchered the guys right on the spot. He got a king's reception when he arrived at the prison.

Sinan was back before he'd even left. He walked into the courtyard without a word, paced a line all morning. He took it real hard every time his transfer petition got rejected. And this time, too, just like when any little thing happened to him, he felt his whole world was crumbling around him.

I went and sat next to him at lunch. I scrunched up and started eating.

"Use a fork," he said.

"I'm gonna eat with my hands," I said.

"Use a fork. You can't eat like that, you'll upset your stomach," he said.

He always told me what to do. Whenever I spoke, he interrupted me and corrected my accent. He told me who I could and couldn't speak to. And he rubbed my peasant roots in my face every chance he got. As if he were carving out his own little kingdom there between those walls. I continued eating. *You shovel in rotten, raw meat with your bare hands, and then you savor every damn morsel, don't you? So why use a fork just 'cause it's cooked?* I was about to say. But I didn't.

"Don't tell me what to do. Gets on my nerves," was all I said.

"You a hood now, are you?" he said. "Since when?"

To him, I could fall right into the class of degenerates and scum at any given moment. I looked him in the face. I should hate him. He had a china chin, delicate as a woman's. The veins on his forehead grew even bluer when he was sad. Tore me up inside. I kept doing my damnedest to be his equal. I started eating with a fork. It wasn't difficult, I simply didn't enjoy it.

"They're going to kill me if I stay here," he said.

"Nobody's gonna do shit to anybody," I said.

"Müfit's got men in here. I gotta scat, and quick."

"No bird flies out of here without the ward ağa knowin' about it," I said.

The ward ağa was a man in his thirties who'd been catapulted to his superior rank as soon as he set foot in here, because he'd killed seven men in a parking lot brawl. He was the man who kept tabs on comers and goers. Next to him, the guards were mere escorts.

The "Müfit! Müfit!" he whined about was the son of the man he'd killed. From what he told me, all hell had broken loose over some broad. Sinan's childhood sweetheart. He had no idea how he slayed that man, the fat sixty-some-year-old daddy who planted himself in their way the night they tried to elope. Both men were certain of their love for Funda. I can't imagine Sinan slapping a punching bag, he's so damn puny. And this Müfit guy told the apartment-building doorman to let Funda know he was on Sinan's ass. Is there really a doorman at the apartment building where Funda lives? Who knows? Hard to separate the bull from the shit when it comes to these stories. Regardless, Sinan thought he was now in the lion's mouth. And he'd started acting extra strange the past few weeks. He couldn't sleep at night, even started praying. He started speaking real fast, like he was mumbling prayers or something. He couldn't sit still. And when he got like that, he'd get more annoyed with me than ever. Yet for years I'd been closer to him than anybody, Funda even.

"Besides, hard for anything to happen with it being this crowded," I said. "Barely room to move as it is."

"Perfect scene for the crime," he replied. "Can't tell who's got whose throat in a crowd like this."

There were men who'd been killed in here by having hot olive oil poured down their ears, or stabbed to death with a shiv. At least, that's what we were told, but neither Sinan nor I had ever witnessed anything of the kind here in the ward. So why did I keep dreaming about killing this guy? I looked in his face like we were two good pals. He noticed, and glanced at me out of the corner of his eye. He was scared shitless, as usual, thinking it was all downhill from here. I should just take care of it for him, I thought to myself. Show him what it's like to be pushed and pulled around at somebody else's whim. Nobody calling after him anyway. Nobody even writes him letters, except for that bitch Funda. How that chick got this loser to clean the crap off her honor, who knows. Ahmet, my boy, you'd be snuffing the life of a whore-mongering motherfucker; you'd rise above the rank of mere mugger and be a whole class above those pickpockets and ass-fuckers—not so bad, huh? And with the ward ağa watching over you, nobody'd make a peep. It'd be an open-and-shut case. The asshole can find out what it means to suck it up while he rots in his grave.

For a moment I thought he sensed what was going through my mind. He was alert like some nocturnal animal, his nostrils flaring wider and wider. I pretended to not give a shit about him, stabbed some meat on the metal plate. Besides, he couldn't actually care less about what I was eating, or how.

It was calm in the ward that evening. I ate alone, sat at one of the tables in the corner next to the dormitory. The doors were long locked. The huge, curtainless window looking onto the courtyard with its pile of snow was nothing but a black wall now. They quickly counted us. The sixty-watt bulb bathed its surroundings in yellow. Beneath its light, the faces of the men sitting at the tables looked more anemic than ever. It wasn't long before the cigarette smoke made it almost impossible to see five feet in front of you. I caught a whiff of another familiar scent there in that smoke. A joint. It was coming from one of the tables by the window. Three men were sitting there sucking it in. They were always together, those three, in the courtyard, in the ward, evenings at the ward coffeehouse. I'd never spoken with them, not once. Sinan, the master, they'd never messed with those guys either. The tall one was shaped like a padlock; huge head, flat body, and virtually no neck. White skin, a little oily. He'd become the leader of the pack, even though he was new to the ward. He always wore a large, checkered dress shirt and a vest. The middle one had small, dark eyes that were pinched together, giving him these broad, open temples. The third one, the tiniest of them, had white skin and gray-blue eyes. I'd heard the big one grew up in Vefa. The other two were from Anatolia.

"In Diyarbakır, they water this stuff with chicken blood to make it sweeter," said the middle one.

It was like each of them was talking to himself. Once the joint had made several rounds, they drank a few cups of tea, which was like tar by then, having steeped in the samovar for hours. It'd gotten pretty crowded around the tables. Like we were all curious to see what would happen next.

Sinan seemed almost oblivious to what was going on as he approached me. He was trying to hide his anxiety, as usual. But then he never was one to get mixed up in crowds. Especially during the day, he never ever walked about. He was in a rush, looking for something to busy himself with. He sat down on his bed, two bunks down from mine, and started writing something in half cursive, half printed letters, and unconsciously flipping through old letters. Probably from that bitch Funda. God only knows. As if that cunt's really yearning for her lover's return, like she claims in her letters. You've nailed her right between the legs the moment she gets a whiff of the dough, there's not a fool who doesn't know that much. At times like this, I wished he'd talk to me instead of taking refuge in Funda's bullshit letters. But just the opposite, he grew even more distant. For a moment I thought of Funda riding him. The smell of her cheap perfume, her cheap panties, cheap lace; the chalky taste of cocaine leaving a tingly numbness in her nose, on her gums; the shadow of Funda's breasts on her stomach under the direct light of the bulb overhead. It really pissed me off. And I was getting more and more pissed off since he'd stopped giving a fuck about me. The place was too narrow to stare into the distance, like a pharaoh's grave. Not like they were going to allot us a fucking chateau, but that's another matter.

Just as these thoughts were running through my mind, he spoke up: "Those are the guys Müfit sent after me."

"How do you know?" I asked.

"That Müfit guy's in the dope business. Sells hash and shit. Can't you see, those guys would sell their own mothers. They're just waiting for someone to give the go-ahead, just look at them." He was talking nonstop, not even pausing to take a breath. There he goes again, thinking every dude who walks in here is his assassin. The idiot, like he's seeing hash and heroin for the first time in his life. Now was the perfect time to play a few tricks, but . . .

"You know them from before?" I asked.

"Nah," he said.

"It's just, it seems to me like they know you."

"No way, this is the first time I've ever seen them," he said. Then he paused. He'd taken the bait. "What makes you think they know me?"

"No, I mean, what do I know?" I said. It was on the tip of my tongue, I'd drop the sinker and walk away. At that moment, I really wanted him to feel the fear, and feel it good. I headed for my bunk.

"I asked you a question!" he barked.

"It's just, I went to see the ward ağa the other day," I said.

"And?" He was drawing closer. I'd snagged him by the roof of his mouth, just like that. Otherwise, I'd have lost him.

"I heard those guys talking with him," I said.

"So what the fuck were they talking about?"

The hook ripped through his palate, *shaack*.

"Don't remember, swear to God. It's been awhile, and you know me, I don't remember shit," I said.

He was at a loss for words.

"I think . . ." I began.

"You think?"

"One of them asked the ward ağa if there was anyone else here besides our Sinan. Since he was saying 'our Sinan,' I figured they knew you," I said.

"What fucking 'our Sinan,' you idiot?"

"I don't know, I just figured they knew you from Istanbul or something."

"Why the hell didn't you tell me this before? Like these guys have been here fucking forever—and you 'forgot.'"

"I swear to God, just figured you knew them. And besides, that thug's not on good terms with the ward ağa anyway, you know?"

He seemed convinced of my sincerity. He'd literally swallowed it, hook, line, and sinker. He exhaled and said something. I couldn't tell if he was just cursing or what, with his teeth pressed together like that. His jawbones, his temples were all fidgety. Thanks to me, he was now absolutely certain that the men after him numbered three, and that they were hot on his tail.

The three guys were completely fucked up by that point. It took less than half an hour before the big one had a cheek against the steamed-up window, his arms spread wide like a frozen image of Jesus, crucified on some invisible cross. Another one they found under his bunk. And the third one they found lying on the floor in the bathroom.

A few hours later everyone had calmed down, the gawkers had dispersed. The smell of ashes and moldy walls gradually replaced the scent of pot. I was in my bunk before the clock even struck 10. I lay down and took a deep breath. I thought about that look on his face that said, *Now I'm fucked*, as I told him the story. If that man gets a wink of sleep tonight, I thought, my name ain't Ahmet.

The ward was completely shrouded in darkness before midnight. The sounds of sleeping men, of snoring, wheezing, teeth grinding, and the scent of polyester shirts reeking of sweat mingled in the air.

I woke up early the next day. I looked for Sinan, but he wasn't in bed. I walked through the bunks, checked the bathrooms upstairs, but he was nowhere to be found. I went out into the courtyard. There he was, facing the ward door. Three men stood before him, with their backs to me. They'd cornered him. I couldn't believe my eyes. The three guys from the night before were in Sinan's face. Man, I was just looking to mess with him a bit . . . How could this be? Or were his suspicions actually right? I pretended to be pacing along the wall, and got as close to them as I could. First I heard them laughing, so I guessed it wasn't anything serious after all. Clearly the leader was talking, and the others were throwing in some laughs for support. But Sinan just stood there, cowering before them. He couldn't leave, and he couldn't make them shut up. He kept puffing on his cigarette, stoking his lungs full of cold air and smoke. The big one spoke up again.

"Ain't nobody in Bomonti ain't poked that chick, and you tryin' to elope with her like she's some eighteen-year-old virgin."

(Sinan remains silent.)

"Dude, you fucking idiot, you go messing with some guy you know nothing about for some three-penny whore?"

(Again, nothing.)

"They didn't teach you back in the army, huh? Khaki outfit, boots, everybody equal, until the day you get your discharge papers. On that day, some guys put on their leather jackets and leave. And other guys, scum like you, they put on ragged-ass jackets all torn at the seams ... Now go on and do your paces, and quit bitin' off more than your runt mouth can chew!"

(Sinan swallows, his eyes wide and rolling.)

"Who do you think you are, trying to stab a man, you fucking piece of shit!"

He didn't even lower his voice when he saw me approaching. I walked right by them. I followed the wall and dove back inside the ward. They dispersed after me. The other two guys were laughing and cussing left and right.

I didn't go near Sinan all day. He didn't talk at all; he didn't eat; he didn't go out to the courtyard. He wasn't angry. He wasn't sad. So what was his deal? He didn't have the usual fever blister popping out of his lip. And he didn't seem like a man waiting for his manifest destiny either. He was cold, motionless, as if all the nerves had been ripped out of him. Was it the comfort of simply knowing what's to come?

Toward evening it started snowing. The men out in the courtyard headed back into the ward, taking cover from the sudden onslaught of slush. I left the crowd and chaos behind and walked up to him.

"What were those guys talking about?" I asked.

No response. He wouldn't talk. He'd erased me, completely. The Sinan who constantly rattled on to me about all his suspicions had been replaced by this mute dupe. I had no idea what he was thinking. What the fuck was going on? He didn't talk, not that evening, not that night. I was dying to find out. But that was Sinan. When he shut down, even his fucking maker couldn't rouse him out of it. I didn't press him any further. The bastard could stew in his own juices for all I cared.

When I woke abruptly early the next morning, I felt like I was about to come. I found myself trying to suffocate the rod beneath my waist, between a pillow clenched between my legs and the rough texture of the cotton mattress. On the verge of explosion, I got up and went to the bathroom. (When I was new to the ward, Sinan had followed me to the dimly lit bathroom a few times.)

It was still pitch black in most of the ward. It took awhile for my eyes to adjust to the darkness, with just a tiny sliver of light seeping in from under the door. As I walked down between the bunks, I glanced at Sinan's bed, but he wasn't there. It was 3 in the morning; all of the doors were locked. Where could he be? I walked toward the stairs leading up to the toilets. When I got to the bathroom door, I heard voices; scuffling and struggling. Slowly, I pushed the door open. There was a pool of blood between the sinks and stalls in their pinkish-yellow glow. I saw the legs of a man, trembling, sprawled out in the pool of blood. The upper half of his body was in one of the stalls. One of his slippers had come off, the other was still on his foot. When I saw his shirt, which had soaked up the blood to the color of rotten cherry, I recognized the broadly checkered design. It was the big guy, the group leader. I took another step inside. Then, above him, I saw Sinan.

He was all over the guy like a spider. He was so agile, stabbing the guy with a shiv, in the neck, in the stomach, all over. The man was nothing but a pulp of muscle and nerves by then. A thin blanket was wrapped tightly around his head. It seemed he'd taken the first hit to the jugular and spurted blood all over the walls. Sinan was rabid, his attention focused entirely upon his prey like some nocturnal animal. He stuck the shiv into the now motionless body a few more times. Then he looked up at the door and saw me.

I took one step back, but I couldn't take the second. I couldn't move. I leaned against the wall. He wasn't at all surprised to see me. He stood up and walked through the pool of blood to the sink. The ice-cold water that ran over his hands and arms was red at first; he rubbed his fingers together until it gradually turned pink, then transparent. He removed his undershirt, now stained with blood. Naked from the waist up, he walked up to me. Then, without a word, and without looking me in the face, he moved straight past me. He was calm, invigorated. And he remained so as he headed out the door and down the stairs. I tried with all my might to move. Finally, I managed to walk down the stairs, silently. It was the longest journey I'd ever taken in that tiny ward. Each step sent a shudder through my body, like a guillotine blow to the neck. I couldn't control my breathing. It was as if my joints had hardened, like all the spaces between my bones were filled with concrete. I struggled to find my way through the darkness. My eyes were popping out of my head, like somebody pumped up on too much shit. I walked by his bed. He was lying there, under the covers, calm as could be. I reached my bunk. Suddenly the damn bunk that I despised waking up in every morning had become the safest shelter. I was surrounded by the noise of snoring. I didn't make a sound. The moment I did, one of those shivs would go splat through my neck. I lay down. And stayed there, motionless.

The next morning they took a count. They removed the body of the big guy. It took at least seven or eight of them to lug it down the stairs. An investigation ensued. Nobody was allowed out of the ward until noon. At noon, Sinan went to the door. He'd hurriedly gathered his dirty underwear and placed them in a bag. He said he was going to the Turkish bath. They let him. They never suspected him since he didn't have any friends, and there was no way he could take out such a big guy.

I would never be his equal. I never talked with him, never approached him again, and never during the night did I look his way . . . and I never made the mistake of ever, ever getting a wink of sleep.

BLACK PALACE

BY MUSTAFA ZİYALAN

Aksaray

I walked down from Atatürk Boulevard, onto Oruçgazi Street, along the wall of Oruçgazi Elementary. That's where I went to school when I was a kid. I ended up in front of the Oruçgazi Apartment Building. You could still see the marks of posters of old political organizations that had once been on the prowl, and had been prowled down like animals, back in the '70s. The windows of the first floor were at eye level.

My mother had died in that building. In Aksaray—in "White Palace." If anything, the world must be bell jar–bottomed, as they say.

The small neighborhood convenience store was still there. The stationery store across from it was too. In its fly-flecked windows were the same books we had used back when I was in school. I was about to go in when a newspaper headline caught my eye: *Scalpel.* I couldn't see the rest. I took the paper, stepped halfway in, and paid the dark-complected, mustached guy behind the newsstand counter. Then I turned around and entered the stationery store.

The owner was still wearing a two-piece suit and a tie. "Ohhhh, look who's here!" he said as soon as I walked in. We shook hands. He sent one of the kids to fetch us some tea from a nearby tea stand. He came closer, as if to share a secret. "No one speaks Turkish around here anymore, sir," he said, with the grimace of a man suffering from heartburn. "Sniffing glue, turpentine, this and that; you name the vice and they deal in it." Then, pointing in the direction of the convenience store with his thumb, "They've taken over, completely."

I didn't ask: *Who? The Kurds?* He had turned out to be another one of those assholes who thought the city was his own personal property. Maybe out of anxiety, out of fear. After all, fear is one ferocious teacher. We made small talk; we drank tea.

That's when I saw the blondie for the first time, just as I was stepping out of the store. He wore some fancy, dark-colored jacket; his arms were folded; he seemed to be scratching his chin. In spite of his years, he had the face of a kid. Good-looking fella. He followed me with faintly squinting eyes. Was there anybody else with me? Where were my hands? Perhaps the fact that I was holding the paper in my right threw him off. He smiled, it seemed, ever so slightly. A fleeting thought: *Is he making a pass at me or what?* Well, there was no harm in that. It once again became obvious to me that I no longer knew the language of the land. The thought gave me an ugly rise. Some sort of fear. For an instant I imagined going straight up to the guy, reaching out with the paper as if to remove some spot of dust from his arm, and then headbutting him square in the middle of his cool smile. I almost took the first step. But then I stopped myself. I winked in his direction. He seemed to be looking elsewhere. I turned around, but made sure not to lose sight of him. I knew as well as I knew my own name that he was keeping me in his field of vision too. So be it. I put some distance between us and turned around for good, and with one ear to the ground listening for steps, started in the direction of Pertevniyal High School. I figured I'd go to the hardware store over there and do some shopping.

* * *

I like hardware stores. They have the remedy for every predicament you can think of. Manning the counter was some boy still wet behind the ears. He did his best to help me out. He found a wire for me, the closest thing he could find to a piano string. I bought some duct tape and a stout hammer handle. A small saw, some sandpaper. I thought of the headline: *Scalpel.* I didn't know the first thing about scalpels. What I did know was that long gone were the days when punks who thought they were hot shit packed straight razors in their shirt pockets. I bought a sturdy box cutter; it fit my hand perfectly. I almost bought a blowtorch too, but then I changed my mind. Truth be told, I'd never really liked the smell of burnt flesh.

Pubs crowded the edges of the neighborhood. I thought I saw the blondie again. But I didn't pay him any mind this time. I went to a pastry shop that had a broken marble counter. I had *börek*. I went to a greasy spoon restaurant. I had vegetable casserole with meat, rice, and *cacık*. Then I ducked into a workers' coffeehouse and ordered rosehip tea. I opened the paper. Let's see what happened when I wasn't looking. The headline said, *The Scalpel Slays Again!* For real. Somebody out there was on a killing spree, knocking off retired civil servants. Nobody had seen or heard a thing. It was almost like some practical joke—saving the retired from their misery! Except it wasn't a joke. And whoever did this was treating the victims like lambs marked for slaughter during the Feast of the Sacrifice. The person, or persons, might very well be in the business of butchering or medicine, the paper said. Well, there is little difference between a butcher and a medical professional, if you ask me. For lack of visual material, they had printed a huge picture of the scalpel; one had been found with each victim. It

was a fancy piece of work: handmade, with some floral ornaments connecting the handle to the blade. *Holy shit, look at
that!* I recall thinking, *Are we seeing the beginning of a serial
killer fad in Turkey? Of all things . . .*

Days passed. I was getting used to the neighborhood. The
neighborhood was getting used to me. I visited the stationery
store every once in a while. I was getting fat on kebabs and *lahmacun.* I recalled the once numerous vendors of firewood, the
yorgan makers, and such. If only I could find a yorgan maker,
I'd stop to watch the cotton spinner. That would help me focus.
But where to find one these days? I went to the barbershop
instead and got an old-school haircut and a very close shave
with a straight razor. That's how I regained my focus. The
razor, glinting like a river snake, reminded me of all the things
I still had to do.

   I wandered about with purpose, before, finally, I dared to
enter Çıngıraklı Bostan Street. It all felt like a dream. Yet I
found the chief's house just like that, as if I'd put it there myself. There it was, still standing after so many years.

I did my best to ignore him, but I couldn't help being painfully
aware of the blondie. To the hilt. He was in the neighborhood,
around me, after me. I was curious as to whether he was following me or not. Maybe he had a number going on in the
neighborhood and he was concerned that I would lay claim
to his stakes, try to scare up a partnership, or wreck his game
somehow. I was picking up a bad vibe from blondie, but whatever his beef, there was no way I'd let him stand in my way. He
had to be handled before I could get down to business.

There was a snack shop selling dried fruits and nuts at the

mouth of Horhor Avenue. One day I was buying dried ole-
aster berries there. The blondie walked by and continued up
Horhor. I grabbed the paper bag and paused to put some distance between us. Now I was after him. The box cutter was in
my pocket. I was about to do some close-range work; it was
giving me a serious buzz.

I don't know if I actually caught up with him or if he
just let me catch up. We were in front of a building; its door
was ajar. I tossed the bag, reached with my left. He turned
then, and I saw his hands were empty. Perhaps foolishly, I
let the box cutter go and pushed the guy, charging into him.
We burst through the door, crashing against its wings. I was
surprised we were still standing. I tried to land a hook on his
face; he moved his head ever so slightly and evaded the blow.
Nice. Very, very nice. There was no one to break up the fight.
My blood was boiling. I saw red the shade of a sizzling iron.
I dove into the atrium of the building and pounced on him.
By that point, he was no different to me than a rabid dog, and I
was a butcher, barging through the gates of the slaughterhouse,
eager to do the deed.

We were sitting on the stairs leading up from the atrium of
the building. We were breathing heavily, good and cranked
up. My knuckles hurt. It felt like I had a few broken ribs. My
nose was swollen. Something warm was dripping down my
face. My vision was off on the left. My brow was beating like
a punctured heart.

As far as I could tell, he wasn't in any better shape. He
turned to me and said, just like that, "We are each worse than
the other, you know." He had a slight accent, like I did. He was
right. We were each worse than the other, in ways both material
and not so material. But I didn't know the half of it yet.

We stepped out, leaning on each other. We ducked into a nearby pharmacy. The pharmacist lady had to hold a scream in when she saw us. Fortunately, the blondie knew what he was doing. We left without having to explain anything to anybody.

We went to a kebab house that I was familiar with, one of several strung from the mouth of Horhor toward the police station. I never figured out the man tending it; I didn't even know his name. He was dark and always wore a black suit. He knew me from back when my mother was sick.

"My oh my!" he said when he saw us. "Did they try to remodel you guys or what?" I would have laughed out loud, if only I'd had the strength. He took us to the back of the store and let us sit at a secluded table. He brought us towels, water, and bags of ice.

Blondie wiped my face with peroxide, then stuffed gauze in my nostrils. "It's not broken," he said. Not that it mattered, really. He fixed my cut eyebrow with some strips. He gave me pills for pain and infection. Then he examined and treated himself in front of a mirror. We grabbed the bags of ice and sat, facing each other, like two geese that had escaped a very close shave by some demented barber.

His name was Pandeli. He lived in Vienna. He was a doctor. Single. He had done his residency training in surgery in Istanbul. Not so luckily for me, he had trained as a kickboxer several years before.

I told him about myself. I lived in New York. I had a car repair shop there. I was single. I had dabbled in tae kwon do in the past. I had come to Istanbul because my mother was sick. I didn't yet explain why I had stayed on, though.

"All right," I said, finally giving in, "so what brought you here, man?"

There was a silence.

"Look, bro," he replied, "to make a long story short—" He took a photograph out of his pocket. It was like stained glass. But black-and-white. A clutch of guys, young and old, looking all pumped up, like they were celebrating something. One of them stared straight out of the photograph, straight at me, smiling brightly. I was reminded of photographs of a lynching I once saw on a Harlem wall; photographs of people smiling as if they had just accomplished some major shit. The guy in the photo had a mustache and a gold tooth in the lower right side of his mouth. He was holding a bottle; I recognized it as olive oil. There was an improvised fuse sticking out of it. There seemed to be a demolished store in the background. I examined the proud crowd in the front. The guy holding the bottle could be seen most clearly. He was young. The photo preserved him, it seemed, best of all. The more I looked at him, the more I examined his features, the more amazed I was. My eyes narrowed to blades. My amazement turned into other things. Into rage. Into disgust. My eyes were like a welding machine gradually finding its focus.

I'll never forget. Never. Damn it. My world went topsy-turvy. Like that. I forgot about my bruised ribs.

I couldn't wait any longer. One evening a few days later, I was on Çıngıraklı Bostan Street again. I knew that the door of the building always stood open, that the superintendent was rarely around.

I ran up those three floors and found the door, easy as cake. I knocked. I knew his wife had died a few years ago. And that he hadn't married again.

He opened the door himself. He looked me over. I imagined pushing my way in, the door smashing his face flat like a tomato.

"I grew up in this neighborhood, *amca*," I said. "I heard that Müzeyyen *Teyze* passed away, so I thought I'd drop by and give my condolences."

"It's been quite awhile since the lady died, son. Where did you hear about it?" Coming from this guy, the word "son" made me sick to my stomach. How? Why? What son?

"I was abroad."

"So our news makes it all the way over there, huh?" He smiled. A hushed, stolen smile, like that of a hyena. Then he relaxed. "Come in," he said finally. "Come on in and sit down." He opened the door for me and stood aside.

It reeked of mold, moisture, perhaps urine inside. It was a crowded condo. There was a chestnut showcase by the entrance full of never-used fine china. The door to the guest room was open; the furniture was carefully covered. He invited me to the living room, where he spent his time when he wasn't in the coffeehouse. He had set up a little corner for himself. It seemed he'd laid the paper he'd been reading on the coffee table before he got up to get the door. His glasses were on top of the folded paper. A pitcher of water, a glass, what appeared to be a saccharine box, his cigarette box, and his lighter were also on the table. Now, where did he keep his service gun, I wondered. Next to the chair hung a calendar and framed newspaper clippings about the chief's exploits, photos of him when he was younger. One of the headlines read: *Anarchist Hunter!* Another: *Peace and Quiet Reign in His Neighborhood!* I didn't recall having any peace and quiet in this neighborhood, but never mind.

He took off his leather slippers and made himself comfortable in that corner of his. *Ağa* to us all. The chief, even if retired. I perched on one of the couches.

"I went to Oruçgazi School back in the day," I said.

"Whereabouts did you live, son?" he asked. That corner, that ağa performance, deserved a proper nightshirt, of the long, flowing, imposing variety. But he was wearing a pressed shirt and pants. Old habits, I thought.

"We lived on Oruçgazi Street."

"Really, in what building?"

"Oruçgazi Building. I'm the son of Asaf *Bey.*"

"I don't think I know him."

My father's name was not Asaf; I hadn't seen my old man in twenty-five years. I decided not to beat around the bush any longer.

"You must know my mother, though."

"What's her name?"

"She passed away."

"I'm sorry. May the remaining live long."

"May everybody . . . She had an injured back. She had to take an early retirement for medical reasons, got to the point that she couldn't even leave the house anymore."

"We should all be blessed with good health. But that's just life, I guess. Things happen."

"Yeah, they happen to some, but not to others. I've always been curious. I mean, I've always wondered exactly how it was she injured her back."

He was becoming visibly uncomfortable. He looked tense.

"Back then, they said she'd injured her foot jumping rope with her students. And then one thing just led to another." He'd swallowed the bait. "Isn't that right?"

"You have such a great memory, amca! How on earth do you even *know* that, let alone remember it? And why?"

"What do you mean 'why'?"

"Did you ever see her around back then? In the street? Here and there? You ever look her in the face?"

That tensed the guy up even more.

"What do you mean, son? Why would we look at a woman like that? Of course we wouldn't, she was a sister to us, here and in the afterlife."

"Right," I said, leaning in toward him. "So would you look her in the face like this?" We were eye to eye. "Like this?" He opened his mouth. But he couldn't make a sound. I let my own voice rip. "Is that the way you treat your sisters, brothers, sons, and daughters? Huh? You two-bit punks?" It was as if a festering boil had burst within me, like the pus was bubbling up, spewing out of my mouth, out of my nose. "Pieces of shit!" My jaws were almost locked with disgust. "Beatings! Thrashings! Honor killings!" I was on him in two steps, an unstoppable surge of words gushing through my mind. A refrain: "Dungeons, tortures, executions . . ."

I strapped him firmly to the chair with duct tape, taking care not to rough him up too much. I gagged him. He was old, too old. I remembered my grandmother. Look at him, look at my grandmother. My mother wasn't religious at all, but my grandmother prayed five times a day and fasted during Ramadan. She was opposed to the death penalty, just like my mother. Back during the coup, during that era known as "September 12," when these guys were stringing people up, my grandmother, may she rest in peace, would say, "They're human beings too, my son; they're our children too, all subjects of Allah." She'd cry silently. A kind of dry, tear-free weeping. Perhaps, being a woman, there were no tears left in her at that age.

The guy stirred as he slowly came to. Once he understood that there was no way he was getting free, he surrendered to the chair.

"Look," I said, "I'll remove the tape, but if you raise your voice, it'll be real ugly for you, believe me." He nodded. I took off the duct tape. He coughed.

"Listen, son, you're making a big mistake. I'm an old, very sick man . . ."

"You are very sick, true, but yours is a different kind of sickness," I said. "And you know what? You've made everybody else sick too. You made the whole damn country *sick* . . ."

"Look, son, the apple of my eye, I'm a retired civil servant of this country."

"I'm not your son, not the apple of your eye, not your anything. And I am nothing to that state of yours. And it's nothing to me."

"Who are you people? Anarchists? Communists? Separatists?"

"What's that? You mean you don't even recognize this little neighborhood bastard? One of many, right? You've fucked yourself up in the head, old man, all hung up like that about those 'illegal organizations'! If *you're* law and order, then hell yes, I *am* an anarchist!"

"Son, I'm telling you, I'm sick, I'm alone, I don't have anybody. Don't you have a conscience?"

"And who do I have? Who did my mother have? Huh? Tell me! I have every bit as much a conscience as you do, no more, no less . . ."

"Don't you have any fear of Allah?"

"Yeah, right. You picked the wrong guy to ask that question to."

"I'm sick, I . . ." He was babbling.

"Wait," I said, "I got just what you need. This'll heal you up for sure." I took out the knife. "Or how about I just carve your prescription into your skin here, how's that sound? That'd make a snazzy tattoo, huh?"

He fell silent. Then he started moaning and praying, mur-
muring the *Kelime-i Şahadet*. I was sure there must be a prayer
book in a bag somewhere, and some holy *Zamzam* water in
the fridge.

I grabbed his face with my left hand, then I took his left,
which was strapped to the chair, with my right. Almost like I
was going to kiss it and put it to my forehead. Right.

"What did you do to my mother? Tell me, blow by blow."

"Who fed you such nonsense, son? There is no such thing!
I swear—"

I squeezed his hand. His bones gently cracked in my hand.
Like pretzels.

"Look," I said, "no bullshit. Why did you take her in?"

He pulled himself together. Then, with some defiance, he
said: "She was muckraking at her school. We heard about it."
My mother had been a member of the teachers' union. She
was a first-rate union organizer.

"What else? Is that all?"

"And a retired colonel from your building came to see
me."

"No kidding? So?"

"They were trying to put together a petition to kick a
whore out of that building. But your mother, she said, 'Everybody has the right to a private life, we have no business butt-
ing in,' and sent the petitioners away."

"How many times I've heard that story. It must've been
sooo fuckin' hard to swallow for you macho assholes, huh? So
what else?"

"She had to be cut down to size. That's just the way things
were back then."

"Back when?"

"Before 1980 . . . Times of anarchy . . . chaos . . ."

"But it's still like that now, isn't it? How was it back then? Tell me, how?"

"She was a divorced woman, she had to be reined in."

"Is that so? 'She was a divorced woman.' Why don't you come straight out and say it: She was a bitch. A cunt. You never had the guts, though, and you still don't, do you?"

"God forbid! I could never say such a thing! No! Never!"

"Well then?"

"I sent my guys for her, and we took her in."

"And?"

"We were just going to give her a good tongue-lashing and let her go." Then he let it slip: "But she was one of those . . . those women. Long on hair . . ."

I knew the saying: "And short on reason? Watch your mouth, asshole!"

"Sorry, I mean, your mother, she started mouthing off about rights, justice, constitution, schmonstitution . . ."

"Ha! You and your schmonstitution. You assholes turned it into a schmonstitution, right? But go on. What then?"

"Then . . . it was a police station, son, every place has its rules."

"Cut the crap! What happened next?"

"The one not helped by berating deserves—"

I knew that saying too: "A beating?"

"Yes. We roughed her up a bit."

"Did you put her on *falaka?*"

"No, I swear to God, we didn't have any such thing at our station."

"Well, where were all those people wrung through falaka then?"

"They'd be picked up and taken away, we sent them away . . ."

"To where?"

"How should I know? I was only a civil servant of the state. How should we know what the state was up to?"

Ah yes, how could they know? So many of my friends were wrecked on falaka, endured suspension, were electrocuted through their genitals, even eyeballs. I'm sure some were sodomized with truncheons or Coke bottles. I was never arrested, never tortured. I was more into mischief and thuggery than all that education, reading, writing, and oration. I never finished high school. I got my college education in coffeehouses and movie theaters. My hangout was a body shop in Dolapdere. I didn't mean shit to the state and its crews. Yet I always heard things from my friends at the coffeehouse in the neighborhood. As much as they could tell, anyway. After all, how could someone talk about such things? I mean, who could you tell? And who would believe you anyway? No way, no human being could possibly do such things to another. I'd always feel guilty when talking to people who had been tortured. I still do.

"Where did you hear these things, son?"

"It's fresh news to me. I just found out . . . Okay, so did you electrocute her?"

"I'm telling you, we didn't have those kinds of things at our station. We didn't know anything about them."

"Did you . . ." His eyes widened. "Stick . . . anything up her?"

"Have mercy! God forbid!"

"Okay, how did she break her foot and her back?"

He was silent again. Then: "She tried to run, fell down the stairs." A pause. "Down two flights."

"And you mean to tell me you guys did not *throw* her down?"

"No, no, I swear."

"And then?"

"We took her back to the neighborhood."

He was silent again. They left the woman on the street. Her legs, her back broken. Up until then, I thought that she'd been taken to the hospital directly from school. At the hospital, those butchers, so-called doctors, somehow failed to see the damage to her back.

"Son," he said, "you're young and still naïve. You don't understand. A divorced woman, her mind up in the air, misguided."

Okay. Either a poor, wretched woman, or a witch. The same old story. Then on with the patronizing, on with the witch hunt. I kept quiet this time.

"Look," he said, "I have money, take it, let me go, I beg you . . ."

I put on my gloves. I went through the apartment. I didn't have to dig around for long before I turned up his service gun, in a closet in the bedroom. A .45 caliber Kırıkkale. And next to it, bullets wrapped in cloth. His truncheon made of black rubber. I pocketed the gun and the bullets. In the same closet I found three bundles of American dollars.

"There must be some fifty, sixty thousand dollars there," he said.

There's a retired civil servant of the state for you! Ha! I didn't bother asking him where he got that kind of money.

"Take it all, just leave me alone now. Go."

That's when I moved behind his chair. I took out the garrote I'd made in my hotel room. I swung it before his eyes. He let out a low-pitched scream. I held the wire by the handles and in a single, swift motion had it firmly around his neck. I leaned in and, my lips nearly touching his earlobe, asked: "How's that? Does it hurt? Here's your chance to see for yourself which is more effective: Palestinian suspension, rope, an oiled noose, or"—I tugged at the wire—"this. You came into this world without a prayer, punk, and now that's how you're gonna go."

I heard the liquid dripping from the chair. He was soiling himself. I remembered my grandmother again. Those times when she was incontinent. I stopped. I thought. They say one nail drives out another, but does it really? Fuck it! Is that the way you're going to deal with this goddamn monster?

I met Pandeli in one of those workers' coffeehouses. I put the photograph on the table and took a good look. Yep, that was him. The police chief. The young hero of those infamous "incidents" of September 6 and 7. As they say, *You can tell the make of a man from his baby shit.* And there he was in his baby-shit days. He must have lost the mustache later. The gold tooth too. He didn't need to be showy. Judging from those piles of bills he'd secretly stashed away, he'd been a virtuoso of the fine art of skimming.

Finally, Pandeli laid it all out there for me, unloading himself like a dump truck. His father's store had been raided during those "incidents." I'd heard a lot about those lootings, which went on for several days, from my mother and grandmother; the excuse was that Atatürk's home in Saloniki had been bombed. They said that you couldn't walk on Istiklal Avenue without stepping on goods from the gutted stores.

Pandeli's father was never able to recoup his business. Nor his head. The family emigrated to Greece. The poor guy killed himself when Pandeli was still young. Pandeli found this photograph among his father's belongings. He recognized their store. Then he read the articles about the chief and saw the photos of him. He recognized the guy and put two and two together. Then, on the fiftieth anniversary of the events, he thought of returning to Istanbul to look into things. It was his first visit back since he'd finished his residency.

We were silent for a spell. Then I told my story. A weird kind of confusion had overcome me when my mother was sick and dying. I don't recall exactly, but I think I believed I was the Grim Reaper or something. I was in a hospital for a while. I heard about the things done to my mother from a friend of hers who visited me there. From Leyla Teyze. The poor woman didn't really have any desire to talk about such things at a time like that, but she was sick and, I think, afraid of dying before she'd had the chance to tell me.

"Okay, look," said Pandeli, "the Spaniards are after Pinochet. But that sort of thing will be a long time coming in these parts."

What could I say? I smiled bitterly.

"So are we just going to let this guy off the hook?"

Good question. We paused and thought for a moment.

"Is there anybody you can think of who knows the city well enough and could find the people we're looking for?" Pandeli asked.

"Yes," I said, "there is, there sure as hell is . . ."

He was right: We were each worse than the other.

I found Pamuk in his coffeehouse in Tophane and convinced him to take a break and come back to Aksaray with me.

"Look," he said, "I'm doing this for your mother's sake, not yours!" Fair enough. We both were Aksaray kids, we went way back; he knew my mother, and he knew other people who had been tortured too.

The three of us gathered at a table back in the workers' coffeehouse. Pamuk looked at me. "So what's your beef this time?" he said.

I was sitting on one side, and on the other Pandeli was leaning toward Pamuk and rattling on in his ear. Pamuk, all serious, was giving him his full attention. Pandeli turned to me. "Let's give him something, at least for his expenses," he said. I gave Pamuk an envelope containing five thousand dollars.

"Finish the job and you'll get another five grand," I said.

"You got it!" he replied. He finished his tea. "Enjoy your teas, fellas. I'll excuse myself now, if I may." In fact, Pamuk was not the kind of guy who asked for permission for anything. He stepped out of the coffeehouse, fading like a huge shadow into the Aksaray evening.

"All right," I said. "Great. What now?"

"Give it some time," Pandeli said. He knew something. Then he told me of his intention to leave for Vienna soon. We kept our goodbyes brief. One never knew.

I was getting restless. I was about to swing by Dolapdere and look for a job. Then one day I read it in the papers: *The Scalpel Slays Again!* This time it had cut up a retired police chief who lived on Çıngıraklı Bostan Street. To shreds. And you didn't have to look too closely to figure out that these were not your ordinary serial killings, not your ordinary serial killer. Some person was clearly rubbing out torturers.

I mailed copies of the newspaper articles to Pandeli in Vienna, just in case. The way he had told it, while looking at the photographs in the papers, he'd remembered some scalpels he had seen during his residency and developed a hunch as to who the killer might be. Then he sent Pamuk, not to do the deed himself, but to tip the killer off that he was in the know, to point the killer in the right direction: in the direction of the chief. Okay, that part I understood. According to this version of the story, the killer had been hanging out at the medical school at some point in the past. Yes, those scalpels were not something you'd forget. Still, how come no one else had remembered them and identified the killer? Was Pandeli the only one close enough to the killer back then to have the privilege of seeing his or her handmade tools? Could the killer be a woman? Was there more than one killer? Could Pandeli be one of them? Was he up to something in Greece too? I didn't understand, I couldn't understand. I was taking that old advice: *Eat the grapes, but don't ask about the vineyard.* But who knows, maybe one of these days I'll swing by Vienna and go to the trouble of looking the man up and asking him.

This time I swung by Pamuk's coffeehouse in Tophane for a change. I drank his tea. I gave him the five grand. I left the Kırıkkale and the bullets with him.

"Haven't you heard, my man?" he said. "Ours is the cool age of glockalization . . ."

Okay, if you say so.

I called Leyla Teyze at the number she had given me. I gave her the remaining money. I kissed her hand. It made her so happy. I didn't know much about these things; I asked her to give the money to some organization dealing with human rights, helping inmates or torture victims. Any way she saw fit. That way that dirty, evil bundle of swiped cash would be put to good use.

I was done with Aksaray, with Istanbul. For the time being, at least. But where to now? I didn't know if I actually had anywhere to return to. I still don't.

I arrived in Brooklyn at an ungodly hour. But Tahir, my partner, was still working in the shop. We embraced.

"Sorry about your loss, bro," he said. "I hope you had a chance to get rid of all those knots."

Well, that's not happening anytime soon, I wanted to tell him—my knots, brother, are here to stay. I tried to deal with death by becoming the Grim Reaper himself; I tried to deal with the monstrosities by becoming a monster myself. But what choice did I have? I'm not part of any political organization or gang or anything. I'm just here, just me, in Brooklyn. One horse, one gun. A retired Grim Reaper. That's it.

As I said, my knots are here to stay.

And as for Aksaray, the "White Palace" of Istanbul . . .

I keep quiet.

Except every now and then, I let go: "You! Damn You! Fucking Black Palace, that's what you are! *Black* Palace!"

SO VERY FAMILIAR

BY BEHÇET ÇELİK

Fikirtepe

Whenever my gaze falls upon the apartment door, where we lingered as she prepared to go without even saying goodbye, I feel her eyes resting on me that one last time—they're looking at me still. Frozen, frightened, confused, but determined. I must have looked confused too. I thought everything was going just fine, I thought for sure she'd come over and take me into her arms and we'd make love again. She pulled the door shut behind her quietly, and left.

Like her, I quietly pulled the door shut, and left. It's around the same time of day that she left. I quickly make my way down the stairs, and then slow as I move through the garden of the apartment complex. I lower my head in polite response to the doorman's greeting.

Are those guys talking about me behind my back? *What does that guy do every night? Where's he going like that?* Is that what they say? So what if they do. Looked like the bastard had a grin on his face when he greeted me. He watched me intently, as if to say, *I know where you're headed, buddy.* How would you know, you idiot? He probably thinks I'm out picking up chicks. If that were the case, I'd take the car. These guys think my car's shit too. They gossip. *He goes on foot 'cause he knows there's no way he can pick up chicks with that lemon.* That's what they say. Goddamn know-it-alls. They can say whatever they want, like I give a shit! The parking lot here's like a car show. Next to all those brand-new fancy vehicles, our car looks like scrap metal. Ours? Those idiot doormen must know by now that there is no "ours" anymore. Maybe they feel sorry for me. Or maybe, if they've had a spat with the old lady that day, they just feel jealous.

It's freezing cold, but at least I can breathe once I'm outside. I can't stand it inside anymore. It's like the walls are collapsing on top of me; television, movies, newspapers, it all makes me sick to my stomach. Forget about sleeping, if I could only breathe I wouldn't set foot outside. I'm managing all right, even if I do wander around like a ghoul every night. But how long can I possibly keep it up? And I've actually come to like going to work. Files, correspondence, meetings all fill up the day. I'm fine when I'm at work, but once I get home . . .

There must be a minibus coming. I can hear it wheezing up the hill. When the weary driver sees me in the distance, he'll be counting his blessings—*Got me a passenger for the last trip of the night.* He'll understand soon enough that he's got me pegged wrong. He'll honk, though, regardless of the late hour. I should walk away from the avenue and go look at that shop window, so he understands that I'm not waiting for a ride. Ugly shit they're selling. And they cost a fortune. I'm sure some folks come in here and try to bargain them down a few *lira*s. We sure did. But I didn't try to cut a deal on the bedroom furniture. If only I'd known! I sleep in the living room now. Can't sleep in the bedroom. It's just one silent scream. But what do you know, same thing goes for the living room.

I should cross the road and head downhill toward the university. It's calmer over there. The minibus route's like a border. They're still going strong on the right side of the road, even at this hour of the night. The left side is nothing but slumber. The buildings on the right are ten, fifteen stories high, but the ones on the left max out at four or five, and usually aren't more than one or two. It's a wonder the contractors haven't ripped into this place yet. They've already started tearing down the ten-story buildings on the right side and putting up bigger and better ones. Actually, this stretch would bring a pretty penny. Either the city won't let them build that high yet, or the plots are too small, divided up into too many units. But anyway.

Are there more streetlamps on the right, or are they just brighter? It's pitch black on the other side of the avenue. Maybe it's the lights in the shop windows that make it so shiny there; here the stores are completely closed down—the metal shutters, the padlocks, the lights, the signs, all tucked in for the night. Shopkeepers probably figure there's no need to keep the place lit up, since there's nobody out here after dark.

A few nights ago there were some young guys hanging out at one of these corners, sitting on a low wall cracking sunflower seeds. Maybe they were drinking beer too. I walked by them without a glance. At first I was afraid; what if they start picking on me, say something, come after me ... But the closer I got, the less scared I felt. In fact, I almost wanted them to try and pick a fight. As I walked past them, I felt the blood rush through my veins, from just below my knees down to my toes (warmed my cold feet up); it was like the stuff wanted to burst out of my body, but it was trapped. When they saw me they went silent and stared. Without even glancing at their faces, I saw that they were looking at me. I just stared ahead and walked right past them, without even seeing the darkness (though, actually, there was a good bit of light shining down from the streetlamp in front of the wall where they were parked). If I run into them tonight, I'm going to turn around and look at them. Let's see if they have something to say. But tonight I am leaving later than usual. Even they are back home in bed by now, I bet. Their fathers probably grumbled about them being out so late and their mothers probably got their beds ready for them while asking what they'd been up to, as if they didn't know their boys were out bumming around on the streets all day.

If I told somebody I spent my nights wandering around these streets, they'd probably think I was nuts. But who would I tell? The other day Ertürk asked me what I did in the evenings. "Nothing," I said. He didn't press me. "We should go drinking sometime," he suggested. "Sure," I replied. But then we never made plans for a specific date or anything. He probably didn't know what else to say after that. What if I got carried away and lost it, or even worse, what if I got weepy? "We should go drinking sometime." That sure took the weight off his conscience. But that's fine with me, it's not like I really want a drinking buddy or anything. I like things the way they are. Walking these streets. Exercise, for the hell of it—for what it, and this body, are worth.

I spot a figure over by one of the cars parked on the left side of the street. Why would anyone be out at this time of night? Unless he's just hitting the streets for no reason at all, like me. He must be headed for the hospital or the police station, can't be anything but bad news at this hour.

Just as I begin thinking I should turn right to put some distance between myself and the shadowy figure, a car alarm goes off. I'm not the only one startled by it. The shadow starts to run. And I after him.

I have to catch him. I can. I will. He's fast too. I've started to catch up, but I can feel the energy draining out of me. So what happens when I catch him? The question doesn't slow me down. What am I going to do, beat him up? Turn him in? I think of something Semih told me. He said for days after his cassette player was stolen from his car, he found his car repulsive. That's what he said. "It was like the car had been defiled, I just couldn't stomach getting into it." I wonder if that's the guy who broke into Semih's car? Well, it was him or someone like him—those pricks are all alike. How many times have I told him, "Rent a place in an apartment complex like ours, the streets aren't safe. You spent all that money on the car, you shouldn't just leave it out on the street."

How much longer can I keep after this fool? What the hell am I chasing him for anyway? He might pull a knife, or maybe a screwdriver; in any case, something sharp, whatever he used to open the car door. All ties have been severed between my brain and my legs; my thoughts don't slow me down; I just keep running, pacing myself like a long-distance pro. I never would've thought I'd be able to run so fast for so long. The benefits of not smoking. As I run I feel this sense of spaciousness, a kind of freshness within; I can almost catch a whiff of mint. Maybe after I catch up I'll just run right past him, make it to the finish line first. The more I run, the lighter I feel. Maybe all the sweating is ridding my body of toxins? My heart is racing, and my head's throbbing just as fast, but my legs couldn't care less, it's like they have a mind of their own.

We're sprinting downhill; if we'd been going uphill, there's no way I could catch up. Here the streets are even darker. He's at most three yards ahead of me. But I can't catch up—we must be running at the same speed. He slows down each time he turns around to look back at me, but it's not enough for me to catch up. He must know these parts well; he never takes a dead end. My legs have started to shake; it's a not unpleasant feeling. I'll be sore tomorrow, but for now it feels good.

I don't understand how it happened. He was trying to jump over a wall just a couple of feet high when his foot got caught and he fell. First I heard a thump, then I heard a moan.

Oh God! The boy's face is covered in blood. He must've hit his head. I feel sick to my stomach. We're unable to speak. We're breathless. He's looking me hard in the face. But his expression is not one of anger, nor of a desire for mercy. He's just looking. Finally, looking at him looking at me, I come to. A hospital, a doctor . . . I take out my cell phone and call for an ambulance. *"Where are you?"* asks the voice on the other end. I don't know. I ask the other guy. He mumbles something, *Cinema,* I think. That's when I realize where I am.

"You know that old cinema? . . . We're over around there." I give the person my phone number.

The boy on the ground groans, trying to drag himself. He'd probably ignore the cuts and bruises and keep on running, if only he could find the strength. "Don't move," I tell him. I sound like the police on TV, yet all I'm really saying is the only thing I know about first aid, right or wrong. He has to keep his head still.

He says something like, *Let me go.* From the frantic beat of my heart, the puffing of my chest, I can't quite make out his words.

"The ambulance," I say, my voice coming out like a whisper, "is on its way."

It isn't long before the ambulance shows up. Thank goodness. We make our way back through the same streets he and I have just run, siren blaring. I sit next to the driver. He doesn't ask any questions, and I don't say a word. We pull up to the emergency room. They put the boy on a stretcher and take him in. Nobody says a word to me. Should I just get out of here? Now they're going to ask me all kinds of questions. Still, I can't bring myself to leave. I'm so worried about the boy. What if they notice me leaving, what'll I say? There's a handful of people waiting in front of the emergency room. A couple of people rush out of the emergency room and over to the glass-partitioned area on the side. I've finally caught my breath, but my legs are still shaking. Should I go over and sit in that glass-partitioned area too? But I can't move. I just watch instead. There's a reception window; that must be where they do all the registering and signing in and stuff. And there are chairs for people waiting on the other side. One person's stretched out asleep, and there's a group of people talking. In the far corner, some bum's leaning back against the radiator; he's holding his grimy head in his hands. He's probably a regular here at night, just moved in; nobody cares.

A middle-aged policeman exits the emergency room. Is he heading toward me or what?

"Which one of you brought in the injured kid?" he yells out.

I walk up to him. I ask him how the boy's doing.

"Fine," he says, and I notice he's holding a small notebook. He's going to ask me something now. How will I answer? Should I tell him the truth? If I tell him I just stumbled upon the boy, he's going to ask what business I had over there at that time of night. Basically, I'm screwed no matter what. Best to ask him some questions first.

"Is he conscious?" I say, surprised at my own ingenuity in coming up with that one.

"Yes, yes he is. Let's go see him."

There are patients waiting on stretchers in the hallway, with friends and relatives standing or sitting next to them. I can hear moaning and weeping coming from the rooms, their doors open. A tired nurse carrying IV fluids walks by. Another is telling one patient's relative something, as if she holds the key to the world's most important secret.

The room we walk into is a grid of curtains. I spot the boy's feet in the first partition. Without realizing it, it seems I've memorized his shoes, his pants. When the policeman opens the curtain, the boy sees me too. His eyes fill with fear when he sees the two of us together.

"He says he fell. Is that true?"

"I think so. I didn't see him fall. I ran out of cigarettes and was looking for someplace open. That's when I saw this boy lying on the ground."

I'm thinking I've provided unnecessary detail when the policeman lets out a yawn and turns to peer at the boy, who shakes his bandaged head yes, without looking at me. For the first time, I get a good look at his face, there in the fluorescent light. At first I thought the mark on his face was a bandage, but upon closer inspection I see it's a bruise the size of a quarter. It's so very familiar. Something from that very last look in front of the door, always there before my eyes—and on her lily-white neck.

THE BLOODY HORN

BY İNAN ÇETİN

Fener

I had opened the window and was looking into the distance, into the blue horizon and the dark, peaceful waters of the Golden Horn. I contemplated this view from high up in my room in Pera Palace. And the view, it howled in warning.

For years I have wondered, in vain, at exactly what point in my life I had gotten off track. How a perfectly orderly life could become so disjointed along the way. Was it because the gates of the past had been suddenly crashed open, in a single violent thrust? I had been scared to death of making a mistake. Fener—complete with its temples of three different religions, its narrow streets, my family, and the house where my destiny was shaped—had always been alive in my memory. If I handled it right, I could fit my whole life into Fener. I was born and raised there. I fell in love there. I left Fener when I was fifteen and returned at the age of forty-five. Istanbul was a city of echoes, where everything—*everything*—resonated with an acute vitality: a historic building, an ornate arch, an ancient tree, streets, bridges, palaces . . . Wherever I looked, deep-seated passions seemed to surface, to come to life, the passions of a fisherman, a woman, a stranger, a thug true to his code. No matter how hard I tried to escape the feeling of belonging, I could not wrestle myself free of the dizzying, blinding nostalgia and longing that held me in their grasp; my memory was digging up details I had never permitted myself to utter, and my mind, on the cusp of a leap, needed to embellish them.

I really used to hate memories. But now my tears were trickling down, hanging from my chin like raindrops from a gutter. I was in Fener, a place that saddens, much like a museum that no one visits. I stood there, just stood there, in front of the Yıldırım Boulevard house where I was born and raised. Some mute color, some shifty darkness had fallen upon me. The building no longer possessed even a shred of the glamour I knew from my childhood; it was but a skeleton of itself. The familiarity of the place failed to return my past to me; alas, it was all lost to time.

All of a sudden I felt so much like a stranger, I had to breathe hard not to cry; I pulled myself together and thought of my family. I wasn't supposed to return to Istanbul, not after all the hell my family had been through. But it was as if I had been unable to tell just what was happening, trapped there in a silent darkness; it induced amnesia, it was indifferent to the past. I had hit the road in a hurry and found myself in Istanbul in no time. Strangely enough.

A long time ago, one morning, contrary to habit, I had woken up before my parents. I didn't dare wake them, so I munched on some food and left. I walked along the shore of the Golden Horn. If I had to describe that walk, I think it best to put it in terms of music. I heard sounds, sometimes sharp, sometimes soft as silk, something between a song and a lament, like the melody of the haziness I was feeling around me for the first time. Yet it was a crystal clear morning, with the sky reflecting on the Golden Horn like a tree shaping its own shadow. But then, it is a difficult business, conveying the feelings that Istanbul evokes.

Without a doubt, though, I had heard that strange melody. Then the noise of cars and fishing boats ruined it all, and I headed back. That morning, a few minutes after coming home, I found my father and mother in bed, completely still, their eyes fixed on the ceiling.

My memories aren't that clear at this point. The bedroom was a pool of gelatinous blood, that I remember very well. Yes, a sea of frozen blood, thawing, trickling, thinning. Even a heart of stone could cease to beat in a place saturated with fear, and though I stood very close, I could not bring myself to touch the bodies. I don't know which I was more afraid of, death itself or the stain it would leave; it was as if I was frozen right there.

Before he was killed, my father had left home late every night for a week. Sometimes he would just pace up and down the street, sometimes he would disappear from view as soon as he was out the door. It wasn't disturbing; in fact, it was rather exciting. I became a bit obsessed with his whereabouts, and so I decided to follow him one night. I left after him. I was like a jinn in human form, burning with curiosity. Where was my father going? Who was he going to meet? He turned toward the Bulgarian church, which looked like a present forgotten there on the shore, wrapped in shiny paper. I went after him, the breeze striking my face as I turned each corner. My father was walking briskly, his head down. Suddenly, he turned around and saw me. He couldn't have heard my footsteps, I was walking so gently.

"Son . . . are you following me?"

I stopped dead in my tracks, my head spinning at the shock of having been caught. I was looking at the gate in front of that silvery church, the marble steps winding up to the entrance, at the dark waters a little further ahead and the

flood of city lights reflected upon them. Gradually, everything
became blurry; everything except for my father's eyes, which
shone in the dark. His face was close to mine.

"You should be in bed at this hour," he said, "let's go
home."

He was so enigmatic, the way he terminated so many of
his relationships so quickly, and how he gave everybody such
a hard time with his stoic stubbornness. In those days, a kind
of mental connection was forming between my father and me.
From the outside, one would have thought that we were just
a father and son who got on well, communicating by normal
verbal means. But the truth was, ours was a silent pact, arrived at somewhere deep down, as if we shared some profound secret.

I spent my whole day in Fener wandering around amongst ruins and run-down buildings. The impression left by the building in which I grew up was quite painful. Still, I had been able
to shake off the listlessness and melancholia, to overcome my
lack of courage. Yet there seemed to be a kind of denial at
the core of the word "life," such that it wouldn't tolerate any
middle-of-the-road options. How can I put it? The shell of
that word was too tough, impenetrable; it was keeping me
out. A language beyond words, an unsound logic had created
such a very private, impermeable realm, even the waves of all
the past that I could possibly imagine whirling about me were
for naught.

The nightlife of the neighborhood was about to begin.
Once darkness had finally descended upon the city, in each
and every sound I heard, I began discerning melodies, which
I recalled very clearly from my past, and which made Fener
that much more real to me. They weren't only sounds I had

heard before, but other sounds too, the imagined voices of people I knew only in name, voices of people who lived centuries ago, and the voice of death, still alive in my mind. They would not be denied, would not be suppressed. It was a world of sounds, a different world, existing in the depths of words, moans, whispers, and silences, a world that did not reciprocate the passion of he who listened and observed with feeling.

Such was my strange emotional state when I arrived in front of the Fener Greek Archdiocese. Perhaps it, too, was infected with the same irrationality. The guard at the door looked me square in the face. I sensed a familiarity hidden in that strange expression.

"Are you trying to find someone?" he asked.

It was a momentary thing, a lie I would never own up to. "Yes," I said, "did you see a tall guy with white hair in a suit and a woman with red hair?"

"No," he replied, "we aren't receiving visitors to the Archdiocese right now. There's no one inside."

The important thing was that I was feeling happy at that moment, and that happiness could be made possible only by means of a lie. Of course, I did what it took to keep the lie from getting out of hand; I turned and walked toward the sea. It was hard to ignore the lie; it was love embracing me generously, and truth seeping into the dark paradise of sadness, through a secret hole.

I returned to my hotel after wandering for a while by the shore. The next morning, I was enjoying the happiness of the seventh day, the day after creation. Solitude, the feeling of security because you are out of the reach, too far away to tend to the intrusions of daily life . . . It was a pleasure. I was having dinner in Fener, in a restaurant with a view of the Golden

Horn. The people at the next table and I were putting on an ostentatious show of mutual respect. What an undeniable blessing these Fener evenings are, we were saying, the world at our command. Dinner took a long time; by the time we finished, the night had engulfed the entire city. We complicated even the simplest of things, especially the simple ones, with our labyrinthine words.

Some men of Fener are night owls; there is no shortage of people coming and going, right up to the moment when the restaurant door is padlocked. As the night wore on, I found myself sitting together with the people from the next table, deep in conversation. We were just about to finish our second bottle of *rakı* and call it a night, when an old man appeared at the door. He stood there and briefly scanned the place before deciding to enter, then he walked straight to our table.

"Good evening, gentlemen," he said with a smile. "Enjoying the fare, I hope!"

Three from our table knew him. They introduced us to each other. A smile broadened across his face and his attention focused on me like a beam. "Vasili, you say! You still speak Turkish like your mother tongue!"

The other men at the table were taken by surprise, and I was too. The man was alert, like a fox, and was obviously eager to hear my response. But I was petrified.

"You are that Vasili, aren't you?" he said. "Son of Yorgo. I knew your father. Do you remember me?"

At that moment, I concentrated upon the calm, serene face of the man, where time, in all its destructiveness, was hiding. His wrinkled face did remind me of something, but it was as if my memory was being swept away by a strong current, a current stronger than life itself, and was struggling to gain a foothold.

"Sorry, can't seem to place you," I said.

Perhaps he had more to say, but he remained quiet. He stood up, extended his arms, and hugged me tightly. His eyes were wet when he sat down. Truth be told, what could I say to him at that hour of the night, with that buzz in my head? Yet it was a precious opportunity; this old man was the first acquaintance I had stumbled upon in my neighborhood, which had been so thoroughly appropriated and alienated by time. He didn't know where to place his huge hands. The heartbreaking zeal of this chance encounter induced a growing sense of disquiet. There was something cruel there in the twilight zone of that dimly lit *meyhane*. My heart filled with an unidentifiable longing, my mind with myriad possibilities.

The busboys, who were no older than fifteen or sixteen, and the middle-aged, mustached waiters were circling us. We ordered another bottle of rakı. The old man (Cevat, that was his name), who had been born and raised in Fener, was talking about how drinking was the only curative he'd been able to find in this city, which so viciously laid waste to human life. He was a man with nine lives, who had managed to survive so many dangers, so many nights, so many miseries, so many adventures . . .

"Your father and I first met in front of the Red Church," he said. "I enjoyed meeting new people when I was young, now I prefer solitude. We remained friends after we met, your father and I. I lived nearby, on Çimen Street, where I still live today. But everything is in the past now. Frankly, that devastating incident did away with it all, all the beautiful memories we had, everything."

I dredged up the courage: "Do you know something?"

He remained silent for a long moment, staring at his plate, before he finally answered: "No, nothing at all. I want to forget all about it, the whole thing."

I refrained from exalting my father, praising his goodness and generosity, but I did give in and let myself get carried away by the memories. I shared a few, though names largely escaped me. At first, my words contained nothing too far beyond the conditions that fate required. It was as if I was in two different times, two different places at once, and that made it difficult for me to speak. In spite of this, words began rolling off my tongue of their own accord; I just kept talking and talking. There are moments when one feels hopeless and does what he can to evade that feeling. But that wasn't my only problem, for it was as if a wall had come tumbling down, and there I was inside the chamber of my childhood. I don't think there could possibly be anything at once so mysterious and familiar as the eternal texture of childhood.

It wasn't easy to keep up conversation with the old man, because he kept interrupting me.

"Come to my home and be my guest tonight," he said, "we have a lot to talk about."

His proposal surprised me; I turned down his invitation with visible mistrust. I suggested meeting the next day. It was late; we got up and left. I took a cab and returned to my hotel.

The following day, at around 2 o'clock, I met Cevat *Bey* in Fener. We sat in a café, we talked very little. It was from him that I learned the name of my father's and mother's murderer: Kenan.

My memories of that time from my childhood were permanently etched in my mind: the decrepit walls of Dimitrie Cantemir's palace, the stone wall of the Red Church, the narrow streets, the muggy, reclusive evenings, a history drunk with glory, and so on and so forth. Yet, for me, none of that was enough to explain away that particular night, and the way the neighborhood's reflection gleamed so ghastly upon the dark waters of the Golden Horn. Cevat Bey finally spoke the words that I didn't dare to say: "Are you ready to face the man who changed your destiny, Vasili?" Though the question sent an unfamiliar rage coursing through my body, I was a coward, frozen with fear. The visible change in Cevat Bey, though, was something else altogether: In that moment, he became a machine designed to resist, a machine built to withstand not only physical attack, but the impact of time. He motioned for me to get up.

We left. The heat, not at all tempered by the night, was unbearable. Later, it was said to be the hottest night Istanbul had had in recent years. I hadn't slept a wink in days. In my exhausted state, I didn't have the willpower not to follow him. Still, I was afraid. Not because I thought everything would be in vain, but because the meeting would drag me to the inevitable, to the very last thing I should do.

We turned into a street on the right, the last one before reaching the Greek Church of Fener. We were both silent. At that moment, Cevat Bey's face seemed devoid of any distinguishing features, except for his huge eyes shining in the darkness. I doubt I looked much different; he must have been as afraid as I was. We went up to the third floor of a bay-windowed building. An old man of medium height opened the door. He was in his pajamas. Seeing me, a stranger, at his door, he peered at me closely, inspecting my face. His expression was one of dread.

"I brought you the son of an old friend," Cevat Bey said. His voice was calm and reassuring.

We entered. The man told us to have a seat, to make ourselves comfortable. There was a grave sadness in his old face, as there is in mine now. I let my imagination wander through the past, through our blood-soaked home, and through Fener. To my mind's eye I summoned the hilly streets of my old neighborhood, its people of different religions, different ethnicities, the flowers on our windowsill, flowers which obscured our view, flowers my mother adored, and pictures of the crucifixion of Christ, and the Virgin Mary holding the Christ Child, her head tilted to one side. It was as if that deluge of blood, which had turned my days and my nights into one long, monotonous, unbearable chain of hours, was seeping out the window that looked upon the Golden Horn, flowing into its waters.

"So why don't you tell me now," the old man said. "This gentleman, whose son is he?"

He was waiting for an answer, his desperation palpable. Cevat Bey gave the old man, who was now sitting on the couch, a solemn glance; then with a bitter smile he alternated, looking at the man, then at the darkness outside, then back at the man, etc. His demeanor was cold and professional.

"The son of a friend of yours, a friend of the past, and of the future," he said.

Without a doubt, the truth could be summarized only in this way. Clearly, we were there to kill my father's murderer. Kenan Bey no longer seemed anxious. He seemed to sense that this summary of the truth was not meant to be ironic or mere insinuation.

"Whose?" he said, smiling.

Instinctively I looked at the man's long, slender old fingers. He could see that I was nervous.

"You tell me, young man," he said. "Cevat's always been like this, he's so fond of suspense."

There, facing my parents' murderer, it wasn't only anger that I felt; I felt sorry for him too. It was a strange feeling.

"Yorgo," I said. "I'm Yorgo's son."

He had heard that voice, my voice, in which he saw his own death, in all its nakedness. The look in his eyes changed. His face transformed, and on it I could see the faint remains of the others' now invisible, lost faces. I will never forget those eyes, the expression on his pale face. We were all, I imagine, thinking of death at that point. The most impatient of us was Cevat Bey. He was staring at me, silently. There was an odd respectfulness in his gaze, tinged with fear and sadness; you could almost inhale it.

I felt the rope in my pocket. At first, I was encouraged by the sense that my sadness was shared by Cevat Bey. But then this feeling dissipated and Cevat excused himself to the bathroom.

My parents' murderer and I were listening to the sound of barking from the street. It was neither close nor aggressive.

"I like this barking sound," he said. "It has a generous, tolerant ring to it."

His neck was stiff when he spoke, however, and he was staring at the window with an unnecessary focus of attention. On a wooden table lay his glasses, medicine bottles, and a book. At that moment, he seemed to me such a miserable character, a second-rate hit man who had squandered his life away. The way he stood there so still and kept looking out the window, apparently lost in thought, all the nonsense he was talking, it seemed like it would go on and on until his fear had finally ceased. What he was saying was irrelevant, because what was about to happen would erase it all.

I didn't say anything.

He continued: "I'm going to make something to eat. Would you help me?"

I wasn't at all surprised. The fact is, people don't really seek answers to all their questions. I followed him to the kitchen. It had a small window, which was halfway open. There were some plates lying facedown and a knife with a wooden handle on the marble counter. It was an unsettling image, the only things missing were the body of a murder victim and blood on the small, dirty rug.

I gripped the rope in my pocket. I was getting ready to strangle him, but then in a mad rage I grabbed the knife instead. The man stared into my eyes. He was petrified, his face was ashen, he couldn't move. He struggled to stand. With his arms he held me in a tight hug. His fear was ferocious. The kitchen reeked of sweat.

That's exactly how it happened. I heard the knife plunge into him and the moans escaping his mouth, which I had covered with my hand. Everything happened very slowly, yet it was over all at once. The act of killing induced a feeling of power, and nausea.

There is only one thing to do in situations like this. It is hard to pull off, but has undeniable advantages: You have to get out of there without leaving any clues behind. But how can one possibly undo what he has done?

Then Cevat Bey, hulking at the door, said in a cautious tone: "Keep the knife, leave the kitchen, I'll take care of the rest." He may have been grieved by this state of affairs, but he looked calm.

I didn't leave the Pera Palace Hotel for two days. Perhaps the guy was actually innocent. I hadn't even considered this. Perhaps, but my situation at that point kept me from considering such a possibility at length. I was anxiously awaiting Cevat Bey's phone call. I had to know what was going on. Whether or not I'd be able to return to Fener or even stay in Istanbul depended on the news he was to deliver. The nostalgia I had felt for the city for all those years had morphed into something monstrous. What was I supposed to do now? That was the question.

On the third day, Cevat Bey and I met. We were walking along the shore and darkness was about to engulf Istanbul. The way he put it, everything was okay. His words weren't burdened by shame or regret; in fact, they seemed almost poetic.

As the city gradually grew emptier, amplifying the background din, Cevat Bey grew silent and withdrawn. Then, perhaps to quell his own uneasiness, he suggested we go to a meyhane. I agreed and we went to the place where we had first met. For some time we successfully skirted the incident that continued to fan my fears. But then, late into night, he said something peculiar: "Destiny made me do it again." I was aware that there was still a lot that I didn't know, but my fear was getting the best of me. I couldn't ask. I just couldn't. I had already decided to return to Greece, yet at the same time I felt I didn't have the right, being as close to unveiling the truth as I sensed I was. It wasn't easy; my memories were drenched in blood, and I was drowning.

As the night wore on, the supposed friend sitting across from me became a dark stain, his lips sealed, often covering his face with his hands. At one point I noticed he was breathing heavily and swallowing hard. When he removed his hands, I was unsettled by the glimmering trail that ran down his cheek and onto his lip—the path of a tear.

"What's wrong?" I asked.

He obviously needed to get something out of his system. Then, finally, he mentioned a connection with an organization. He had been in jail for a while in his youth. His brother had been killed. He choked up while telling me about those dark days. I searched his gestures, his behavior, for signs that might shed some light, but all I saw was death, and the fear thereof. It wasn't only his brother who had him so distraught; tears continued to well up in his eyes.

"I can't get that night out of my mind," he said.

"What night?" I asked.

He looked at me with sorrowful yet determined eyes, then he told me, the words falling slowly from his mouth: "The night the decision was made to kill your father."

At first, I didn't want to believe him. If I was going to hear the truth, it had to be the whole truth; I asked him to tell me everything.

"The three of us were members of the same organization, your father, Kenan, and me," he said. He continued to drink as he talked. "Your father didn't like what the organization was up to, for a lot of reasons, and so he split. That was betrayal, and the punishment for betrayal was death."

I asked as nonchalantly as I could, "What kind of an organization was it?"

He hung his head, then called the waiter and ordered another drink. He seemed to want the rakı, which had already numbed his body, to rub him out for good, obliterate his very existence once and for all. His eyes were damp and bloodshot and he began mumbling. His face was covered with deep lines, like the threads of a spider web. He was trying to console himself with the din of his own words, but I couldn't make out what he was saying.

Then he went silent.

"Is that it?" I asked.

"No," he said. "Organizations, politics, you know . . . The hard part, once you've made all the pieces fit together, the hard part is really grasping what it is you're fighting for."

The past was consumed by an unquestionable void. But no, it wasn't empty; whatever was there was definite and intimidating. Cevat Bey took another sip of his rakı and leaned back. He thought I'd understood everything, from his eyes I gleaned that much, but I hadn't understood a thing. For a moment, I thought it would be a friendly gesture to take him home and tuck him in, but my curiosity got the best of me.

"So who ordered my father's murder?" I asked.

He leaned against the table and drained his glass in one gulp.

"I did," he said.

His eyelashes weren't moving, he wasn't breathing. It was dreadful. An amorphous, indescribable moment. Then he stood up, calmly; he was no longer crying.

"Vasili, my son," he said. "Let's take a walk in Fener. You can take me wherever you want."

A WOMAN, ANY WOMAN

BY TARKAN BARLAS

Yenikapı

An old friend and I are on the ferry, deep in conversation, washing the old days down with a few cups of tea. We talk about our junior high days, looking for movie theaters where they'd pepper the karate flicks with porn, and how lucky we, two smooth young boys, were to have survived those catacombs unscathed, and we laugh. Some of our tastiest memories have to do with our laying in wait for a girl, any girl, to practice the things we'd risked life and limb to learn about in those dark theaters. Tea helps the memories go down more smoothly, makes them easier to swallow. We were waiting for a girl. Any girl . . . Our kingdom for a girl . . .

It's a deep conversation, of words and glances. I keep looking at my friend. The memories compound as we laugh. I recall that I hardly laughed at all back in those days though. I feel another sinister joke rising in my gut.

Just then, a guy who knows my friend from college walks up to us. We change the subject. I have a hard time taking interest. The man's conversation is dull. Politics, the difficulty of making ends meet, earthquakes, and whatnot. My attention wanders away from the conversation and onto the waters outside the window. If I weren't in the ferry, but on an open boat, I'd be throwing *simit* crumbs to the seagulls right now, I think. The weather outside is beautiful, the man sitting next to me is not. He's a depressing rain cloud, interrupting and darkening my day.

Mercifully, we approach Yenikapı. On the pier I see men with hands like ropes. They look like they could grab a ship by one end and haul it in with their bare hands. Their job is a matter of life and death, and so they are animated yet earnest, running to attend the scene like surgeons, readying the pier for docking in the nick of time. I move quickly, dragging my friend away from the boring guy and onto the pier. Having extricated ourselves, we take to the streets.

Silently and swiftly, we make our way to the tiny bar beneath the railway, cramming ourselves into an already packed sardine can. We turn into two dirty beards, gawking at an erotic flick on a twenty-inch TV screen, lined up on high stools underneath fluorescent lights. Even though it is filthy and flickering, holding on for dear life, it's still too bright for a place this obscene, I think. It is on to announce to the outside world that in here, everything's all right.

A man eating rice pilaf with chickpeas from a street vendor, probably taking in a quick dinner before he heads home for the night, is glad that everything's all right; he takes a peek inside the bar as he shovels down his final spoonful of pilaf, and relaxes upon seeing that the other members of his sex are not up to anything new. They're just like he left them, right where they belong. *Rakı* is still the belle de jour. He wipes his greasy hands on his pants and disappears, leaving behind a cloud of cigarette smoke. Now you see him, now you don't . . .

Inside the bar, the volume of the conversation is low. Eyes are squinted. The TV murmurs on. Droopy lips and gaping mouths stare at the small screen, where a couple is shown in compromising positions, until a train passes overhead, sending a quake through the bar and prompting the viewers to regain their tight-lipped composure.

My friend and I leave the bar. We go our separate ways, postponing a stroll by the water to another time. As I walk alone on the cracked sidewalks, I feel a desire to find a woman, to make the night bearable, to pour my heart out in the filthiest hotel room in the world. I see a figure standing next to the road. Someone whose back is turned to me, someone with long hair. Even the way I walk becomes more erect. I check my pocket to make sure I have enough cash on me. I croak out a hello with all the courage I can muster. When the figure turns around, my knees almost give out. It doesn't have a face, but a deep, dark void, with pitch black eyes, eyes that are beastly—not human. What I had mistaken for hair is a black pelt enveloping its body from head to toe. I am scared shitless. It approaches, floating, feetless. A chilly vapor precedes it. And a muffled scream. Then a sobbing sigh. I lower my head, covering my face with my hands. I quickly turn away and start to run.

Without quite understanding what I have just seen, as if not yet feeling the pain of dismemberment, I slow to a walk. I'm stunned. I know it is following me, I can feel the cold vapors on my sweating back. I speed up again. I want to leave it behind, I want it to disappear. I want to be left alone with the snack shops and their garishly colorful signs, with that dark, wilted guy selling sunglasses on the corner.

Suddenly I get my wish; I look behind me and it's no longer there. Relieved, I continue along my way. I greet the guy selling glasses, and then pick up some sunflower seeds at the snack store, savoring the normalcy of a cliché exchange with the greasy-bearded guy at the counter. I try to reassure myself that everything's all right. But still, I can't shake that feeling.

Pounding the sidewalk, I start to get the shivers. There's something strange going on. It's like certain things are out of place on the street. Like certain things are missing. Like everybody's so distracted by details they fail to notice that the huge building at the plaza has been removed, and because they can't see it, I'm afraid of noticing it too. It feels weird, and creepy. I look around and notice that there don't seem to be many women. I take a second look and realize that there are in fact *no* women. But I was just here yesterday and there were plenty of women; hailing cabs, returning from weddings with their husbands, sitting with their boyfriends in hamburger joints, whispering gossip and laughing boisterously. Girls revealing tattoos to one another, replicating vapid Hollywood banter, cursing their fathers. Of course, not all of them were lookers, but at least they were there, where they were supposed to be. I glance up at the apartment buildings, but there isn't a single woman dangling a basket to the downstairs grocer. Could this whole thing be a curse? I prefer to blame the rakı. But I'm just not convinced.

The more I walk, the drier my lips get. I pass a crowd waiting for the bus. The crowd reeks, almost of death, and I turn the other way to avoid the smell. A huge, frowning eyebrow of hairy bodies. Just yesterday, this place was totally different. How can this be? I'm searching for a woman who's looking to go somewhere. With me, without me, it doesn't matter anymore. I'm growing tired, starting to feel strangled. It's like the oxygen's being sucked out of the air.

I want to go home, to run into some girl, any girl, from my neighborhood. With a tram full of guys, I go up to Beyazıt Plaza. The Istanbul University dorms are up here. There must be some female students around. Some of them must be out getting a bite to eat, cramming with friends at a café, preparing for the next day's exam.

Walking along the plaza, my disappointment only grows. There isn't a single female student. It's like I'm on a film set. Like this is *Candid Camera,* and somebody somewhere is watching me and laughing his ass off. But this is too much. Nobody deserves this. I continue along my way, like a radar beam, beneath the harsh lights of shops selling meatballs, grilled sandwiches, and *döner.* I swiftly pass the hole in the wall that sells tripe soup—slim chance of seeing a woman in there—and try to find the girl who works in the next shop, selling colorful jewelry and posters of landscapes. She looks you in the face when she talks, makes you happy you're alive. Every time I stop by her shop, I do my best to charm her. My speech becomes more refined, my laughter takes on a different tone. Not because I expect anything from her. But because she gives me the energy to make it through the rest of the day.

But when I reach the shop, what I find hits me with the force of a fist to the face. The girl has been replaced by a beady-eyed brute who's clearly let the place go to seed. He's removed all those bright pictures of Istanbul, which the girl had taken such great pains to display, and carelessly stacked them behind his chair, turning the charming little store into an ugly warehouse. Disgusted, I turn and leave, the memory of the bead girl trailing after me, morphing into a hundred other men unable to forget her smile, suffocating their longing in cigarette smoke.

I'm looking for a woman, any woman. I couldn't care less about sex. I just want to pass a woman on the street. Sevim *Teyze*'s café comes to mind. I think of going there, to chat with Sevim Teyze, to relax and have some tasty pastries and coffee. But what I really need is to hear the sound of her sweet, soothing voice.

Drenched in sweat, I reach what should be Sevim Teyze's

café. I don't recognize a thing, and it sends a chill down my spine. I look at the flower pot next to the door, there in its rightful place, but it has a wad of phlegm in it. And two cigarette butts. Some guy with sausage-shaped fingers is manning the counter. As I walk through the door, I wish with all my might that everything would snap back to normal then and there. But it doesn't. I approach Sausage Fingers, in fear.

"Isn't Sevim Teyze in?"

"Who's that?"

"The owner of this place."

"I'm the owner of this place!" His answer comes crashing down on me. He tells me he's been there for years, that he doesn't know anything about any teyze, and that he has no desire to either. The woman was here just yesterday, I am absolutely certain of it. Sweat's pouring out of me as I look around, and this other world is sucking me in deeper and deeper. The cute wooden chairs have been replaced by dirty white ghosts of cheap plastic. The tiny lamps with the soft lights are gone. There are glass vinegar holders smudged with fingerprints on the tables. I want to lift those fingerprints and track down everyone responsible. This place has become just like all the others. Those sausage fingers can't be bothered with delicate matters; they are busy stuffing baloney in a shoe-sized piece of bread.

I rush back outside. I walk toward the gate of Beyazıt Mosque and Çınaraltı. But that spacious plaza now stifles me. The huge plane tree, once a cool oasis where you could enjoy your tea in the open air, has turned black, its dry leaves crackling, dead and withered. A stiff pigeon falls to the ground in front of me. In a panic, I look around for a delicate hand, but all I can see are hairy knuckles, dirty nails, and callused fists gripping the dainty tulip glasses.

An unbearable stench reaches my nose; it's coming from the Sahaflar Gate, the antique book bazaar. The used book stands have lost their exquisite, yellowish scent and now reek of dead mice. The windows are full of books bound in black. There are no names on the books. They're a monotone, monochrome choir cloaked in black. I lean closer to the window, straining to find a name, and the choir breaks out in a ghastly chant. I am searching for the name of a woman, but the books have no authors, male or female.

I leave the Sahaflar Gate, desperate to forget what it is I've been looking for. A crowd has gathered next to the street in a commotion of ear-piercing cries and police sirens. There is a man on the ground, bleeding to death. Blood gushes from his throat. Everybody is busy telling everybody else what happened while the man lies there dying. I hear them say that the man was stabbed over a girl, and I become delirious with hope. I couldn't care less about the man who's been stabbed—I want to see the girl, to see the girl and put an end to this nightmare. I stare into the police car, hoping to see her. Surely they would take her into custody, into safety. But there is no girl. Not in the car, not anywhere.

I hear whispers in the crowd: Two men were out on the town. One man made a remark about the other man's girlfriend, and got stabbed in return. He said she was "beautiful." Perhaps what they call his girlfriend is not what I envision. Perhaps he is in love not with a girl, but with a piece of fabric—a piece of fabric that he airs out every once in a while, before putting it back in the closet.

My mother—I need to find her. I rush down the narrow empty road leading from behind the university toward my home. I want to believe that this will all be over soon, that girls on their way to class will fill the plaza in droves the next day. Without a doubt, I would embrace every single one of them. I imagine a horseman storming through the grandiose gate of Istanbul University to read aloud some imperial decree, explaining the reasons for this temporary calamity and apologizing for any inconvenience.

I make my way home, convinced that tomorrow I'll be back to yesterday and everything will be fine. My father is sitting in the living room in his underwear, cleaning his nails with a pocketknife. I have never seen my father in his underwear, nor have I ever seen him with a pocketknife. He burps loudly, his eyes glued to the TV screen. This can't be our home; it must be another catacomb of my nightmare. My flesh is creeping as I try to find my mother. But then I change my mind and decide to wait. I don't have the courage to look for her. I'm too afraid of what I won't find. My father mills about like a bear marking his territory. He claims to be looking for an ashtray. His black socks are hanging from the couch.

I have to find her. I check the kitchen, but my mother is nowhere to be found. My suspicion snowballs into an avalanche.

"Did Mom go to bed, Dad?"

"What did you say?"

I repeat my question.

"What's the matter with you, boy?" he says, his eyes glazed over.

I insist on an answer. He seems to feel sorry for me. He looks me straight in the eye, and talks to me like I'm suffering from some kind of amnesia or something.

"You never had a mother," he says. "You know that. She never was. She never could be."

Don't say that, Dad! Don't talk like that! Don't think like that!

He doesn't explain. He just stares at me as if to say that

I should know that there is no such "thing." The glint from his knife stabs me in the eye, blinding me. And so I listen, straining to hear the sound of my mother—a word, any word that's been captured in the walls, a scream still hanging from the curtains. I want to grab onto it before it flies away, caress it, shelter it in my ear. But I can't hear a thing, except for the grunting of the man pretending to be my father. I'm looking for my home. I leave, distraught and angry. I wait on the street until sunrise. To witness the return to normalcy.

Morning comes, but the darkness doesn't leave, it only fades to gray. Dark gray. Walking through the pungently male clusters of students on the plaza, I start to abandon all hope. I enter the Covered Bazaar. It's like a scene out of *One Thousand and One Nights*. I'm the main character in a bad fairy tale. I want to succumb to the beckoning young buck apprentices and buy a pair of *şalvar*, not as a souvenir but to wear in earnest. I want to buy a *tesbih*, not as decoration but to click in my hand. I want to wander into the Oriental Café and get hooked on a hookah. I wander through the labyrinth of the bazaar, hoping to get lost, when one of the arched entrances catches my eye. It's completely black, a hole leading to nowhere. I delve inside, wishing for the worst, hoping to hit rock bottom.

Suddenly, I find myself in one of those movie theaters that shows the karate flicks with the porn interludes. The place reeks of semen. The floor is sticky. I see a sliver of light in the distance. I run, my feet clinging to the gunk on the floor. The insidious goo rises and rises, until I'm in the stuff all the way up to my knees. My whole body throbs. I'm in terrible pain. I finally make it out. I reach the light.

I'm on the ferry, sitting next to my friend and that boring guy, who's still talking. I look outside; everything seems normal. I watch the brunette woman across from me licking her ice cream with gusto, another girl down the row courting the boy next to her. I now realize just how wrapped up I've been in whatever it is that boring guy's been saying. I've been hostage to his drivel for a full half hour, the cramp in my stomach growing more and more crippling the longer I listen.

He talks like he's seen, done, knows it all. He has a small store where he sells religious books. I try to envision the bookstore. It smells of rose oil, and men dressed in şalvar, men from another century.

"The people are waking up, though, slowly but surely," he says.

"Waking up to what? The benefits of literacy?" I ask.

He leans back and smiles. He's so sure of himself, it's repulsive.

"That too," he replies, "but what I really meant was that they are waking up to the fact that they are living in sin. The most remarkable thing about it is that they can't see just how immersed in sin they themselves really are, how this sickness has infected them—and so they need to be told. They have to be taught a lesson." They can't fathom the consequences of skimpy skirts, he claims.

"What kind of a state is this anyway?" he scoffs. "They tax believers, use the money to open rakı factories, support the *meyhane*s, ban the headscarf. It's ridiculous. But now they're finally being taught a lesson, if only they could open their eyes and see it for what it is."

He holds up the newspaper: the Gölcük earthquake. Thirty thousand deaths—crushed bodies, crushed hopes, a country in mourning. But for him, the tragedy is a punishment. "Punishment by God," he says.

So he means to say that tens of thousands of people had

forsaken their religion, had reaped what they had sewn. According to him, Istanbul was next—the sinners were being weeded out. This guy built his happiness on the ruins of thousands, on the despair of millions.

"It's not just about the veil," he says. "Covering your head is not enough. Every one of those who perished in the quake were people gone astray, people who abandoned their religion."

I have to get out of here.

The man turns to me, about to deliver the darkest chapter of his sermon. But I stand up, leaving him speechless. He is looking not in my eyes but at the seat of my pants now. Finally, a real savior appears. A girl I know from work. She nods in greeting, and I respond—I've never been so happy to see anyone in my entire life.

We reach Yenikapı. Outside, I see men with hands like ropes.

PART IV

GRIEF & GRIEVANCES

ORDINARY FACTS

BY RIZA KIRAÇ

4th Levent

At the funeral, together with my brother's comrades, I raised my left fist into the air, I yelled out slogans, and I sang marches.

When my brother's corpse, the three bullet holes in his body plugged with cotton balls, was brought into the mosque, I, like everyone else, fell silent. Rather than join the congregation as they performed the funeral *namaz*, I stood proudly in the corner with the young comrades.

Following the namaz, the coffin was lifted onto shoulders once again and everyone walked to the cemetery. Two neighborhood women stood on either side of my mother, their arms linked in hers, trying to hold her up.

I was walking next to Haldun *Abi*. Every now and then he'd put his hand on my shoulder, keeping me next to him. Everyone was crying, everyone but me. I just couldn't. Not because I didn't love my brother, I loved him dearly. I would have done anything for him. He wasn't just my brother, he was a father to me too.

Seeing that I wasn't crying, Haldun Abi said to me, "Your brother would be proud of you, the way you're standing tall."

After we'd buried my brother, every day for a month, my mother walked all the way to Sanayi Mahallesi—the "industrial" neighborhood—to visit his grave. For the first two weeks I went with her, so she wouldn't be alone. And for the next few days after that, I'd go to the cemetery after school and walk back with her. She just stood there in front of his grave, sobbing silently. Every once in a while, she'd reach down with her cracked and callused hands and caress the earth, as if touching her son's skin.

The only thing I could do to console her was stand by her side. There was nothing else I could do; there was nothing I could say.

For several days after my brother's funeral, my father came to the house to make sure we had everything we needed and to play host to those who came to offer their condolences. Later, he'd stop by after work and sit with us. We hardly spoke a word. Eventually, my father would get up and go, leaving us and our silence behind for his new, peaceful home, his urban, educated wife, and my stepsister.

The neighbors' daughters would come over and light the furnace, sweep the house, cook us some food, and then go home. If it hadn't been for them, it never would've occurred to my mother or me to light the furnace, or to eat, or to take care of any other trivial daily necessities. Those bites of food that we reluctantly put in our mouths at the dinner table remained stuck in our throats, day and night.

Once it was dark out and we'd turned the house lights on, we'd sometimes hear gunshots coming from down by the streams that flowed toward Kâğıthane. When the sounds drew closer, to just a few streets over, I'd switch off the lights and sit my mother down on the floor.

The following day there would be another funeral, this time in Gültepe, or Yahya Kemal, or Çeliktepe. Again left fists would be raised and marches would be sung, or a crowd proclaiming *Allahuekber* would rain curses down upon the Communists.

One morning about two months after my brother's death, I went to wake my mother up and I found her dead.

We buried her next to my brother. I stood before their graves and looked at the people around me, all of them poor, all of them hopeless, all of them angry, and all of them sick of what was happening—whatever it was.

There was no way I could stay in the house alone. How could an eleven-year-old boy live on his own in a rickety shanty?

We emptied out the house, gave our stuff to the neighbors. All I had left was a bird cage and a pair of canaries flitting around inside it. My father didn't want the birds; he thought they brought bad luck. I placed the cage on my lap and sat in the center of the living room. My father gave in. We walked from the steep hill of Yahya Kemal to the Gültepe bus stop, the first stop of the line. There wasn't a bus yet, so we waited. The bus eventually came, and we got on.

While everyone else was going back to their shanties after work, I was headed for a new home, an apartment. I was leaving behind the place where I had been born, the graves of my brother and mother, for another neighborhood, another street, another life, the home of a woman and her daughter, neither of whom I knew. My father was carrying two small plastic sacks and my school bag, and I was carrying a cage with two canaries flapping around like crazy, frightened by all the noise.

The bus arrived at the Neyir stop, which lies at the intersection leading to Büyükdere Avenue. Some people called this the factory stop; some just called it Neyir after the textile factory on the corner.

We were listening to the news broadcast on the bus driver's transistor radio. It was more like the newscaster was reading a list of names: those who'd died, those who'd been arrested; the prime minister, ministers of state, soldiers, the president . . .

I started looking out the window to escape the gloomy atmosphere of the bus; the workers were leaving the pharmaceutical, ceramic, lightbulb, and textile factories on the east side of Büyükdere Avenue and heading home. Behind the green hills of the west side were the villas of the rich and famous, and huge construction sites of apartment blocks in the making.

It was at that moment, at that corner, that I began crying.

For the first time in my life, I felt that something was changing, but I wasn't sure what. I'd started sobbing when my father peered at me with a look of fear on his face that I'd never seen before.

"What's wrong, Sadık?" he asked.

I couldn't tell him; I didn't know. It could hardly be a coincidence that the avenue dividing the rich from the poor, the luxurious apartment blocks from the shanties, the city from the village, had been named Büyükdere—the "large brook." But I didn't really know what that meant, so I banished all my confused thoughts to the dark recesses of my mind.

I was on the thirty-fifth floor of the skyscraper, facing the avenue. Between the city and me was a two-way mirror, separating the accused from the witness. But which of us was which, I couldn't tell.

To my left was the factory stop, where I cried as a child, in its new guise: a main thoroughfare clogged with traffic, despite six lanes and an underpass at the intersection. And on my right, a mesmerizing Bosphorus view, enough to drive one to obsession.

Some spirit was whispering my brother's last words, which

were stuck in my child's mind like a rusty knife. Back then Büyükdere Avenue was still long, but it didn't have much traffic; you could amble across it, from one side to the other.

"Take a good look at this avenue, Sadık," my big brother had said to me; I was just starting elementary school. "It's a border, a border that shows which class you belong to."

The only kind of class I knew about was the one where I'd learned to read and write and do arithmetic. I didn't understand what my brother was trying to say, not until much later, when I enrolled in the police academy.

The pain of those memories was always with me. Years later, I finally understood what my brother was trying to tell me, but it was too late; I felt classless.

The Bosphorus side of the avenue was full of luxurious apartment complexes, paved roads, fancy playgrounds, and glamorous shopping centers. The east side—Gültepe, Çeliktepe, and Sanayi Mahallesi—was a dump where the hopeless, the poor, laborers, immigrants from villages near and far, and Gypsies took refuge. It was a black hole.

I didn't stay long in that apartment with my father, stepmother, and stepsister. Two years later I moved in with my aunt in Ankara. Ankara was heavy, it was stone; it weighed upon me.

The door opened. İlhan *Bey*, a tall man in his fifties, with short hair and a bony, smiling face, walked in. He approached me with quick steps that hardly suited a man of his stature.

"I'm sorry to have kept you waiting, Sadık Bey," he said as he shook my hand. "We're so busy these days, and unfortunately I've got another meeting that I must attend in just a few minutes."

I simply smiled in response. His hands were like ice, and I felt oddly unnerved; I'd never felt like that before.

He invited me to sit at the long conference table.

"What can I do for you?"

His tie was sticking out of his jacket; he tucked it back in. It was just the two of us sitting next to each other, but for some reason it felt like all the other chairs at the table were occupied too. My eyes wandered over the empty chairs and up to the cameras. İlhan Bey was smiling. I kept waiting for him to look at the watch he was covering with his right hand, but he insisted on focusing his attention elsewhere.

"I wanted to talk to you about the body found on the twelfth floor four days ago."

İlhan Bey didn't budge. He just kept looking at me, silently.

"You knew him, didn't you?"

"Of course I did," he replied. "Murat Bey and I worked together for years on the board of directors. I don't know what to say. You never know when your time will come." He was still wearing the same expression as he said these words.

"You probably have your suspicions about who killed him, don't you?"

"Killed him?" he asked. He didn't seem surprised by my question, though. He didn't look angry or agitated either.

"That's what we think, sir. And I did a background check on you."

"You needn't have gone to the trouble," he said, smiling. "All you had to do was ask; I would have told you whatever you wanted to know."

"It must be a tough job, being vice president of the firm."

He finally raised his arm and looked at his watch. "I'm sorry, Sadık Bey, but I don't have much time. Can you please get to the point?"

"I could've called you in to the station. In fact, I could take you in right now. So please don't make a fuss if I take a few extra minutes of your time."

"I'm trying to be reasonable. I'm happy to hear you out. But there is no way you are taking me anywhere. You can be sure of that." The determined look in his eyes seemed to imply that he had friends in high places.

"You were born in Çeliktepe. You attended Robert High School and then . . ."

"I graduated from Bosphorus University. Did my doctorate in America. Worked with some of Turkey's biggest business magnates. I know my own life story, Sadık Bey."

I smiled.

"Do you know who *you* are?" he asked, his voice calm as could be. He continued: "*I* know who you are, Sadık Bey."

"Really?" He was mocking me.

"Yes, I do."

"Well, all you need to know is that I'm a policeman and you're a suspect!"

"So you say. But the truth of the matter is, I couldn't care less about Murat Bey's death, and you can't pin a thing on me, Sadık Bey. Let's be frank. If there's something you have to say to me, just come out and say it. I'm wasting precious time here."

There was plenty to say, but at that moment I felt it was still too early. I stood up. İlhan Bey peered at me for a moment before rising to his feet as well.

"Thank you, İlhan Bey," I said, extending my hand.

"Is that it?" He seemed a bit unsettled.

"That's it," I said.

I shook his cold hand again, and he thanked me. He walked to the conference room door and opened it. As he started to walk out, I called after him.

"That makes five murders," I said. "I'm not going to let you get away with a sixth."

His hand was still on the door handle. He squared his shoulders and his face flashed red with anger. He looked arrogant. He closed the door and took two steps toward me.

"I knew your brother, Sadık Bey. He was a few years older than me, and he was *my* big brother too. When he pointed a gun at someone, he fired; but you—you're just trying to corner me with a pistol of blanks. I really don't know how it is that we didn't meet when you were a kid. There was something your brother used to say: *If you're going to do something, do it with your body and your soul.*"

I took a long look at his face.

I left the skyscraper through exit number four and walked toward a fountain flanked by ugly, stylized lion statues. I lit a cigarette. I could tell I was being followed; I could feel it.

My cell phone rang. It was Faruk. "Where are you, sir?" he asked. I told him to go on home. My hotel was nearby.

It was starting to get dark. I began walking, up the stairs and to the top of the hill. I remembered this place. We used to come here to fly kites or play ball sometimes. It was a soccer field of natural grass, but once we found a woman's body here; the grass was yellow and her head had been smashed with a stone.

I made it up to Büyükdere Avenue; there was an iron rail that ran between two lanes to keep people from crossing.

I walked toward the bus stop, where a group of people were standing waiting. I killed some time glancing around at the towering buildings and skyscrapers. I had five bodies, five skyscrapers, and one suspect who really shouldn't even be called a suspect. I didn't have a shred of evidence; all I had was a hunch.

I kept my eye on the bus stop across the street, the factory stop
. . . Faruk had told me they call this place "Silicon Valley" now.
I took the stairs leading down from behind the stop, and then
walked through the underpass and along the dirty dimness of
flickering fluorescent lights and the reverberating drone of traffic, before emerging on the other side and heading up another
set of stairs. The old Neyir building had been turned into a
courthouse, restored complete with black windows to give it a
modern air. The pharmaceutical factory was still there across
from the new courthouse, but with a few added stories and an
annex in the rear. As I walked toward the factory stop, I was so
sure of the footsteps silently trailing after me that I didn't even
turn around to make sure they were really there.

Faruk was blabbering about something he'd read in the paper. "Sadık Bey, they say that if all the toilets in the skyscrapers
on this avenue were flushed at the same time, Istanbul's entire
sewage system would explode," he told me, laughing.

"We'd really be up shit creek then, wouldn't we?" I said.

"Somebody ought to test that theory," Faruk replied, still
laughing.

As I made my way toward Mövenpick Hotel in 4th Levent,
I could still feel the pair of eyes behind me. The road used
to be lined with all kinds of factories, big and small, but now
the corporations had taken over and it was one long series of
buildings fronted by black glass, all postmodern, all tightly
guarded by private security companies, all rigged with cameras in every corner.

About ten minutes later I reached the lot where the bus
terminal used to be, before they tore it down. Somebody
would want to erect a skyscraper here too; it was just a matter of time. I crossed the street at the Çeliktepe intersection.

When I reached an iron curtain surrounding a new skyscraper still under construction, I turned around and looked behind me, hoping to see the eyes that were following me.

When I entered the hotel lobby, my head was spinning from all the noise and the strange melancholy I had picked up on the avenue. The woman at the reception desk greeted me with a smile and handed me the card key to my room.

I was planning to have a cup of coffee in the lobby and then head out to grab a bite to eat. But then I noticed that a man sitting by himself in the lobby was watching me. A blue halo of cigarette smoke encircled his head. When he saw me look at him, he put out his cigarette, stood up, and walked toward me. "Hello Sadık," he said, with a confident smile on his face.

I gave him a quizzical expression. "Hello."

The look on his face was eerily distant. He was a big guy—big-boned, that is, though with a bit of a paunch and chubby cheeks; he must have been in his mid-fifties. I couldn't place him.

He continued to smile as he shook my hand.

"I could imagine you growing up to be just about anything but a police officer," he said, still polite as could be.

Maintaining my air of formality, I responded to his words—which seemed more an expression of surprise than a compliment—with a slight smile.

"I didn't expect you to remember me," he said as he sat down. "My name's Haldun, I was a friend of your brother's."

I tried to look him in the eye. There was something there, something hidden. But nothing about him reminded me of the man from thirty years ago, nothing but a subdued tone of compassion in his voice that made me think of my brother's funeral.

I just stood there, frozen, while he continued to smile. "Why don't you have a seat?"

We sat across from one another. I felt sheepish and guilty, the way you feel when you run into someone, especially someone older than you, and you just can't place them. Though my body may not have followed suit, I knew that my soul was crouching in some corner.

Haldun Abi and I left the hotel and walked toward the factory stop. He talked the whole time, as if he was desperate for conversation, but I don't remember a thing he said.

We reached Kanyon, a high-class mall, and he said to me, "I can hardly take someone like you out just anywhere, now can I?"

He passed through security like a ghost, as if nobody even saw him. The security officer walked up to me. I showed him my police ID and he took a step back.

As we walked through the broad corridors of Kanyon, Haldun Abi asked me, "So, how are things in Ankara?" He said it like he needed a breather; tired of kicking the ball around by himself, he decided it was my turn now.

My response added up to less than a minute of trite clichés, and Haldun Abi reacted by giving me an odd expression. Actually, it wasn't really so much odd as it was angry.

We sat down at a restaurant. I ordered for both of us. Haldun Abi lit a cigarette. I could read the annoyance in the dull look on his face.

"I'm waiting for you to ask," he said all of a sudden.

"Ask what?"

"Why I came to find you after all these years."

How could I? I remained silent.

"I talked with İlhan. He said you went to see him this afternoon." He sounded irritated. "That's why I came to the hotel. I'm telling you this because, even though we haven't seen each other for years, you're important to us. No matter how old you are, we have to look out for you; you're his little brother. You understand?" His questioning eyes were fixed squarely upon me.

I nodded. I could understand him trying to protect me, but protect me from what, I had no idea. If there was anyone who needed protecting, it was İlhan, not me.

"With everything changing as quickly as it is, there are certain things we have to do to stay afloat. You're a policeman, you have certain obligations to the state."

I'd heard this kind of talk before, and I could sense where it was leading.

The waiter brought us our food. He looked tense for some reason. He left a huge plate of pasta with seafood and a glass of dark beer in front of Haldun Abi. I'd asked for *mantı*.

Haldun Abi put out his cigarette and started digging into his food. He paused and looked me straight in the face. "You're going to end this investigation and go back to Ankara. If you try to mess with İlhan, they'll kill you," he said.

Blood rushed to my head, and I knew that if I didn't keep my composure, I was going to say the first words that came to mind, and that I would regret it later.

"You have no right to order me around like that, Haldun Abi. Especially when it comes to a matter like this. Take it any further and I'll have to bring you in," I replied.

He began to laugh. It seemed my words had put him in a good humor. He laid down his fork, which was still wrapped in spaghetti, and covered his mouth with a napkin. The color was back in his chubby cheeks.

"I know more about those guys who died in the skyscrapers than you do."

"As much as you've heard on the news," I said.

He picked up his glass and took a sip. He leaned back, relaxed, it seemed.

"I knew every one of them," he said.

"You trying to get me to cough up some info about the investigation, Haldun Abi?" I asked.

"I don't need to. Like I said, I know more than you do."

"What do you know?"

"Every one of them was on the board of directors at the firm where he worked. These aren't ordinary, unconnected murders. I'm going to tell you why, but first you have to tell me why you suspect İlhan."

"I can't," I said.

"Yes, you can. If you don't, then I can't tell you who's next."

I looked at the plate of mantı in front of me. I felt bloated, though I'd only had a few spoonfuls. I motioned for the waiter. I asked him to take my plate and bring me a beer.

I turned and stared at Haldun Abi. "How can you help me?"

"If you tell me what you know, I'll answer all your questions. Now let's start with İlhan," he said.

I had a slight headache. I undressed and took a shower. When I got into bed, I couldn't erase the image of Haldun Abi's scornful smile from my mind. I picked up my phone from beneath the bedside lamp and called Faruk, waking him. I told him to come to the hotel for breakfast in the morning with all the files on the murders with him, and to pick up a copy of *The Communist Manifesto*—a legitimate one—on his way over.

* * *

Once we'd finished our dinner, we moved to the restaurant bar. I wanted to go back to the hotel, but Haldun Abi said that he hadn't yet told me what it was he really wanted to say. I couldn't possibly grasp the real reason he wanted me to go back to Ankara, he said, and he didn't know what he had to do to make me understand.

"Just cut to the chase then," I said, "and tell me."

He began tapping out a rhythm on the glass of beer in front of him; he seemed to be mumbling a tune to himself. "Have you read *The Communist Manifesto*?" he asked.

"Back when I was in the police academy, yes," I said with a smile.

"Good, then maybe you'll recall how it starts: *A specter is haunting Europe . . .*" He began to laugh. Either he was shitting me or he was testing me. "Marx came up with this theory, shortly before his death, that the center of the world revolution had moved to the east, and everyone thought that meant Russia." He looked at me silently, with an earnest expression on his face, as if his words held some profound meaning. "These skyscrapers are built on the bodies of revolutionaries. These deaths aren't murders, they're revenge." His face was red now, but it wasn't from all the beer, it was because he was in pain; tears had welled up in his eyes and he was trying hard to keep them in.

"So is a leftist organization responsible for this? Or is someone bigger behind it?"

"No, no. I knew you wouldn't understand."

I woke the next morning to the ringing of my hotel room phone. I felt like I'd been roused from a nightmare just in time.

"I'm in the lobby, Sadık Bey," said Faruk.

A corner of the breakfast table was covered with files, and on top lay a copy of the *Manifesto*. I picked up the book and flipped past the prefaces. The book started just as Haldun Abi had said.

I went ahead and began eating my breakfast in silence. I could see from Faruk's face that he had a million and one questions that he was dying to ask me.

"So what do you think about the murders?" I asked.

"There are so many questions I just can't get my head around," he replied. "You know the old cliché about how there's no such thing as the perfect crime? Well, these five murders are perfect! For now, at least. The officer handling this case before you, he and I talked about it a lot. Every single person we tagged as a suspect proved where they were and what they were doing at the times of the murders. We couldn't find any sort of connection between the murder victims and the suspects we took in. We weren't able to turn up a shred of concrete evidence."

"Was there any abstract evidence?"

Faruk was trying to understand what I was getting at, but I knew he wouldn't be able to.

"I mean, did you encounter anything that seemed beyond reason?"

"Yeah, five bodies," he said, chuckling.

My cell phone started ringing. I looked at the number and handed the phone to Faruk. "Will you take it? It's the police department."

Faruk grabbed the telephone and answered. A few seconds later he hung up. "The chief wants to see you at 3 o'clock," he said.

There were five of us in the room: the police chief, the vice chief, director of Istanbul intelligence, Faruk, and me. I'd turned in a written report just two days before, but they wanted to have a face-to-face. In my report I'd written that we didn't have nearly enough intelligence, and that the only thing the victims seemed to have in common was that they were all over fifty years old and they were all corporate executives. But this was stuff they already knew. In other words, they weren't satisfied.

"You've made no progress," the police chief scolded me.

The fresh-faced kid from intelligence was quick to put forth his self-defense. "The files we sent in were as thorough as could be; we didn't leave out a single detail."

The finger-pointing hardly befitted such a high-level meeting. For a moment, I wondered how they would react if I told them what Haldun had told me the previous evening. I had no choice but to insist that the investigation up until then had been inadequate.

"Either we haven't gathered enough evidence or we've got a serial killer on our hands who knows how to carry out the perfect crime," I said.

Then, whether to provoke me or to intimidate me, I'm not sure, the wise guy from intelligence chimed in: "So tell us, which building do you think is next?"

I didn't even have to think about it. "Kanyon," I said confidently.

"How can you be so sure?" the police chief asked.

"It's just a hunch," I said. "Someone's getting back at the capitalists."

I went to my father's that evening for dinner. I hadn't been able to sit down and have a real conversation with him, my stepmother, and my stepsister since I'd arrived in Istanbul.

At first we mostly talked about the past, about the good

parts; they didn't bring up how withdrawn I'd been as a child. My father had never wanted me to go to Ankara.

I still felt like a stranger when I was with them.

We had left our places at the dinner table and settled in the sofas in the sitting room. My stepsister moved to the kitchen to make coffee.

My father wore a contented smile on his face. I sensed what he was thinking, but I had other things that I wanted to talk about.

"Do you remember Haldun, Dad?" I asked.

"Haldun from the old neighborhood?"

I shook my head yes.

"Of course I do. How could I forget him? He was a good kid, may he rest in peace. I'm surprised you remember him, you were so young."

I asked the next question not out of surprise, but out of fear.

"When did he die?" My voice was quivering.

"They arrested him after the coup. It was 1982, I think. He died during interrogation. They said it was suicide. Who were we to question the military? They buried him next to İlhan. They were such good kids, the both of them. It's a shame."

"İlhan?"

"You know, İlhan, he used to live on the other side of the brook. You don't remember him? He was the only blonde in the neighborhood, curly hair, the kid was like an angel. He died before Haldun did. They shot him, threw his body into the brook. It turned up two days later in Kâğıthane."

My stepsister brought our coffees and then settled down into one of the sofa chairs. "Can't we forget about all those bad memories for a while? We only see each other once a decade as it is," she griped.

"Can you take me to their graves tomorrow?" I asked. My father nodded.

The small mosque next to the graveyard in Sanayi Mahallesi had grown immensely, like a piece of fruit pumped full of hormones. When we moved through the gate to the grave- yard, Faruk asked, "Which way?"

"Downhill and to the right."

We stopped next to my mother's and my brother's graves. I hadn't been to visit for nearly ten years. My father held his palms facing upwards in prayer. I opened my hands and mum- bled something that I thought sounded like a prayer.

Once he'd finished praying, my father wiped his hands over his face. "It's not far," he said.

We walked for a few more minutes until we reached a pair of graves surrounded by an iron fence. They looked like holy tombs where pilgrims came to pray. On both stones were written the words, *Martyrs of the Revolution*.

I turned and faced Faruk. "You remember this name?" I asked.

He looked carefully at the name on the gravestone. "It's just a coincidence, two guys with the same name."

"No," I said. "That's not it. The guy knew me."

Faruk was smiling as we rode up in the elevator. This time I'd asked to have someone come with me. We got off on the thirty- fifth floor and walked down a long corridor and through a glass door. The secretary stood up to welcome us before let- ting İlhan Bey know that we were there. A few minutes later, we were ushered into his office.

A slightly cross-eyed man wearing metal-framed glasses stood up when we entered the room. He was short and chubby.

Faruk looked at me, I gently shook my head.

He motioned for us to have a seat at the conference table.

"How can I help you, Sadık Bey?" he asked.

Faruk was glancing around anxiously. "I came here two days ago, but they took me to see someone else on this floor by the same name," I said.

İlhan Bey smiled. "That's impossible! There's nobody here with the same name as me."

"But I was here. In this conference room."

"Well, I'm the only İlhan on this floor," he said with a smile. "I'm sure I would know if there was anybody else here with the same name!"

A cell phone started to ring. Faruk grabbed his phone and headed for a corner of the room so as not to interrupt us.

"Where did you go to college, İlhan Bey?" I asked.

"Bosphorus University. I studied computer engineering," he said.

Just then Faruk approached and whispered in my ear: "They found another body a few minutes ago. At Kanyon this time. They're waiting for us."

I did my best to give İlhan Bey a smile; after all, it was probably the last time I'd be seeing him.

BURN AND GO

BY SADIK YEMNİ

Kurtuluş

"It was you who pushed him. Then you made some kind of pact to keep quiet about it."

I was so shocked, on so many levels, I couldn't respond.

"Kevork told me. He said it was an accident, an accident that became a source of lifelong agony."

Anfi pushed back her long hair, which, though white now, was the feature most reminiscent of her younger days. Her large brown eyes were exactly like those of her son Yani; they were full of sorrow. They weren't accusatory. There was no hate in them. For now, at least.

"When did he tell you that?"

"Two months ago, when I bumped into him on my way back from shopping. He's changed the least of all. Still has the same thick red hair, square face, large, timid eyes."

"I was eighteen the last time I saw him."

"You know what they say, coincidence is a fickle thing. Just five more minutes and I would've missed him. He was looking for me. He was shocked at how much the neighborhood had changed in the last forty years, just like you were. He'd knocked on my door, but there was no answer, and so he was about to leave. Clearly, some part of him was thankful. That the past hadn't opened the door. He jumped when I called his name. You should have seen how he hugged me though. We could've been models for some ad. One part of him didn't want to find me. But the part that did was deeply shaken."

And Anfi had had no trouble finding me. "Google knows everything, *maşallah*," she had said. She had found Avram first, then me. She was very sick. Her days were numbered. She wanted to see us all one last time.

My schedule at the university was flexible. I'd been separated from my wife for two and a half years. My dog Ganz had died of old age. I had been involved with one of my students and caused something of a scandal. I'd lost all desire to complete the piece I needed to turn in to gain full professorship. I accepted Anfi's invitation and immediately booked my Vienna–Istanbul ticket over the Internet. The part of me that was afraid of changing its mind quickly took care of plans for the trip, before I had time to lose my resolve.

We were supposed to meet at 2 o'clock, but my plane was delayed and we had to postpone until that evening. It had been thirty-seven years since I'd seen either Kevork or Avram. We had parted ways when I left for college in Ankara, and chance hadn't brought us together since. The only place that could possibly reunite us had quickly built bridges, thanks to Anfi.

"Yani liked you best of all."

"It was an accident, Anfi. I was pushed into that same hole at least half a dozen times myself. It was just soft, squishy soil, full of worms. You'd be scared, you'd get scratched up here and there, but that was it. How could I have known? I loved him. You know that."

"Why didn't you bring him home right away? To me, to the pharmacy . . . You might have saved him."

It was then that the mental block I had erected to keep myself from dwelling on that moment cracked wide open, and the image of Yani lying motionless in the hole forced its way into my mind. His eyes were half-open. He wasn't breathing. I thought he was faking it. The sand covered the blood on his neck. He let out a scream when he fell, the way we all did. We'd already started walking away. Such was our routine. If you fell in a hole or some trap, you'd follow after the rest of the gang and give them hell once you'd caught up. Finally, we stopped and waited, and when we realized he wasn't coming, we went back. We couldn't see that he had a huge piece of glass rammed in his stomach and that his jugular was sliced open. It wasn't until I'd gone down into the hole and grabbed his shoulders, until I'd seen how his eyes had already gone dull . . . My gut froze. He wasn't faking it . . . I saw the fear, the finality of it all, in the faces of Avram and Kevork. Yani was no more. Our lucky charm was gone. Mourning the death of our closest friend was like a two-way mirror, our cursed faces crying and smirking at the same time. In retrospect, how disturbing that we made a pact with hardly a word. Like the plan was already there, in our minds, just waiting to spring. We would pretend we'd never seen it.

That's what we did. We kept quiet.

"It was at least ten minutes later when I went down into the hole. He wasn't moving. He wasn't breathing, Anfi. Just imagine how scared we were. We didn't grow up with all those gory horror films like kids do today. It was such a heavy, bizarre burden. We were terrified. We felt guilty. And not just for pushing him into the hole."

Anfi, sighing, looked away. She fixed her eyes upon her long, wrinkled fingers, giving me time to unwrap our crime of thought. She was like a young woman, her slim body shrouded in a somber brown dress. Everybody envied Yani. Especially the boys. We were his buddies. We got to know luck at its source. He was the only one whose mother had a college degree. Anfi was a pharmacist at Life Drugstore. It wasn't the best-known pharmacy in the neighborhood, but still, it was the place where we dropped our pants to get those painful injections in our butts. Anfi was intimately acquainted with our behinds, our rashes, and the secrets of the neighborhood women.

Later, I developed this kind of habit, where every time I lowered my underwear in the presence of a woman, I'd think of those fingers feeling for just the right spot to stick the needle in and then quickly rubbing away the hurt with an alcohol swab. Sometimes the image of a kid lying at the bottom of a pit, gazing at the sky with hollow eyes, would attach itself to these thoughts and spoil the fun.

Yani was an only child. He was fair-skinned like his mother. He was a smart, lively, and kind kid. He wasn't rough, he didn't curse or connive or sneak into movie theaters for free, or drop frogs or crickets into girls' shirts, or take a piss in inappropriate places like we did, but he'd pretend he did all of it. *Accept me the way I am,* he'd say. And we did. His greatest asset was his luck. In games of chance, he always won. If a wasp stung somebody, that somebody would never be Yani. The neighbor whose window was smashed by a soccer ball would never make out Yani among the group of children. His mischief, his mistakes never lingered long in the collective memory. It was the same in school. He wasn't always on his best behavior. He'd tattle, copy, cut class, things like that, yet he was always considered innocent as an angel. His innocence was his cross to bear. Yet with time, it became something of a burden that he imposed upon us, his closest friends, to bear in his stead. Until now, I've never thought of it in those terms. It's true, though, that it was a burden. We were the ones shouldering it. It was exhausting. And maybe we just grew sick and tired of it. Even that part of me that still believes I'm making excuses for our envy concedes this point. Such was his luck, that shadow of his innocence. So that his luck might prosper, *we* had to face the lack of it.

"Has this room changed much?"

I looked at Anfi. A new expression had appeared in her eyes. I didn't know what to make of it. It was like a moment of decision.

"It's the same as far as I can recall."

"Can you say what's on the windowsill without even looking?"

I hadn't even glanced in that direction since I first walked in. But I knew.

"A small coal-heated iron, a dark blue kerosene lamp, a miniature icon of Virgin Mary, and one of the Virgin Mary with Jesus. Let's see . . . a small box with a blue bow, and inside of it—"

"You were always the one with the best memory. A kind of blessing. Now tell me, what's in that box?"

"Yani's hair."

"You left him to the vultures. They didn't find him for two days. His eyes, ears, nose, fingertips were all eaten away. Two days. It could have been five, or ten."

I thought of saying something like, *Hair holds up really well though,* but then decided to keep it to myself.

"It was the barber from the next street over who dumped that glass into the hole. Everybody knew. A car drove by and scattered a bunch of stones, that's how it broke. It was a big deal. Nobody forgets a window glass that size."

"Anfi, is that why you invited us here? To talk about these things? It was an accident. I regret it. And I'm sure Avram and Kevork do too. It happened a long time ago."

"We'll have another coffee, won't we?"

I looked at my watch. Quarter to 9. Anfi had said that Kevork and Avram would be here at 9. I had been looking forward to seeing them and rehashing the past, but now I wasn't so sure. The idea of topping off the night in a *meyhane* still beckoned, though.

Google knew us, indeed. Avram was the producer of a popular television show in Canada. He lived in Ottawa. He was the honorary president of a gay club called The Diamond Gator. Kevork had studied interior design. He had lived in New York for several years before moving to Rome. He had his own studio. It seemed he'd made it big time. I had learned all of this within fifteen minutes, just after Anfi first called me a week ago.

"Let's have our coffee. Come to the kitchen."

I followed her with a resignation similar to the one I used to have when pulling down my pants in anticipation of a big, thick needle.

I was surprised when I saw the same beaded curtain still hanging at the kitchen door after all those years. It let out a surreal tone as Anfi passed through it. She had done her best to freeze everything as it had been forty years ago, but she couldn't help the modern kitchen appliances: an electric kettle, a new oven, an electric lighter.

Anfi put water, sugar, and coffee in a *cezve,* which she then placed on the stove. Both of us were having our coffee with lots of sugar. As she stirred it in silence, I ran my hand over the curtain of beads. My senses perceived in its sound a cryptic message. Had I forgotten something? This thing that was happening, was it a moment of the past, lodged some-where in my memory, thrashing, struggling to right itself in the present? A sliver, a shard, a splinter of a memory? When, after several seconds, the revelation failed to appear, I removed my hand.

"I replaced it twice. Fortunately those things became touristy, so they're not hard to find."

Though still relatively large, the kitchen felt smaller than it had in my childhood. I took a step inside and saw the black-and-white photograph hanging on the left wall. It was in a wooden frame, protected by glass. I knew it well, because my mother, too, had had a copy of the same photo. Four of the five women in the picture were grinning at the camera, with babies in their arms and several older children standing in front of them. March 1951, Tatavla. Barely two months old, I was the youngest of them all; Avram and Kevork were six months old. Yani was looking at the photographer from the bosom of his mother, wide-eyed. How new to the world we were.

"So, your mother died two years ago, huh? I remember when she moved to join her siblings in İzmir, after your father passed away. To think that was twenty years ago! She was a helpful person, very sincere, from the heart. She made a mean fava. Reminds me of those fava bean festivals, haven't thought of those in a while. You never did care much for fava beans . . . So why didn't you have any children? Your mother so desperately wanted a grandchild, as you know."

"That's just the way things happened. Monique, my wife, had two miscarriages. And then we never . . . And now we're divorced . . ."

Anfi nodded sympathetically. "There aren't many of us left from that photograph. Avram's mother Rosa died five years ago. You remember the woman next to her, right? Rachel. She was so young when she died, the poor thing. From a brain hemorrhage. She just collapsed in the street. On Papaz Street.

She was coming back from a visit to her cousin. Kevork's mother was as healthy as a horse. You should have seen how she used to hike up Tatavla slope at that age of hers. And then she died too, of pneumonia. About three years ago. Maybe even four now. And those two boys, I forget their names. That blond one, and the one with those sparkling eyes . . ."

"Metin and Kirkor."

"Right. They went into business together. Import, export. They kept it up for quite some time. Business was good. They stayed in Kurtuluş, in luxury apartments built on the old gardens. They had a two-story shop in Valide Çeşme. They always remained true to their roots. Their money evaporated during the crisis of '99, though, so they took a third partner. Turns out the guy was connected with the mafia, and he killed both of them. In Bodrum. In public. In broad daylight. That girl to the right in front of Rachel married a Spaniard. I heard that she drowned somewhere near Barcelona. I didn't know her family very well. She was just a girl next door who showed up whenever there was a camera around. Anyway, that's fate for you."

Our eyes met, and I waited for her to go on. The ill-fated girl's name was Semra. She always gave us gum when we were little. She didn't have a father, and her mother was always passing out. It was from her that I first heard the word *vagina*. I decided not to mention that just then. Anfi silently continued stirring the liquid, which was building to a bubbly cream at the top.

That unforgettable Sunday a black Buick had driven through the puddles and splashed mud on us. Our clothes were ruined. But Yani remained spotless. He just stood there with a grin on his face; he was holding a purple plastic water gun he'd won in a scratch-off a few minutes earlier. A single five-*kuruş* scratch-off and he of course got the biggest prize. Meanwhile, we'd emptied our pockets and won nothing but a few stale candy bars.

That was Yani for you. When my hand pushed him, it was on behalf of all of us. It was an act of envy. After all, he'd just fall in, make a face, and then come chasing after us with that water gun, right?

That the hole happened to be filled with glass delivered our most deep-seated wish. The barber, that son of a bitch, had turned our fantasy into reality, though in our heart of hearts we never would've wanted for it to come true. Those shards of glass cut a life short, relieving us of that cross we bore, the cross of Yani's good luck, only to burden us with something much heavier. A can of regret, a can of worms.

While Anfi was splitting the froth between our cups, I thought about how I hadn't been wrong in imagining that Yani's death would profoundly alter the future of his close circle. I checked my watch. Five after 9. I was sure Avram and Kevork would agree. Together we had learned just what it meant to pass the days without Yani. Everything had a different tone now: daylight, colors, the sweetness of little white lies, the thrill of mischief, the marvel of jokes, heads sent spinning by movie reels . . . The change was potent and palpable. It couldn't all be due to feelings of guilt alone.

"Would you like some liqueur?"

"What kind?"

"Tart cherry. I made it."

"Sounds good."

Anfi put two slim glasses on the same tray she had set the cups on before, took an unmarked bottle from a lower cabinet, and filled one of the glasses to the brim with a cherry-colored liquid. Then she stooped and took another bottle, presumably of the same. There were three clean glasses on a dish rack to the left of the sink. The liquor was being downed fast around here, I thought.

I took the tray from her and proceeded to the living room. We sat down. Anfi raised her glass, and I responded in kind.

"Here's to the good old days."

When I saw her drain her glass in a single gulp, I followed suit. I have a sensitive palate. Whenever I go out with friends, I'm always prompted to be the first to try the wine. I noted some subtle flavor in addition to the cherries, alcohol, and sugar. It wasn't bad. A kind of spice, perhaps.

Anfi looked into my eyes, smiling. "For a moment there you looked so much like your father. A taller version of him, of course. He had a temper, but he also had a heart of gold. During the riots of September 6 and 7, for two days he stood guard in front of the passageway where our store was and wouldn't let anybody through. He took off time from work to do that. And he sent a friend to mind the pharmacy, God bless him. You wouldn't remember. You were four years old then."

"My father used to talk about those things when he was drunk sometimes. Yani stayed at our place for two days. I still remember, because we gave him my bed."

"So you remember that too. And then . . . well, our stores were still standing at the end of it all. We picked up where we had left off."

The way she paused and sighed at that moment clearly indicated, to me, that they in fact *had not* picked up where they had left off.

"Fifty years, just like that . . . Good thing you were late. It gave me some time to think . . . No, not to think, but to see things anew. Come with me."

When she stood up I automatically followed. My head was feeling a bit heavier. I remembered that liqueur often had high alcohol content. I didn't exactly have a good tolerance for alcohol, and to top it all off, I was drinking on an empty stomach. I looked at the cups of coffee, which we hadn't even touched.

"Let me show you."

It was an intensely emotional moment. At first I figured she meant the photographs. We went into the hall, and I thought I had assumed correctly. We were going to Yani's room. She opened the door, the first to the left. The curtains were drawn and it was dark inside. She turned the light on. It took me a few seconds to grasp what I was seeing. The icy fingers of terror began stroking my neck. My instincts told me to run. But I couldn't.

Clearly, we would not be able to address the matter of this Yani Museum, in nearly pristine condition after some forty years. Two adult males were stretched on Yani's bed, faceup. The redhead's eyes were slightly open. He had a black jacket and a burgundy shirt on. Avram, totally bald now, had closed his eyes tight, as if cringing from a blow. His goatee was matted with dried vomit. His right pant leg was rolled up to the knee. The feet of both men were extending out of the bed by ten inches or so; both had their shoes on.

"They arrived at 2 o'clock sharp. We talked. I served liqueur to them too. Enough Seconal and risperidone per person. It was a painless journey to the other side. I got rid of the pharmacy eleven years ago, but my apprentices, bless them all, never fail to show the proper respect."

"The second bottle."

She nodded. "Do you still remember Nejat?"

"Nejat with the pencil mustache."

"Good memory! He never married. I turned my pharmacy over to him. After my first brain hemorrhage. It happened two more times after that, but I survived. Seeing these days was in my stars."

"But Anfi, why?"

"It's rather difficult to explain, that whole process. The pressure of those moments when the darkness within strains to get out. And does. One might say . . . Now, how are you feeling?"

My knees couldn't carry me anymore. The nausea I'd been feeling since I laid eyes on the bodies was beginning to subside, but I was about to collapse.

"Come and sit. There are some things I want to tell you before the last page is turned."

She took my arm. For the first time I sensed her body odor overpowering the lilac scent she was wearing. Those two yards to the chair felt like an eternity. I put up no resistance. Though she tried to hold me up, I collapsed onto the chair in a heap. My head snapped back, but fortunately did not hit the wall too hard. Pain was a volatile liquid, evaporating fast.

"You really have gotten heavy. You are okay, aren't you?"

Her face was very close to mine. Breaking free from the fear that I was about to slide into the dark hole of my demise, I nodded. She smiled, her eyes full of compassion. Of all the women in my life, nearly every one that I had picked myself resembled Anfi, in one way or another. I thought about telling her. But I couldn't.

"Why? Why all this . . . ?"

She eyed the two on the bed, sighed, and sat down at the foot. The bed gave a jolt, and the bodies moved, as if to make room for her.

"Kevork came. Two months ago, I told you. His only daughter had died of liver cancer. His wife had become an alcoholic. He was very sad. He told me, 'It's like we're all cursed or something. We have to put an end to it.' He was a little tipsy, he'd been drinking vodka that day, but he was still making sense."

"It was an accident, Anfi."

"The only two people left from that photograph. They are in this room."

"There is a whole world out there beyond this room."

"That's right. If you'd made it this afternoon like the others, there would be three of you lying on this bed now. But since you were late, I had time to weigh the consequences of my actions . . . and . . . I changed plans. You remember the gardens, and the *meze* sellers in this neighborhood, don't you? I was a baby during the fire of 1929. My father's two shoe shops burned down in that fire. I'm told my mother used to pray every day at Hagia Dimitri Church over in Feriköy. I once took you and Yani there on Christmas. You were five. You kept insisting that you light each and every candle. You threw a tantrum. I didn't know what to do. Everything changes so fast and . . ."

Barely conscious, I struggled to make connections between all the things she was saying.

"When Yani passed away, I soon lost my ability to deal with all the changes happening around me, the way everything was becoming so dirty, so vulgar. It even kept me from properly mourning the death of my husband. He was an only child. His death marked the death of this home. Your mother used to say, 'The childless home neither laughs nor cries.' That's true. I could no longer feel, not like I used to.

"You were the first to agree to come, you know. They just

followed. If you had refused, they wouldn't have come, either. This meeting hinged on you."

I remained silent, at a loss for words, and so she continued.

"All three of you came from abroad to meet with Anfi, an old woman already north of seventy-five. The lengths one goes to, to appease such long simmering guilt, right? And now fate beckons. It's impossible to resist. A most definite rendez-vous. You come, and you meet your end."

"The arrangement in the photograph is a coincidence. That everybody . . . that everybody except the two of us is dead . . . it's your doing . . ."

"I was the one who gave you the volumes of *Les Pardaillan* and *Fantômas* to read. You had the gift of language. Yani didn't like to read as much as you. You were always good at math too. Your envy of Yani didn't stem from any lack of yours, it was because you were so self-centered."

"What about the hands, the hand that placed the glass in that hole, Anfi?"

"If it hadn't been for the glass, you would've come up with something else."

"That's terrible, Anfi. We were kids. We'd all have gone our separate ways to college . . ."

Anfi ran her hand through her hair and sighed again, then she stood up and left the room. I imagined myself making an effort toward the door. But my legs were like putty. I peered helplessly at the corpses on the bed. It was true, Kevork had not changed at all. Over the years, since I'd last seen him, he'd put on perhaps a couple of pounds for each year, but otherwise looked the same. His red hair was as thick as before. Avram, though, was a different story. I probably wouldn't have recognized him at all. But then they might have said the same about me, of course. I'd lost a lot of hair, and I'd grown a paunch.

Yani's desk was exactly the way I remembered it, with its marble top, his snowball, his brass pencil case. It was then that I realized once more what a curse a strong memory can be. I couldn't help but envy those with a more permeable sieve.

Anfi came back, this time with a glass made of china. I couldn't tell what was in it. She took her place. Lifeless legs strained to move again.

"How unrecognizable this Sopalı Hüsnü Street has become, hasn't it? It took Kevork a full hour to find the house. Oh, do you know what they brought as presents? Avram brought some luxury chocolate thins, and Kevork brought chocolate with cherry liqueur. Chocolate for the old Anfi. It reminded me of High Life Bakery. You boys used to go there for ice cream. That was the first thing Avram said. He hadn't changed one bit. He summarized all his problems in a single breath. His boyfriend had left him for someone younger. Canada was a very boring place. He'd return to Istanbul in 2020 for good, and so on and so forth . . ."

I remained silent. Anfi took a few sips from the liquid in the glass and continued.

"Presents of quick, easy consumption, perfect for someone with both feet in the grave. Only you brought something for my heirs. For distant relatives. They'll just sell everything and be on their merry ways. The fact that you brought an engraving of alpha and omega means a lot, doesn't it? An implied suggestion to turn the page, yes?"

She was right. I nodded.

"You all wanted to become tram conductors when you were kids. Do you still remember? A second-class seat in the tram was five kuruş. A first-class seat was ten. All those shenanigans you boys did for a free trip used to scare me to death."

"Yani used to pay and get on though. And then watch us."

"He looked up to you guys so much. Too bad you didn't have more time together ..."

"That's not why Kevork came to you, Anfi."

"When he entered this room, he cried, and then he hugged me, sobbing. He told me how much he regretted it. Maybe a hundred times."

"He lost his only daughter. He was devastated."

"So he knew what it meant to lose your only child. It was his idea to organize this ritual, this communal confession."

"This is no ritual."

"What is it then?"

"It was an accident."

Anfi murmured something I couldn't make out and then finished what was left in the glass. She held the glass, pressing it against her face, and looked at the bodies. Then at me.

"What did you come all the way here for? To hear me say that I forgive you? And that Yani forgives you too? And that he's happy now, up in the sky? Is that what you came to hear?"

"What did their deaths change, Anfi?"

"As you know, Yani is resting in Feriköy Cemetery. I visited him this morning. One last time. Like everything I did today ... one last time."

I looked at the glass she still held against her face. I thought she must have taken sleeping pills too. In this room, we were closing the book. Meanwhile, I'd grown even more drowsy. There wouldn't be any drinking with Avram and Kevork at some neighborhood bar. No veiled pissing matches about who had more money or power. Most importantly, we wouldn't be laying it on the table, dissecting that incident we never ever talked about, never even alluded to, in all those six years we were together afterwards. You pushed. We fell. If only you hadn't pushed . . . It was your turn. When the time came, you let it all out. Well, you shouldn't have kept quiet then. If you hadn't, you wouldn't all be lying here now like bags full of shit.

"When Yani was born, our cat Sarman gave birth too. To three extraordinarily beautiful kittens. It was their first week. But then one morning, Sarman was extremely restless. One moment she'd be dashing toward the door, and then the next she'd be leaping at the window. It was like she was trying to tell me, *Open it, I'm leaving.* She just kept meowing and meowing. I finally gave in and opened the door. She stormed out and got run over by a car a few seconds later. Traffic was heavier than usual. But it's like that when your time comes. It's a meeting that you can't postpone. I tried to feed the kittens milk with a dropper, but it didn't work. They were too small. They died too."

I had heard this story from Anfi before. Hearing it again at that moment, in that context, the impact of the omen was intense.

"If only you had opened the door five seconds later and . . . if only there hadn't been glass in the hole."

Anfi offered a smile that was half appreciation, half regret. "That's not the point. It's an irrelevant detail. He'd just be pushed again and again, until there was glass in the hole. And the door would be opened again and again."

"Your logic, it's flawed," I said, in all sincerity. "It's a biased expectation. Life, experience, they change the way we look at things. And now, what use is it, all of this—"

I stopped and looked into her eyes, the eyes of a woman who had left her mark on every phase of my life. And it was she who had determined its finale. I was amazed at the overwhelming power of that part of me ready to go along with it. For a moment, I wondered whether or not Monique would be sad when she heard about my death. She was the one I hurt most and argued with most, yet she was also the one I was once happiest with. Such is the human mind, a timepiece of fascinating inner workings.

"Don't worry. There's been a slight change in plans. Only you will wake up. In a couple of hours. You'll have a light headache. An upset stomach too. Everything is ready in the storage room by the front door. Cans of kerosene. Set the house on fire and go. It should start in this room . . . There's one more thing I want you to do before you go, though. I want you to promise me that you'll bury that small box with Yani's hair in it on top of his grave. That's the only thing I want. If you had arrived on time, I wouldn't have had the chance to tell you that I know, that I knew, how very capable you boys would be of feeling regret, and remorse. We are even now. Burn and go, okay? Don't worry, the fire won't harm anyone else. There's just a condemned building to our left, and a garden with some old, dried-out fruit trees behind us."

I don't know if my mouth said anything to Anfi. I was on the verge of sleep. My eyes were no longer open to the room. My thoughts were scattering like a harem of women at the sight of a strange man. As darkness fell upon my mind, in spite of everything, my will to live and see the flames was letting out its final, weak roar.

Unfortunately, regrets, however strong, cannot roll back time.

THE HAND

BY MÜGE İPLİKÇİ

Moda

I n a *dolmuş* on the way to Moda. That's where twelve-year-old Nazlı's story begins. Nazlı, a delicate name for my delicate little girl.

Her mother and I separated early. It just didn't work out between us. Yet we were so in love! Or at least that's how I remember it being, at the beginning. I always wanted Nazlı to remember things that way too. That day, we had met at the Kadıköy piers and were making our way to the Moda dolmuşes when Nazlı asked me if people got married for love or money. Why? I asked. Because I'm in love, she said. At that moment I felt a twinge of pain, deep down. Like any father of a daughter, I was a little shaken up at first. I felt very clearly then and there that I was not prepared to share her with any other man, but I kept this sentiment to myself. Love is important, I said, but you have to have money too. I said it like it was some trivial remark. Like I usually did. And which I would so desperately regret later. She was a little angel. A little girl. This time, though, I decided to play down my hopelessness. Actually, dear, I said, it's not about money; love is all that matters.

Just then, the early afternoon sun, shining from above Kumkapı, way over across the Bosphorus, struck our faces—the trees were up to their tricks again. We crossed the street. Eight-person dolmuşes had largely become a thing of the past, but I insisted that we wouldn't board anything but. All right, buddy, the steward at the dolmuş stand told me, just hold on. So it seemed they hadn't yet become completely obsolete. It wasn't long until it arrived. A yellow, beat-up old thing. It was something like this, right? I asked Nazlı. Yes, Daddy. I latched onto her hand, and onto that moment when she boarded an eight-person dolmuş from Kadıköy to Moda, to see her grandmother. Her hand was cold. My heart beat unevenly, and with a wrenching at my gut, I told her that I felt chilly. There was a crisp nip in the air that winter. Warm me up, Daddy, she said jokingly, and then kissed me on the cheek. We settled into the very back seat. You sit by the window, Daddy, she told me. No, you sit by the window, I said, and look outside, so I can see outside and watch the sun shining off of you at the same time. Oh, you're such a romantic, Daddy! she said. And then with a roguish smile: He's just like you!

Nazlı was still smiling, there in her plaid pleated skirt and red plush coat. And the time sped by, as the dolmuş swayed its way toward Moda.

The dolmuş took the coastal road for a while before veering inland. I just sat there, Nazlı's hand in mine. Again I felt that I loved her too much to share her with anyone else. Whatever it was that I had felt toward the rotund little baby in the nurse's arms at that very first moment, that's what Nazlı was. A miracle. Inhaling the scent of my twelve-year-old girl, I would whisper in her ear, telling her that she wasn't alone. And she, she would laugh. Always. She knew that her grandma had baked a fabulous cake to go with the tea, over which the two of them would chat about politics and whatnot. As my mother's first grandchild, Nazlı had a special place in her grandma's life, and she milked it for all it was worth. Both of them were fully aware of this, and neither had any complaints.

How wonderful that you're with me, Nazlı, I said, out of

the blue. The dolmuş was making its way up Moda Boulevard, past the flower shop and the toy store. I got a few strange looks from the people around me. But Nazlı was there, with me; I could see the tiny veins on her neck, her hazel eyes gleaming from beneath full brows.

I didn't need any more memories of those eyes reflecting off the windows of the passing cars. I needed Nazlı, only Nazlı. My daughter; she was twelve years old.

I'm so glad you're with me, Nazlı!

For those sitting near me, I was just some guy mumbling to himself, one passenger out of eight sitting in a dolmuş headed toward Moda. A father searching for the past in a heap of odd recollections. To think that it had happened just two years ago. And now there I was, a man left with nothing but a few pathetic memories, all his miracles wrenched away, especially . . .

Earth to Daddy, Nazlı might have said. Don't mind me, I would have replied. The dolmuş was passing by the Kadıköy Girls' School just then. Back when I was in my early teens, we used to come here a lot after school, to pick up girls. I was going to tell Nazlı that, but then I changed my mind and sank a little further into the dolmuş's threadbare seats.

I had a girl on my mind, a girl from two years ago. It was a winter day, and late afternoon was turning into early evening. She was running late to her afternoon tea. The light was different then; twilight was already setting in. I wasn't with the girl on that day. It was another man who sat next to her. The same man, with his dark face and skittish eyes, that I would later grow sick and tired of seeing, first in the newspapers, in sketches based upon witness testimonies, then in photos, and finally in the flesh. But on that day, at that hour, he was still just a traveler en route to Moda, sitting next to a girl. Another man among men. Except he wasn't. In gray police files he was known as the "Ümraniye psycho," a man who raped children in secluded corners of the city, then killed them and carved his signature, deeply, into their tender young necks. But still, he looked like anyone else: he was ordinary, common, his eyes dull and distant.

Twenty-four hours after the incident, the Moda *muhtar* at the time gave a press conference in a corner of the apartment-building courtyard where the girl's body had been found, describing the incident as "the degenerates' invasion of Moda" and avoiding other questions posed by the press; it was just too close to election time.

The girl was so young. Her breasts had just budded the previous spring. She had a few pimples, but her face was still that of a child, her dimples still those of a baby.

When the eight-person dolmuş had taken off two years earlier, the girl had felt a slight tingle on her right leg. At first she assumed that it had something to do with the way the space between the seat rails was sucking her in. Sitting on a seat of shriveled, gray animal hide, a piece of skin wrinkled and bitter, she stretched her leg down to feel for the floor beneath her plaid skirt. The tingle, however, continued. Sliding back and forth on the seat, her skin on the skin of the seat, it seemed to her that the tingling was about to pass. But soon it was replaced by another discomfort. A heaviness. As if something had been added to her leg. A third skin. At that moment, she could not fathom why on earth the third skin might be there. Her head was, at best, in the clouds. That's what her grandmother would have said, and then chuckled.

Her grandmother must have been waiting for her then, with the tea brewing. There would be meaty *pide* to go with the tea, and her grandmother's scrumptious lemon cake.

Maybe the weather was to blame. They hadn't yet had a proper winter that year. Or maybe it was Moda's fault. Moda was so wonderful, so beautiful and dreamlike, and in her mind's eye it would forever remain that way. Or so the girl hoped. One thing was for sure: Within this idyllic landscape, there was no such thing as a stranger. For her, at that time, a stranger—or *el* as her grandma would say, using the more old-fashioned word, incidentally the same word for "hand"—was something far away and unknown, foreign and distant, far in the future. Like growing pains. Like blood. Like pus. Like death even. All of it unbelievably distant and strange. And that was how it was supposed to be. But next to her the breathing grew grunting and putrid.

There was a girl on my mind, a girl who was gradually fading away. She was alone.

What's wrong with you today, Dad?

It's Nazlı. My beautiful daughter. My beautiful twelve-year-old daughter.

Nothing, I'm fine!

Again I get the strange looks, pleading for the ride to be over as soon as possible, so that they can finally be rid of me.

My hand is in Nazlı's. Hers the hand of a child.

There was a girl on the man's mind. Her heart beat so quickly, like the hearts of all children.

It would take awhile for the girl to grow certain that the heaviness belonged to a living hand; by then, the dolmuş had made the second turn inland, away from the Marmara shore. The hand continued. It slid, slowly, a little further. Gradually making its way down the twelve-year-old right leg, the hand was clammy with sweat by the time the dolmuş passed the rundown police station. And the girl was sweating too. Not a good day to be wearing such a heavy coat! Not a good day to be running late! Sweat trickled down the girl's legs; she was unable to move. The hand paused, before suddenly starting up again, gliding along the girl's young skin. To the very depths. On the right side of her neck the girl sensed a drawn breath, a breath grown hoary, aged before its time. She herself breathed quickly, sharply, through her nose, her nostrils gaping like two big eyes on her face. Someone, a passenger, asked to be let off on Moda Boulevard, where the toy store and the flower shop would open up a couple of years later. The girl felt weighted down, pinned to her spot by the heaviness of the door to her left—a door that could not be opened. First she would try to rest her head against the bottom of the window. How could she possibly shut her ears to the sound of the man's breathing? The stench of his breath mingled with the diesel fumes, singeing her nostrils. Her child's body sank lower into the seat of the dolmuş, as she sought to understand the route of the hand sliding up her thigh.

The huge iron gate of the Kadıköy Girls' School, Kolombo Kabob, Ali's Ice Cream, gaunt trees at the top of the hill leaning against dim streetlamps. And then the fork in the road, and the dolmuş's waddling veer to the left.

The girl sat straight up. Stiffly. Waiting. The hand had to be removed from her body. Immediately. She struggled to think about what she should do in a situation like this. The nap of her red coat scorched her neck, and her face flushed red from the heat.

Taking the dolmuş up to Moda meant going to Grandma's, to safety. Her father would come later. Today was her first time taking the trip alone. Her father had a project he needed to finish up before he could leave work. The next stop, the girl repeated to herself. At the next stop, she would finally be able to wrest herself from the sinister hand. She was terrified of her eyes meeting those of the man sitting next to her and breathing so forlornly.

An early twilight had descended by the time they finally arrived at the last stop. The door opened, and soon the auspicious sound of footsteps broke the evening silence. Two people, a couple of rare visitors to Kemal's Tea Garden, were heading for the dolmuşes, and thus home, having had their fill of hot tea and heated conversation for the day. Rushing out of the dolmuş, the girl wanted so badly to call out to them. Her eyes sought theirs—anything but the disconcerting gaze of the dolmuş driver, his eyes seeping, damp from the diesel. But for some reason she could not call out; her voice got stuck in her throat.

It was at precisely that moment that she felt it. The hand that had been stroking her right leg throughout the journey had transformed into something else, something humungous, and she sensed that it would pursue her, chasing her to her death. The hand was a person, it was a shadow, it was a nightmare. It had thick knuckles and pudgy palms. A limb marked by dirt and sweat, by the unknown and the groundless. It was a wordless organ; the rhythm of its breathing did all the talking. It was some *thing*—filled with rage toward the past that had spurned it, cold-blooded in the face of fear, eager to dismember.

The hand, which had assumed myriad forms in the reflections and projections of shadow play with her father, now became something else altogether; growing heavy and awkward, it became another name. It was a complete stranger, so different from the shadows her father projected onto the wall, shadows that she likened to rabbits and wolves, dragons and flying dinosaurs. This hand was something completely different; it was the ghost of the wolf, the dragon, the flying dinosaur. It was a colorless jinn possessed by and emanating fear. It was a shadow merging with other dreadful shadows, growing giant and amorphous. It grew and grew. In it the girl could see ghouls with eyes, eyes that stirred as they looked into the deep, endless, pitch-black darkness. The girl felt it, the breathing of the hand, right next to her now, and in the very pulse beating in her neck.

She should run, run away.

And so the girl ran, but not toward her grandma's, and not toward Kemal's Tea Garden; she ran down the hill, past Koço, and toward the stairs. She then made her way, stumbling, along the shore, where the sand turned to gravel, and old caïques docked next to the new. She pushed on, into the heavy wind, until her lungs finally gave out. With all her might she struggled, resisting the vulgar hand as it breathlessly closed in upon her from behind. Panting, in a vindictive voice, the hand told her how much it enjoyed watching lonely young girls die lonely deaths on romantic shores in winter. A knife emerged and was pressed to her neck. Its possessor, the hand, grabbed her roughly and pulled her beneath it. It leaned toward her ear and then, wet and warm, so unlike a hand, so unlike a ghoul, stuck its tongue deep inside her ear. The pervert's tongue slid around her eyes, into her nostrils, over her chin, her dimples, over her cheekbones, onto her neck. In her every joint she felt the other body weighing down upon hers as the hand nearly choked her. Her red coat, it ripped open as a deep silence seemed to descend upon the shore; there was no longer a body of a young girl to be concealed by the coat, the sweater, the lace-lined undershirt with its sewn-in training bra, or the panties with their matching lace; now, there was nothing but a body doused in its own blood. With its fingernails, the hand dug into her flesh, and with its knife, it sliced her open. The girl was barely conscious. She thought that now, finally, it must be over.

She was wrong. At that moment, she met with another invasion altogether. It entered between her legs and jarred her entire body with a deep, searing pain. Againandagainandagainandagain. The hand's eyes pierced the darkness. It loosened its grip on the knife for just a few moments, allowing the girl one gasp for breath. In that instant, she felt that she saw death, and it became clear to her that she would have to fight to survive. With a final spurt of energy, she grabbed some sand and threw it into the hand's eyes. The knife fell; the hand relaxed its grip. The girl knew that this was her chance. She thought of when she and her father used to play tag during the summer. Run, she said to herself, run away as far as you can.

She ran. As far as she could. She ran and ran, her coat in tatters, her undershirt ripped, her underwear in shreds, and her body bleeding and bleeding and bleeding, along the dark shore lined with burnt-out lamps. When she reached the steps leading up to Bomonti, she didn't look back; she just told herself to run, run. You're it—run! And she ran. As far as she could. Knowing that she would get caught. Her father always caught her; knowing that full and well.

The girl always got caught. If it were her fate, she would know it. And she did.

And so she would succumb to the hand when it found her this time; this time, she would not put up a fight. He would take her down to the furnace in an ordinary apartment building. Using a piece of the coat, the hand would gag her before tying her hands and feet together. Finally, the girl would feel the knife entering her throat, and with it, a searing pain. Her mouth stuffed full of red plush and soaked with her own red blood, she would emit a sobbing sound—the kind only children make at night in their sleep.

Three hours after the girl was found, the old woman said to be her grandmother spoke her last sensible words: If this is what happens in the heart of Moda, then we are done for.

Last stop, the driver would say.

Go on, Nazlı, go straight to your grandma's house, the man would say, his hand still inside that of his daughter.

I'll never leave you alone again, Nazlı, he would say to her.

He would find his daughter, in her red coat, beautiful and untouchable.

There was an aura of loneliness about the man who stepped out of the eight-person dolmuş at the Moda stop. He walked downhill, toward the stairs, toward Koço, toward the sea. Meanwhile, not far away, a monotone silhouette of synthetic prosperity reflected upon the water; at the Moda Maritime Club, grandiose preparations for a wedding were underway.

TURKISH PRONUNCIATION GUIDE & GLOSSARY

a as in f**a**ther
c as in **j**am
ç as in **ch**icken
e as in p**e**t
g as in **g**oat
ğ (soft g) a silent letter that elongates the vowel preceding it, as in nat**io**n
ı as in p**i**ano
j as in the "s" in trea**s**ure
o as in g**o**at
ö as eu in the French fl**eu**r
r somewhere between the English and the Spanish r (**r**ight and pe**r**o)
ş as in **sh**ip
u as in f**u**ll
ü as in the "ew" in f**ew**

abi: colloquial for *ağabey*.
abla: older sister, ma'am.
ağa: man wielding clout, feudal lord.
ağabey: brother, older brother.
Allahuekber: "God is great, God is almighty."
amca: uncle, used also as a term of endearment and respect.
bayram: Islamic holiday, usually either Holiday of Sacrifice or Holiday of Sweets, as they are called in Turkish.

Bey: Mr., used after the first name.

börek: pastry, usually with some savory filling, which comes in baked or lasagna-like varieties in different sizes.

cacık: side dish, a kind of cold soup (akin to the Indian *raita*) made of yogurt, diced cucumbers, and sometimes garlic; *tzatziki* in Greek.

cezve: Turkish coffee pot.

dolmuş: shared taxi, which usually operates between two fixed destinations, very possibly an invention of Istanbul.

döner: dish of meat, a kind of kebab, roasted on a spit at a vertical grill, akin to a gyro or *shawarma.*

falaka: torture by beating the soles of the feet.

gılman: male servant in paradise.

Hanım: Ms., or Mrs., used after the first name.

huri: female servant in paradise.

imam: religious (primarily prayer) leader of a congregation and/or mosque who may be a volunteer or an appointed civil servant.

kaşar: pale-yellow cheese akin to Italian *caciovallo* and Greek *kasseri.*

Kelime-i Şahadet: the Muslim creed of belief; professing it is a prerequisite for adopting the Muslim faith; it is recited in the face of death.

kuruş: Turkish penny; one-hundredth of a *lira.*

lahmacun: circular, thin-crust pastry (akin to an individual pizza), usually with a meat topping.

lira: Turkish currency.

lodos: south or southwest wind.

mantı: dish of boiled dumplings (akin to ravioli), usually served with yogurt.

maşallah: an exclamation meaning, "Wonderful!" or "May God protect you/him/her from evil!"

medrese: building or group of buildings used for teaching Islamic theology and religious law, usually including a mosque; an important part of Ottoman architecture.

mevlit: celebration involving the chanting of "Mevlit," a poem by Süleyman Çelebi celebrating the birth of the Prophet Muhammad, and passing out hard candy special to the occasion, usually held to celebrate an event or to commemorate the deceased.

meyhane: cross between a bar and a restaurant where *mezes* are served.

meze: food prepared in small portions (akin to *tapas*) to be savored with liqueur, primarily *rakı*.

muhtar: elected head of a neighborhood or village.

namaz: Islamic ritual of worship consisting of certain gestures, movements of the body, and prayers, performed five times a day.

pastırma: cured meat; first dried and then slathered with a cumin paste. It is found pretty much throughout the Middle East and Balkans, including Armenia and Greece. The word is said to be linguistically related to pastrami.

pide: generally flatbread, but comes also open-faced with a topping (akin to pizza) or filling (akin to a calzone).

rakı: the "national drink of Turks," an anisette and licorice flavored liqueur (akin to Greek ouzo), which turns cloudy-white when mixed with water.

reis: skipper of a fishing boat, chief.

şalvar: loose trousers.

simit: ring-shaped, crunchy, savory roll (somewhat akin to a pretzel), usually sprinkled with sesame seeds; a popular street snack in Turkey.

sucuk: spicy, garlicky sausage akin to chorizo.

tesbih: prayer beads, worry beads.

teyze: aunt, used also as a term of endearment and respect.

tulumba: dessert made by pouring dough from a pastry bag, frying and dunking in a sweet syrup (akin to *zeppole).*

yorgan: comforter.

Zamzam: holy water from the Well of Zamzam located in the Kaaba in Mecca, Saudi Arabia.

ABOUT THE CONTRIBUTORS

Sıtkı Murat Coşkun

YASEMİN AYDINOĞLU was born in İzmir in 1968 and has a degree in Chemical Engineering. She is temporarily residing in New York. "One Among Us" is her first published story.

Ahmet Tozar

TARKAN BARLAS was born in 1970 in Istanbul, where he grew up, attending Saint-Benoît French School and the Istanbul University Department of Journalism and Public Relations. His short stories have been published in *Varlık* and *Adam Öykü*. He received the 2006 Everest Publications First Novel Award for his novel *Lanetli Oda*. His second book, *Huzursuz Ruhlar*, a story collection, was published in 2008. Barlas works as an advertising copywriter.

Uluç Özcü

MEHMET BİLÂL was born in 1962 in Istanbul. He studied sociology at Istanbul University and Germanics and Political Science at Stuttgart University. He has worked as a reporter and editor and is currently an advertising copywriter, scriptwriter, and songwriter. He is the author of two novels and a collection of essays on Turkish pop music.

Şadiye Narin

BEHÇET ÇELİK was born in 1968 in Adana, Turkey. He graduated from the Istanbul University Faculty of Law in 1990 and had his first short story published in *Varlık* in 1987. His stories, essays, and translations have been published in various publications. Editor for *Virgül*, a journal of literary criticism, Çelik is the author of five story collections, the most recent of which, *Gün Ortasında Arzu* (2007), won the prestigious Sait Faik Short Story Award.

Özer Sayın

İNAN ÇETİN was born in 1966. He has worked in libraries, bookstores, and the publishing industry. His first published short story appeared in *Adam Öykü* in 1995. Since then he has published literary criticism and essays, two story collections (*Bin Yapraklı Lotus*, 2003, and *İçimizdeki Şato*, 2005), and a novel (*İblisname: Bir Hayalin Gerçek Tarihi*, 2007).

Yücel Tunca

İSMAİL GÜZELSOY was born in 1963 in the town of Iğdır and grew up in Istanbul. His articles and stories have been appearing in literary journals since 1987. His first book, consisting of (in his own words) a series of "micro-novels," was published in 2000. A second novel, *Ruh Hastası*, was published in 2004. More recently he has published a trilogy, the *Banknot Üçlemesi*. Güzelsoy still lives in Istanbul, where he has worked as a guide in the city and other regions of Turkey.

HİKMET HÜKÜMENOĞLU was born in 1971 in Istanbul. His first novel, *Kar Kuyusu*, was published in 2005, and his second, *Küçük Yalanlar Kitabı*, in 2007. Hükümenoğlu also writes short stories and scripts, works as a translator, and dabbles in electronic music.

Ruşen Çakır

MÜGE İPLİKÇİ was born and raised in Istanbul. She received the Yaşar Nabi Nayır Award (for writers and poets under the age of thirty) in 1996 and a Haldun Taner Award in 1997. She is the author of four story collections and two novels, and is the editor of two works of nonfiction. İplikçi is currently the chairperson of the Turkey PEN Women Writers' Committee.

Ayşa Karısoy Kıraç

RIZA KIRAÇ was born in 1970 in Istanbul, where he grew up. He studied cinema at Dokuz Eylül and Marmara Universities and has worked as director, assistant director, and writer for documentaries, commercials, and TV programs. His short films and documentaries have been shown at various national and international festivals. His stories have been published in a variety of literary journals and anthologies. He is also the author of two story collections and four novels.

Marc Viaplana

LYDIA LUNCH continues to bitch, moan, insult, attack, purr, and squeal thirty years after her initial outburst. Her exhibitionist tendencies are manifested in the written, spoken, or sung word, through photography and film, and most often in live performance. Her first book, *Paradoxia: A Predator's Diary*, was published by Akashic in 2007. In 2009, Akashic will publish her next book, *Will Work for Drugs*.

Hugh Pope

JESSICA LUTZ was born in the Netherlands in 1962 and moved to Istanbul in 1989. She works as a reporter for various Dutch media as well as CBS radio, *U.S. News and World Report,* and BBC radio. She has written two books: *De Gouden Appel* (2002), about modern Turkey, and *Gezichten van Istanbul* (2008), about Istanbul. A short story of hers was published in *Tales from the Expat Harem* (2005).

Mehmet Demirtaş

BARIŞ MÜSTECAPLIOĞLU was born in 1977 in İzmit-Kocaeli. He is the author of Turkey's first fantasy fiction series, the four-volume *The Legends of Perg,* as well as the novel *Şakird.* His most recent work is an ongoing series of illustrated children's books and he is currently writing a novel that will be published in 2009. Müstecaplıoğlu has also been working as a human-resources specialist in various firms for the past eight years.

Tevfik Göktepe

ALGAN SEZGİNTÜREDİ was born in 1968 and works as an author, graphic designer, painter, and translator. He has two published detective novels, *Katilin Şeyi* (2006) and *Katilin Meselesi* (2007). Both novels feature the handsome, charming knucklehead Vedat and his partner, short, squat Tefo, the brains of the crime-busting duo.

Dilek Akdemir

AMY SPANGLER is a native of small-town Ohio and moved to Istanbul upon graduation from college in 1999. She still lives in the elusive and amorphous Istanbul, where she works as translator, agent, and editor. She is the translator of Asli Erdogan's novel *The City in Crimson Cloak* (Soft Skull, 2007) and coowner of AnatoliaLit Literary and Copyright Agency (www.anatolialit.com).

Orhan Cem Çetin

FERYAL TİLMAÇ was born in 1969, in Adana, Turkey and studied Economics at Boğaziçi University. Her short stories and essays have been published in numerous literary magazines in Turkey. She is the author of the story collection *Mevt Tek Hecelik Uyku* (Okuyan Us Publishing, 2007) and won the Altkitap Short Story Prize in 2006. She lives in Istanbul.

Jan Banning

SADIK YEMNİ was born in Istanbul and has resided in Amsterdam since 1975. His writing combines myriad genres and styles: detective fiction, drama, paranormal, horror, science fiction, metaphysics, and humor. He is the author of nine novels published in Turkish, as well as a variety of short stories, essays, plays, and film scripts.

Murat Eyuboglu

MUSTAFA ZİYALAN was born on the Black Sea coast of Turkey. He worked as a general doctor and coroner in a rural Anatolian village and now lives and practices psychiatry in New York. He has worked with torture victims, prison inmates, delinquent children, pathological gamblers, and people with AIDS. His poetry, short fiction, and essays have appeared in many literary periodicals, anthologies (most recently in *New European Poets* from Graywolf Press), and books.

Also available from the Akashic Books Noir Series

PARIS NOIR
edited by Aurélien Masson
300 pages, trade paperback original, $15.95

All original stories from Paris' finest authors, all translated from French.

Brand new stories by: Didier Daeninckx, Jean-Bernard Pouy, Marc Villard, Chantal Pelletier, Patrick Pécherot, DOA, Hervé Prudon, Dominique Mainard, Salim Bachi, Jérôme Leroy, and others.

Paris Noir takes you on a ride through the old medieval center of town with its intertwined streets, its ghosts, and its secrets buried in history . . . But *Paris Noir* is not only an homage to the crime genre, to Melville and Godard, it's also an invitation to French fiction.

ROME NOIR
edited by Chiara Stangalino & Maxim Jakubowski
300 pages, trade paperback original, $15.95

Groundbreaking collection of original stories, all translated from Italian.

Brand new stories by: Antonio Scurati, Carlo Lucarelli, Gianrico Carofiglio, Diego De Silva, Giuseppe Genna, Marcello Fois, Cristiana Danila Formetta, Enrico Franceschini, Boosta, and others.

From Stazione Termini, immortalized by Roberto Rossellini's films, to Pier Paolo Pasolini's desolate beach of Ostia, and encompassing famous landmarks and streets, this is the sinister side of the Dolce Vita come to life, a stunning gallery of dark characters, grotesques, and lost souls seeking revenge or redemption in the shadow of the Colosseum, the Spanish Steps, the Vatican, Trastevere, the quiet waters of the Tiber, and Piazza Navona. Rome will never be the same.

BROOKLYN NOIR
edited by Tim McLoughlin
350 pages, trade paperback original, $15.95
*Winner of Shamus Award, Anthony Award, Robert L. Fish Memorial Award; finalist for Edgar Award, Pushcart Prize.

Brand new stories by: Pete Hamill, Arthur Nersesian, Ellen Miller, Nelson George, Nicole Blackman, Sidney Offit, Ken Bruen, and others.

"*Brooklyn Noir* is such a stunningly perfect combination that you can't believe you haven't read an anthology like this before. But trust me—you haven't. Story after story is a revelation, filled with the requisite sense of place, but also the perfect twists that crime stories demand. The writing is flat-out superb, filled with lines that will sing in your head for a long time to come."
—Laura Lippman, winner of the Edgar, Agatha, and Shamus awards

LOS ANGELES NOIR
edited by Denise Hamilton
360 pages, trade paperback original, $15.95
*A *Los Angeles Times* best seller and winner of an Edgar Award.

Brand new stories by: Michael Connelly, Janet Fitch, Susan Straight, Héctor Tobar, Patt Morrison, Robert Ferrigno, Neal Pollack, Gary Phillips, Christopher Rice, Naomi Hirahara, Jim Pascoe, and others.

"Akashic is making an argument about the universality of noir; it's sort of flattering, really, and *Los Angeles Noir*, arriving at last, is a kaleidoscopic collection filled with the ethos of noir pioneers Raymond Chandler and James M. Cain."
—*Los Angeles Times Book Review*

HAVANA NOIR
edited by Achy Obejas
360 pages, trade paperback original, $15.95

Brand new stories by: Leonardo Padura, Pablo Medina, Carolina García-Aguilera, Ena Lucía Portela, Miguel Mejides, Arnaldo Correa, Alex Abella, Moisés Asís, Lea Aschkenas, and others.

"A remarkable collection . . . Throughout these 18 stories, current and former residents of Havana—some well-known, some previously undiscovered—deliver gritty tales of depravation, depravity, heroic perseverance, revolution, and longing in a city mythical and widely misunderstood." —*Miami Herald*

TRINIDAD NOIR
edited by Lisa Allen-Agostini & Jeanne Mason
340 pages, trade paperback original, $15.95

Brand new stories by: Robert Antoni, Elizabeth Nunez, Lawrence Scott, Oonya Kempadoo, Ramabai Espinet, Shani Mootoo, Kevin Baldeosingh, elisha efua bartels, Tiphanie Yanique, Willi Chen, and others.

"For sheer volume, few—anywhere—can beat [V.S.] Naipaul's prodigious output. But on style, the writers in the Trinidadian canon can meet him eye to eye . . . Trinidad is no one-trick pony, literarily speaking." —Coeditor Lisa Allen-Agostini in the *New York Times*